D0969230

Pirate Ghosts
Ghosts
Of The American Coast

WITHDRAWN

Pirate Ghosts

Of The American Coast

Stories of Hauntings at Sea

Edited by Frank D. McSherry, Jr.,
Charles G. Waugh, and Martin H. Greenberg

August House / *Little Rock*
P U B L I S H E R S

HoR
P667gh

©Copyright 1988 by Frank D. McSherry, Jr.,
Charles G. Waugh, and Martin H. Greenberg
All rights reserved. This book, or parts thereof,
may not be reproduced in any form without permission.

Published by August House, Inc.,
P.O. Box 3223, Little Rock, Arkansas, 72203,
501-663-7300.

Printed in the United States of America

10 9 8 7 6 5 4 3 2 1

LIBRARY OF CONGRESS CATALOGING-IN-PUBLICATION
DATA

Pirate ghosts of the American coast : stories of hauntings at sea /
edited by Frank D. McSherry, Charles G. Waugh,
and Martin H. Greenberg. — 1st ed.
p.   cm.
ISBN 0-87483-077-X (pbk.) : $8.95
1. Ghost stories, American. 2. Ghost stories, English.
3. Sea stories, American. 4. Sea stories, English.
5. Pirates — Fiction. I. McSherry, Frank D. II. Waugh, Charles.
III. Greenberg, Martin Harry.
PS648.G48P57 1988
813'.0872—dc 19   88-26302
                                                            CIP

First Edition, 1988

Cover illustration by Jan Taylor Weeks
Production artwork by Ira Hocut
Typography by Diversified Graphics, Little Rock, Arkansas
Design direction by Ted Parkhurst
Project direction by Hope Norman Coulter

This book is printed on archival-quality paper which meets the
guidelines for performance and durability of the Committee on
Production Guidelines for Book Longevity of the Council on
Library Resources.

AUGUST HOUSE, INC.   PUBLISHERS   LITTLE ROCK

Acknowledgments

"Before I Wake" by Henry Kuttner, copyright ©1944 by Henry Kuttner. Reprinted by permission of Don Congdon Associates, Inc.

"The Blue Spectacles" by August Derleth, copyright ©1949 by *Weird Tales*. Reprinted by permission of the agents for the author's Estate, Scott Meredith Literary Agency, Inc., 845 Third Avenue, New York, New York 10022.

"The Digging at Pistol Key" by Carl Jacobi, copyright ©1947 by *Weird Tales;* renewed ©1975 by Carl Jacobi. Reprinted by permission of Kirby McCauley, Ltd.

"No Ships Pass" by Lady Eleanor Smith, copyright ©1934 by Lady Eleanor Smith. Reprinted by permission of Aitken & Stone, Ltd., London.

"The Red Swimmer" by Robert Bloch, copyright ©1939; renewed ©1967 by Robert Bloch. Reprinted by permission of the Scott Meredith Literary Agency, Inc., 845 Third Avenue, New York, New York 10022.

"Seven Turns in a Hangman's Rope" by Henry S. Whitehead, copyright ©1952 by Henry S. Whitehead. Reprinted by permission of the agents for the author's Estate, Scott Meredith Literary Agency, Inc., 845 Third Avenue, New York, New York 10022.

"The Terrible Old Man" by H. P. Lovecraft, copyright ©1926 by *Weird Tales*. Reprinted by permission of the agents for the author's Estate, Scott Meredith Literary Agency, Inc., 845 Third Avenue, New York, New York 10022.

"A Vintage from Atlantis" by Clark Ashton Smith, copyright ©1953 by *Weird Tales*. Reprinted by permission of the agents for the author's Estate, Scott Meredith Literary Agency, Inc., 845 Third Avenue, New York, New York 10022.

Contents

Introduction

. . .*By the flames,*
Decked out in crimson, gemmed with syenite,
Hailing their fellows with outrageous names,
The pirates sat and diced. Their eyes were moons.
"Doubloons!" they said. The words crashed gold. "Doubloons!"
— **STEPHEN VINCENT BENET**

Pirate gold! Doubloons, pieces of eight!

Buried treasure!

A black ship sailing under a golden Caribbean moon, flying from its topmast a black flag with skull and crossbones — the Jolly Roger.

Scarlet-coated pirates dueling with cutlasses on sands white-hot under the glare of a tropic sun, for a sea-chest full of gleaming jewels, seized from Spanish galleons.

And dimly heard in dreams pirate voices chanting: "Fifteen men on the Dead Man's Chest — / Yo-ho-ho and a bottle of rum! / Drink and the Devil have done for the rest — / Yo-ho-ho and a bottle of rum!"

These are among the most exciting and exotic images of boyhood — pirate tales of adventure at sea and on land.

Now, these romantic and exotic scenes were based on real pirates, colorful people who did remarkable things. There were Henry Morgan, terror of the Spanish Main from the Panama Coast and its silver trains to Cartagena, to the Windward Islands, who later became

9

Royal Governor of Jamaica; Captain Kidd, who buried his pirate treasure somewhere along the coast of Long Island Sound and died on the gallows without revealing the treasure's location; Jean Lafitte, the pirate who led his gunners to the aid of General Andy Jackson at the Battle of New Orleans, dealt the British Army one of the most lopsided defeats in all its long history, and disappeared mysteriously off the coast of Yucatan a few years later; and Captain Edward Teach, self-named "Blackbeard," who terrorized his victims by tying firecrackers in his beard and lighting them. There were even lady buccaneers, like red-headed pirate queen Anne Bonny, who defeated a Spanish force more than three times the size of hers in a fleet action in 1720 off Walker's Point.

Their adventures are the basis for some of the great works of literature. Who can forget the thrill of first encountering *Treasure Island,* Robert Louis Stevenson's exciting novel for young people (of all ages) about Jim Hawkins, Long John Silver, the one-legged seacook with a green pet parrot on his shoulder, and their trip to the tropical island where pirate Captain Flint's treasure is buried? Then there's *Porto Bello Gold* by Arthur D. Howden-Smith, a long novel telling how Flint's treasure got there in the first place. *A High Wind in Jamaica,* by Richard Hughes, tells how captured children aboard a pirate ship are changed by pirate life. And there's Rafael Sabatini's *Captain Blood,* about one of the great romantic figures of historical adventure, riding off the pirate coast in his blood-red ship the *Arabella.*

Ghost pirates? Tales of the supernatural?

Yes indeed.

For strange, inexplicable things happen at sea. Why not?

Three-quarters of the whole world's surface is ocean, nearly all of it unexplored. Who knows what lies below in the depths, and may rise to the surface from time to time? Or move secretly through ocean fogs?

Ship after ship has been found in good condition, but

with no soul aboard. The *Mary Celeste* is the classic case, found off the Azores in 1872, yawing, no hand at the wheel. There was no trace of violence, no mention of trouble or storm in the ship's log — but no trace of crew or captain, or captain's wife and baby daughter.

Nor was that the only one. In 1921 the schooner *Carol A. Deering* ran aground at Diamond Shoals on the North Carolina coast, with food on the galley stove, again no trace of violence or damage — and not a soul aboard. In 1940 the British West Indies yacht *Gloria Colite* was found abandoned in the Gulf of Mexico, in fine shape; in 1956 the U.S. yacht *Connemara* was found equally deserted near Bermuda. (There's more; see *Among the Missing* by Jay Robert Nash.)

Not to mention the ships that simply disappear. In 1918 the U.S.S. *Cyclops,* aircraft carrier-turned collier, set out from the West Indies and vanished into thin air. The Danish *Kobenhavn,* a training ship for officer cadets, disappeared without a trace in 1928 in the South Atlantic. The U.S.S. *Poet,* a 12,000-ton grain carrier, vanished in 1980 near Delaware. "It is extraordinary," said Capt. Alan Villiers, "how ships, big and small, can go out of port fit — apparently — for any conditions they might meet, move for a day or two or for weeks among other ships, and then disappear as utterly as if they had never been." (Villiers's book, *Posted Missing,* lists many others.)

And — who knows? — just as there were real pirates to base fiction on, these stories of the supernatural at sea may well be based on more than lore and legend. Only now is humanity beginning to realize how little it knows of the universe into which it is starting to step — "stars, sun, sea, light, darkness, space, great waters," says Joseph Conrad, novelist of the sea, "the formidable work of the seven Days, into which mankind seems to have blundered unbidden. Or else decoyed."

The eerie sea stories in the present collection are by such well-known authors as Robert Bloch, creator of *Psycho,* whose grim and shivery tale "The Red Swimmer"

11

has never been reprinted in the U.S. and only once, in a rare edition, in England; H.P. Lovecraft, modern master of the macabre, whose tales of horrors from the sea have the chill of ocean fog in them; John Masefield, professional seaman, novelist, and later Poet Laureate of England; Henry S. Whitehead, minister assigned to the West Indies, master of supernatural horror, who heard tales of pirate ghosts in the Caribbean from those who experienced them firsthand — and others.

We hope you enjoy them.

And remember — they're just fiction. Skilled, convincing, eerie fiction, to give you again that romantic thrill and shiver that everyone had when first reading about pirates. And that's the real pirate gold — the aura of adventure and romance they left behind, a literary treasure.

It *is* just fiction. Isn't it?

Frank D. McSherry Jr.

No Ships Pass

LADY ELEANOR SMITH

I am glad, thought Patterson, that I've always been a damned good swimmer . . . and he continued to plow his way grimly through the churning, tumbled argent of the breakers. It seemed hours, although it was actually moments, since the yacht had disappeared in one brief flash of huge and bluish flame; now the seas tossed, untroubled, as though the yacht had never been; and the boat containing his comrades had vanished with such swiftness as to make him think that it must have been smudged by some gigantic sponge from the flat, greenish expanse of ocean. The strange part was that he was able, as he swam, to think with a complete, detached coherence; he was conscious of no panic; on the contrary, as he strove with all his might to gain the strip of land dancing before his eyes, his mind worked with a calm and resolute competence.

"I always thought we'd have a fire with all that petrol about . . . Curse all motor yachts . . . I wonder if the others have been drowned? . . . Good job I gave the boat a miss . . ."

He was not even conscious of much regret as he thought of the probable fate of his comrades — his employer, his employer's son, the members of the crew. Already, as he swam on and on through gently lapping waves, the yacht and those who belonged to it had become part of the past, remote and half-forgotten. The present and the future lay ahead, where a long line of sand shimmered like silver before his eyes. Yet it was funny, he mused; there had been no sign of land seen from aboard the yacht, and it was not until the actual panic of the fire that he had noticed the dim shape of this island, "near enough to swim to," as he had cried to the others, but they swarmed into the boat, taking no notice of his cries. And so he had embarked alone upon this perilous adventure.

He was a strong swimmer, but he was growing tired. Were his limbs suddenly heavier, or had the sea become less buoyant? He clenched his teeth, striking out desperately, then floated for a while, lying on his back, the huge arch of the sky towering a million miles above him like some gigantic bowl, all fierce hydrangea-blue. When he turned to swim again, he was refreshed, but more sensible of the terrors of his situation. And yet, was it his fancy, or had the shores of the island loomed nearer during the moments of this brief rest? At first he believed himself to be suffering from hallucination, then, as he looked again, he realized that he was making remarkable progress . . . He was now so near that the beach glittered like snow in the tropical sunshine before his eyes, and the sands dazzled him, yet he could perceive, lapping against them, a line of softly creaming surf, and above the sands there blazed the vivid jewel-green of dense foliage. The gulls wheeled bright-winged against the brighter silver of sea and sand. Then he was prepared to swear that his ears distinguished, sounding from the shore, a harsh and murmurous cry that might have been — for he was very weary — something in the nature of a welcome for the creature trying so desperately to gain this sparkling and gaudy sanctuary.

And then exhaustion descended upon him like a numbing cloak, and his ears and his brain whirled. His limbs seemed weighted, and his heart pumped violently and he thought he must drown, and groaned, for at that moment life seemed sweet and vivid, since life was represented by the island, and the seas were death.

"Well, now for death," he thought, and as he sank, his foot touched bottom.

He realized afterwards that he must have sobbed aloud as he staggered ashore. For a moment, as he stood ankle-deep in warm, powdery sand, with the sun pounding fiercely upon his drenched body, the surf curling at his feet and the cool greenness of a thickly matted forest cresting the slope above his head, he still thought that he must be drowning, and that this land was mirage. Then the silence was shattered by a shrill scream; and a glowing parrot, rainbow-bright, flew suddenly from amidst the blood-red shower of a tall hibiscus-bush, to wheel, gorgeous and discordant, above his head. Dripping fire-colored blossom. Loud, jangling, piercing cries. The island was real.

Patterson fainted, flopping like a heap of old clothes upon the smooth, hard silver of the sand . . .

When he came to himself, the sun was lower and the air fragrant with a scented coolness that seemed the very perfume of dusk itself. For a moment he lay motionless, his mind blank, then, as complete consciousness returned to him and he rolled over on his face, he became aware of a black, human shadow splashed across the sands within a few inches of where he lay. The island, then, must obviously be inhabited. He raised his eyes defiantly.

He could not have explained what he had expected to see — some grinning, paint-raddled savage, perhaps, or else the prim, concerned face of a missionary in white ducks, or, perhaps, a dark-skinned native girl in a wreath of flowers. He saw actually none of these, his gaze encountering a shorter, stranger form — that of an elderly, dwarfish man in what he at first supposed to be some

15

sort of fancy dress. Comical clothes! He gaped at the short, jaunty jacket, the nankeen trousers, the hard, round hat, and, most singular of all, a thin and ratty pigtail protruding from beneath the brim of this same hat. The little man returned his scrutiny calmly, with an air of complete nonchalance; he revealed a turnip face blotched thick with freckles, a loose mouth that twitched mechanically from time to time, and little piggish, filmy blue eyes.

"Good God," said Patterson at length, "who are you, and where did you appear from?"

The little man asked, in a rusty voice proceeding from deep in his throat:

"Have you tobacco?"

"If I had it'd be no use to you. Do you realize I swam here?"

"You swam? From where?"

There was silence for a moment, a silence broken only by the breaking of the surf and by the harsh cry of birds, as Patterson, more exhausted than he had first supposed, tried idiotically to remember to what strange port the yacht, *Seagull*, had been bound.

He said at length:

"I — we were on our way to Madeira. The Southern Atlantic. The yacht — a petrol-boat — caught fire. And so I swam ashore."

"Petrol?" the man replied, puzzled. "I know nothing of that. As for the Southern Atlantic, I myself was marooned on these shores deliberate, many and many a year ago, when bound for Kingston, Jamaica."

"Rather out of your course, weren't you?"

The little man was silent, staring reflectively out to sea. Patterson, naturally observant, was immediately struck by the look in those small, filmy blue eyes — a singular, fixed immobility of regard, at once empty and menacing, a glassy, almost dead expression in which was reflected all the vast space of the ocean on which he gazed, and something else, too, more elusive, harder to define, some curious quality of concentration that, refusing to be classified, nevertheless repelled. He asked:

"What's your name?"

"Heywood. And yours?"

"Patterson. Are you alone here?"

The narrow blue eyes shifted, slipped from the sea to Patterson's face, and then dropped.

"Alone? No; there are four of us."

"And were they also marooned?"

As he uttered his last word he was conscious that it reflected the twentieth century even less than did the costume of his companion. Perhaps he was still light-headed after his ordeal. He added quickly: "Were they also bound for Jamaica?"

"No," Heywood answered briefly.

"How long," Patterson pursued laboriously, "have you been here?"

"That," said his companion, "is a mighty big question. Best wait before you ask it. Or better still, ask it, not of me, but of the Captain."

"You're damned uncivil. Who's the Captain?"

"Another castaway, like ourselves. And yet not, perhaps, so much alike. Yonder, behind the palms of the cliff, is his hut."

"I wouldn't mind going there. Will you take me?"

"No," said Heywood in a surly tone.

"Good God!" exclaimed Patterson. "I shall believe you if you tell me they marooned you for your ill manners. I've swum about eight miles, and need rest and sleep. If you've a hut, then take me to it."

"The Captain will bide no one in his hut but himself and one other person. That person is not myself."

"Then where do you sleep? In the tree, like the baboons I hear chattering on the hill?"

"No," Heywood answered, still looking out to sea. "I've a comrade in my hut, which is small, since I built it for myself. A comrade who was flung ashore here when a great ship struck an iceberg."

"An iceberg?" Patterson's attention was suddenly arrested. "An iceberg in these regions? Are you trying to make a fool of me, or have you been here so long that your wits are going? And, by the way, tell me this: how do you try to attract the attention of passing ships? Do you light bonfires or wave flags?"

"No ships pass," said Heywood.

There was another silence. It was almost dark; already the deep iris of the sky was pierced by stars, and it was as though a silver veil had been dragged across the glitter of the ocean. Behind them, on the cliffs, two lights winked steadily; Patterson judged these to proceed from the huts mentioned by his companion. Then came the sound of soft footsteps, and they were no longer two shadows there on the dusky sands, but three.

"Hallo, stranger!" said a casual voice.

Patterson turned abruptly around to distinguish in the grayness a sharp, pale face with a shock of tousled hair. A young man, gaunt-looking and eager, clad normally enough in a dark sweater and trousers.

"And this is a hell of a nice island, I don't think," the stranger pursued, thrusting his hands into his pockets. He had a strong cockney accent. Patterson was enchanted by the very prosaicness of his appearance; he brought with him sanity; walking as he did on faery, moon-drenched shores, he was blessed, being the essence of the commonplace.

"Name of Judd. Dicky Judd. I suppose you're all in. Been swimming, ain't you?"

"Yes. And this fellow Heywood won't take me to his hut. Says it's full. Can you do anything about it?"

"You bet," said Judd. "Follow me, and I'll give you a bite of supper and a doss for the night. This way — the path up the cliff. We'll leave Heywood to the moon. Come on."

Ten minutes later, Patterson was eating fried fish and yams in a log-hut, with an open fireplace and two hammocks swung near the rude doorway. He had noticed, as they climbed the slope together, a grander, more commodious hut built a few hundred yards away among some shady palms. This, he surmised, must be the home of the elusive Captain. No sound came from it, but a light burned in the narrow window. As he ate his food he speedily forgot the existence of these fellow-castaways. He asked instead, gulping down water and wishing it were brandy:

"How did you come here, Judd? With the others?"

Judd eyed him swiftly. For one second Patterson imagined that he detected in the merry greenish eyes of his companion the fixed, almost petrified expression that had so much perplexed him in the gaze of Heywood. If he was right, this expression vanished in a flash, yet Judd seemed to withdraw himself, to become curiously remote, as he answered coolly:

"Not I. I came here after them — some time after."

"Do you mean that, like me, you were the only survivor from your ship?"

"That's about it," Judd answered, with his mouth full.

"Tell me about it."

"Oh, there's nothing much to tell. She was a great liner — I had a berth aboard her — and she struck an iceberg in mid-Atlantic. There was not room for me in the boats, so I jumped . . . But she was a lovely ship, and big as a city. *Titanic,* they called her."

"You're pulling my leg. And for heaven's, chuck it — I've had about enough for one day."

"S'trewth, I'm not!" Judd told him energetically. "But no matter. You don't have to believe me."

And he whistled, picking his teeth.

Patterson asked with a shiver:

"Look here, joking apart, do you mean to tell me that you honestly believe you were cast ashore from the wreck of the *Titanic?*"

"On my oath," said Judd. He added, jumping up: "Bugs is bad here at night. Wait, while I swat a few."

"Just answer this," Patterson interrupted. "Why in heaven's name, when you think you were wrecked in mid-Atlantic, should you have landed here on a tropical island off the African coast? Bit of a miracle that, wasn't it?"

Judd was silent for a moment, flicking at the mosquitoes with a palm-leaf fan. He said at length, sucking his teeth:

19

"Not being a seafaring man, I take it, you don't happen to have heard of a fairy-story told among sailor-boys all the world over — story of a mirage island that floats about the seas near wrecks bent on collecting castaways?"

Patterson thought desperately:

"This man's as mad as Heywood, and that's saying a lot . . . And I've got to live with them . . ." Aloud he said: "No, I've never heard that one. But there's one other thing I'd like to ask you . . . Who's this Captain Heywood was talking about? Has he been here for many years?"

"I'll give you this goatskin for a blanket," said Judd, "and you can doss near the doorway, where it's cooler. So you know about the Captain?"

"I've only heard his name. I asked you, has he been here for a very long time?"

"Many years," answered Judd, with a peculiar inflection.

"Tell me more about him."

Judd laughed.

"You don't half want to know much, do you? You'll clap eyes tomorrow on Captain Thunder, late of the bark *Black Joke,* well known (he's always boasting) from Barbados to Trinidad and back again. But you may whistle for the Captain tonight!"

Patterson was sleepy.

"Sounds like a buccaneer," he muttered into the goatskin, and was soon unconscious, oblivious even of Heywood's noisy entry into the hut.

By early morning the island's beauty seemed more exotic even than the radiant plumage of the parakeets darting to and fro in the dim green light of airy tree-tops. Patterson was refreshed after a good night's sleep, and consequently less depressed. He bathed with Judd, leaving Heywood snoring in his hammock. The beach was a shining snowdrift, the sea a vast tapestry of hyacinth veined and streaked with foam, glowing, glittering in the brilliant sunlight.

They swam for twenty minutes and then lay basking on the sands.

"Hungry?" Judd inquired.

So delicious was the morning that Patterson had quite forgotten the eccentricity manifested by his comrades the previous evening. Rolling over on his stomach, he was about to reply in enthusiastic affirmative, when he surprised once more in his companion's gaze that bleak, fey look that had already disconcerted him. He could not understand it, yet it was as though a somber shadow fled across the beach, obscuring this gay and vivid world of amber sunshine, creaming surf, tossing sea and glowing, brilliant blossom. Beauty was blotted out when Judd, the commonplace, looked like that; he felt suddenly lonely, humbled and scared.

"Judd," he said suddenly, and Judd wrenched his eyes away from the horizon.

"Judd, listen and please tell the truth. Just what are our chances of getting away from here?"

Judd eyed him thoughtfully.

"If you want the truth, we haven't any. Sorry, and all that, but there it is."

"Rubbish!" said Patterson. "A ship will surely pass one day. Just because you've had bad luck . . ."

"No ships pass," Judd told him.

"Rubbish again! Look how close mine came yesterday. The trouble with you, Judd, is that you've been here too long, and got into a rut. I don't believe you care much whether you're rescued or not. Now, I do. And I'll tell you my plans — "

"Listen a minute," said Judd. He propped himself up on his elbow, avoided his companion's eyes, and resumed: "You might as well hear it now. No sense in keeping it from you, although you'll think I'm pretty nutty. Listen, then, Patterson. We're here for keeps. Get that? Look at the Captain and his friend; look at Heywood. If I told you how long they'd been here you wouldn't swallow it, and I'd not blame you. But you've got to know some time — we're here *for ever*. Now I feel better."

Patterson shuddered in the blazing sunlight.

"Do you really think we've got to stick this until we die?"

Judd flung a pebble at a pearly cloud of seagulls.

"Worse than that, Patterson. Worse by a long chalk. I told you last night this island was mirage, magic. Stands to reason it is, floating round the world picking survivors from shipwrecks in all the Seven Seas. Well, there's something worse than that — much worse — and I'm going to tell you what it is. There's no death on this island. Death forgets us. We're here for all eternity."

Patterson laughed nervously.

"You should be in Bedlam, Judd. I suppose a few years' desert-island does that to one. But look here, now I've come to join you, we'll get away somehow, I promise you that."

Judd slipped on his trousers.

"You don't believe me, and small blame to you. I was like that once. But it's true. I swear to God it is. There's no death here. For the animals and the birds, yes, or we should starve. But not for us. We're here for all eternity, and you may as well make the best of it."

Patterson, trying to dress himself, found that his hands were trembling. Yet he tried to be reasonable.

"Look here, Judd, what put this crazy idea into your head?"

"Do you know," Judd replied, "how long Heywood's been here? Of course you don't; I'll tell you. He was marooned in eighteen-twenty-five. As for the Captain, he's had a longer spell. He was a pirate, one of those Spanish Main fellows I read about when I was a kid. His crew mutinied in July seventeen-ninety-five."

"Very interesting," Patterson commented idiotically.

"Don't you imagine," Judd continued, "that we haven't all of us tried to escape in the past? We've built rafts and boats — they've always been chucked back here on the beach by mysterious tidal waves or tempests. Then we've tried to kill ourselves and one another — we've been wounded and lain sick for weeks with mosquitoes battening on our wounds, and our wounds have festered, but we've pulled through. Now we don't do that any more. Too much pain for nothing. You always pull through in the end. We've tried to drown, and swallowed quarts of water, but always we've been flung back on the sands here. Death's not for us — we've jolly well found that out. And so we make the best of it. It's all right after a time. You live for eating and sleeping, and you blooming well don't think. Sometimes you go mad, but in the long run you get sane again. And you kowtow to the Captain, who's got twice the guts of anyone. And, oh, yes, your clothes last just as you last. Funny, isn't it?"

"What about breakfast?" suggested Patterson.

"I knew you'd think me loopy," said Judd. "All right, come on back to the hut."

They scrambled to their feet, and there was an awkward constraint between them. Then Patterson pulled Judd's arm.

"What's that? Look, over there! Is that just another confounded mirage?"

Judd screwed up his eyes. Beside the rocks, where seaweed flourished like green moss, a woman stood, skirts kilted in her hand. She was barefoot, and sprang from one rock to another, with the grace and agility of a deer. She was gathering mussels. As she worked she sang, and the drowsy, bell-like sweetness of her voice was wafted faintly to their ears all mingled with the cry of seagulls.

"Oh, that," said Judd. "Well you better remember to act respectful when she's about. That's Dona Ines, the Captain's girl. She was a prisoner; he had her with him on his boat when the crew of the *Black Joke* mutinied, and they were cast up here together. At least, they both say so. First she hated him, then loved him for forty years or so, and since then, for about a hundred years, she's been fed up, but he's still keen on her. So keep away, that's my advice. Once Heywood went snooping about her, and the Captain cut his throat. He'd have died elsewhere, of course, and he suffered the tortures of hell, he told me. He'll show you the scar if you're interested."

"Wait," said Patterson, "you've given me a turn with your crazy talk, and she's coming toward us. There's no harm, I suppose, in speaking to her?"

"None, as long as you're respectful."

They waited there on the beach while the woman

approached them. She was young, about twenty, and extremely handsome. She wore a stiff, flowing skirt of burning crimson, and a little jacket of orange. Her dark, rippling hair hung like a black plume down her back, and her oval, vivid face was delicately modeled, with high cheekbones, a mouth like red blossom, and immense velvety-brown eyes. She was Spanish, of course, and well bred; her wrists were fragile, exquisite, her bare feet slender and arched. Her body was lithe, graceful, and voluptuous; she moved swiftly, as though she danced, and as she drew near to the two men, a sudden soft breeze blew a lock of floating ebony hair across the fire and sweetness of her mouth.

Patterson was dazed; he had encountered much superstition during the course of the morning, his stomach was empty, and he was but ill-prepared for such beauty. Dona Ines said gaily, speaking fluent, attractive English:

"Good morning to you, *señor*. I heard last night of your arrival, but was not allowed to greet you, as I so much desired. Please forgive my execrable manners. We shall see so much of one another that it would be as well to start our acquaintance on friendly terms."

Patterson pulled himself together and kissed her hand, a long, delicate hand all dusty-tanned with the sun. A huge diamond glared from her third finger.

"Morning, Ines," said Judd casually. "Where's the Captain?"

"Micah?" She became suddenly indifferent. "Waiting for his breakfast, I suppose. I must go to him. Shall we walk up the hill together?"

And so they went, and the Dona Ines moved lightly between them, all bright and flaming in her gaudy clothes, and told Patterson that he must accustom himself to this idea of eternity. After the first hundred years, these things mattered little enough.

"As well be here, laughing and walking in the sunshine, as in our graves. Don't you think so, *señor?* And I, who am talking to you, have so much experience of these things. Why, haven't I lived here with Micah Thunder for near on a hundred and forty years? And it might be yesterday that he sacked Santa Ana, he and his fleet, and took me prisoner when I was on my knees at Mass, and swore that I should be his woman. And so I was, both here and on his ship. But I have almost forgot the ship, and Santa Ana, too. Now there is only the island, and yet I am not a stricken woman, am I, nor yet a day older than when cast up on these shores?"

And so she prattled, her dark eyes flashing like jewels, until she and the two men came to the clearing where were the two huts, and there, in front of the smaller one, sat Heywood, surly as ever, eating.

"Good-by, *señor*," said Dona Ines. "We will meet later, when I have fed my Captain."

Patterson sat down on the ground and said nothing.

"Here's orange juice," said Judd, "and custard-apples, and some cornbread I baked myself. No butter — we don't rise to that — but, all the same, we'll dine on oysters."

Patterson ate in silence. He supposed himself to be hungry. And he thought that he was in a nightmare, and would wake soon with the steward shaking him, and find himself once more in a gay, chintz-hung cabin of the *Seagull,* with bacon and eggs waiting in the dining-saloon. But he did not wake.

"I'll help you rig up a tent after breakfast," said Judd. "I've got some sailcloth. It'll last you for a few days, and then you can build a hut for yourself."

Heywood, eating ravenously, said nothing, but eyed him in silence.

"I wish," he thought desperately, "they wouldn't stare at me like that."

And suddenly he knew of what their fixed eyes reminded him. They were like dead men in the way they gazed. Glassy and vacant, their eyes were as the eyes of corpses. Perhaps their fantastic stories were true, and he had in reality been cast for all eternity upon a mirage island.

"Oh, Lord," he thought, "I'm getting as crazy as the rest of them. And yet the woman, the Spanish woman, seemed sane enough, and she believes their tales."

After breakfast he worked at putting up his tent, sweating in the copper glare of the sun, while Heywood went on fishing and Judd vanished into the woods with a bow and arrows. No sound came from the other hut. When he had finished erecting his tent, Patterson lay down in the shade inside of it, and found himself craving a cigarette with a passionate, abnormal longing. It was stuffy in the tent, and mosquitoes clustered round his hot face. He shut his eyes and tried to sleep, but sleep evaded him. And then, as he lay quietly in the oppressive darkness, his instincts, already sharpened by twenty-four hours' adventure, warned him that someone was watching him. He opened his eyes.

Outside, regarding him impassively, stood a small, slim man in dainty, dandified clothes of green-blue shot taffeta. These garments, consisting of a full-skirted, mincing coat and close-fitting breeches, were smeared with dirt, and seemed to Patterson highly unsuitable to desert-island life. The little man wore cascades of grubby lace dripping from his wrists, and rusty buckles on his pointed shoes. He bore himself like a dancing-master, and had no wig, which seemed odd to Patterson, who gaped at the gingery, close-shaven head revealing glimpses of bare skull like pinkish silk. The face of this man was long and narrow and candle-pale, with thin, dry lips and pointed ears. His flickering, expressionless eyes were green as flames; he blinked them constantly, showing whitish, sandy lashes. His hands were long, blanched and delicate, more beautiful than a woman's, and he wore on one finger a huge diamond ring, the twin to that other stone blazing upon the finger of Dona Ines. Patterson, disconcerted by the cold, unwavering eyes, scrambled to his feet and held out his hand. It was ignored, but the Captain bowed gracefully.

"Captain Micah Thunder, late of the *Black Joke,* and at your service."

He spoke in a high, affected, mincing voice.

"I have already," Patterson told him, "heard talk of you, Captain Thunder, and am, therefore, delighted to have this opportunity of meeting you."

"You're a damned liar," replied Captain Thunder, with a giggle. "My fame, I understand, has not, through some absurd mischance, been handed down throughout the ages, or so Judd informs me. They talk, I hear, of Flint and Kidd — even of Blackbeard, most clumsy bungler of all — but not of Thunder. And that, you know, is mighty odd, for without any desire to boast, I can only assure you, my young friend, that in the three years preceding the mutiny of my crew I was dreaded in all ports as the Avenger of the Main, and, indeed, I recollect taking during that period more than thirty merchantmen."

He sighed, giggled once more, and shook out the lace ruffles of his cuffs.

"Indeed, sir?" said Patterson respectfully. To himself he thought, in a sudden panic: "I must humor this man; he's worse than any of them."

For the Captain, with his conical, shaven head, his long, pale face, his deprecating giggle, his cold, greenish eyes and high, affected voice, seemed as he minced there in the sunshine most terribly like an animated corpse coquetting, grotesquely enough, in all the parrot-sheen of silken taffetas and frothing lace. This creature, this little strutting jackanapes, so bleached and frozen and emasculated, looked, indeed, as though a hundred and more years of living on the island had drained away his very life-blood, leaving a dummy, a vindictive, posturing dummy, clad in fine raiment, staring perpetually out to sea with greenish, fishy eyes. And something, perhaps the very essence of evil itself, a breath of cold and effortless vice, emanated from him to stink to Patterson like a rank and putrid smell. The odor of decay, perhaps; the very spirit of decay, for surely, in spite of sanity and common sense, this man should long ago have rotted, not in a coffin, but rather from a gibbet on Execution Dock.

And Dona Ines, creeping up softly behind him, seemed brighter, gayer, than a hummingbird, in contrast to her pale pirate. Receiving a signal from her eye, he knew that he must make no mention of an earlier meeting.

"My mistress, Dona Ines Samaniegos, of Santa Ana," announced the Captain, with a flourish.

"Your servant, madam," said Patterson formally.

And the lady, very grave and beautiful, ran her hand lightly over the Captain's sleeve and swept a curtsy, deep and billowing. She was not merry now, neither was she barefoot; she seemed haughty, and had shod herself in high-heeled, red shoes.

"This flower," said Captain Thunder casually, indicating his paramour with a flick of a white finger, "springs from a proud and splendid Castilian family. Is it not so, my heart? I took her when my fleet sacked Santa Ana, finding her myself, when my hands were steeped in blood above the wrists, praying in terror before a waxen, tinseled image of the Virgin. She was sixteen, and very timid, being fresh from convent. Before I wooed I was forced to tame her. When I had tamed her, I was still enamored, and for four years she sailed the Main as queen of my fleet. The *Black Joke,* my ship, and the Black Lady, as they called my woman (being accustomed to flaxen peasant maids from Devon), those were all I prized in life. My ship they took, my woman I have kept, and will continue to keep whilst we remain here."

The drawling voice was icy now, and the light eyes had become green stones. Patterson realized he was being warned. He answered lightly:

"And may I congratulate you, Captain, upon a lovely and most glorious prize?"

"Do you mind," said the Captain to Dona Ines, "when that little ape, Heywood, tried to take you, and I slit his throat?"

She nodded, her eyes very dark and lustrous.

The Captain turned to Patterson.

"There is no death on this island, sir, as you will discover for yourself, but it is possible to fight, and, fighting, to inflict wounds. A sorry business, very. I declare I regretted it, when I saw the poor creature gurgling in mortal agony. He was sick for many days. But, sooner or later, we all heal. However, I'm soft-hearted once my rage is appeased. And you will pray excuse me while I seek the shade. I'll leave madam here to entertain you for ten minutes. A change for her, a pleasant interlude for yourself. In ten minutes, then, my dove?"

Bowing, he retreated, walking away with pointed toes, more like a dancing-master than ever.

When he was out of earshot Patterson said impulsively: "I'm not enamored of your Captain!"

"And I," she said thoughtfully, "was once enamored of him for forty years."

"And now?" Patterson wanted to know.

"Now?" She scooped up some sand and let it sift through her fingers. "Oh, my poor young man, does anyone remain in love for all eternity? Do you really believe in that pretty legend?"

"Then you hate him?"

"Hate? No. You can neither hate nor love for a hundred years. I have suffered both, so I know, and tried to kill myself three times. Oh, yes, there is not much that I cannot tell you about love. One does not live as long as I have lived without learning wisdom."

"And please tell me, Dona Ines," begged Patterson, "what you have learned about life in a hundred and forty years."

"A hundred and sixty," she corrected. "I was twenty when cast up here. What have I learned? One thing above all — to live without emotion. Love, hate, tedium — those are all words, very unimportant words. They are nothing. I like to eat when I am hungry, sleep when I am tired, swim when the sun is hot. All that is good, because it is just enough. I used to think — I never think now. I was mad, you know, for a little time, five years or so, because I thought too much. But soon I was cured. That was when, having both loved Micah and hated him, at last he sickened me. I imagined I could not bear that. But you see I was wrong."

She laughed, shaking back a tress of her hair, and he knew that, with death, she had also lost her soul and humanity. She was, as she had said, empty, drained of all

29

emotion; she was as sterile mentally, this lovely lady, as the parakeets chattering above her head. But she was very beautiful.

"And the Captain?" he inquired. "Is it rude to ask what his feelings are toward you?"

"Indeed, no!" And she laughed again. "The Captain is still a man, although he should have been dead long ago. Being a man, he has need of a woman sometimes. Being a man, he is determined that other men shall not take that woman. That is all. Apart from that, like us all, he is petrified."

And then, although the ten minutes were not up, she heard Judd coming up the hill and slipped like a bright shadow to her own hut.

Days passed slowly on the island. One day was like another. Always the sun poured brilliantly upon sapphire seas, gleaming sands, jeweled foliage. Macaws flashed like darting rainbows through the dusky green of jungle arches, the fruit hung coral-bright from trees whose blossoms flung out trailing creepers gayer, more gaudy, than the patterns of vivid Spanish shawls. And yet it seemed to Patterson after two months that all this radiant beauty was evil and poisoned, like a sweet fruit rotten at the core. What should have been paradise was only a pretty hell. Slowly, reluctantly, he had been forced to accept the island for what it was according to his comrades. He now believed, although shamefacedly, that Thunder and Dona Ines had lived there since the mutiny of the *Black Joke,* that Heywood had been marooned in the last century for insubordination, that Judd had emerged from the wreck of the *Titanic.* And yet, obstinately, he still clung to the idea of escape. And then, once away from the island's shores, he would regain mortality, he would wrap mortality about him like a cloak.

Meanwhile, he noticed one or two curious facts. His clothes, after eight weeks' rough living, were almost as good as new. It was no longer necessary for him to shave more than once a week. And, once, Judd, climbing a palm in search of coconuts, had slipped, crashing on his head to what seemed certain death fifty feet below and had been picked up suffering from nothing worse than slight concussion. This accident shook his faith more than anything else that he saw.

They lived comfortably enough on fish, home-baked bread, fruit, coconuts, and the flesh of young pigs found in the jungle. Patterson learned to shoot with a bow and arrow, and to tell the time by the sun and stars. He learned to be patient with Heywood, who was halfwitted, and he learned to search for turtles' eggs in a temperature of ninety-nine in the shade. He learned, too, to treat Captain Thunder with respect and Dona Ines with formality.

Sometimes, the Captain, a reserved, sour-tempered man, would unbend, and fingering his cutlass, tell stories of life as a buccaneer of the Spanish Main. Terrible stories, these, vile, filthy, sadistic stories of murder and vice, plunder and torture, and fiendish, cold-blooded, ferocious revenge. Told in his drawling, affected voice, they became nauseating, and yet Dona Ines listened peacefully enough, her dark eyes soft and velvety, her red, silken mouth calmer than an angel's. Sometimes she would look up and nod, and say:

"Oh, yes, Micah; I remember that, don't I? I was with you then, wasn't I?"

"You were, my dove, my heart. If you remember, I burnt your hand in the flame of my candle until you swooned, because you affronted me by asking mercy for those dogs."

And she would laugh.

"I was foolish, was I not, Micah? For what did it matter?"

Patterson, loathing these conversations, was, nevertheless, forced to listen because at night there was really nothing else to do. Always before in his life he had accepted books without question as being quite naturally part of his life; now that he had none, the lack of them appalled him. He tried to write, scratching a diary on strips of bark, but the effort was not successful. Nor did his companions do much to ameliorate the loneliness of his situation. He preferred Judd to the others because Judd was young and gay, and comparatively untouched by the sinister, dragging life of the island, yet there were times when even Judd seemed to withdraw himself, to become watchful, remote, secretive. Patterson learned to recognize these as the interludes when his friend, pitifully afraid, thought in a panic of the future that lay ahead for him.

Heywood was sulky and monosyllabic. The Captain, so cynical and depraved, with his vicious mind, his giggle, and his will of iron, had revolted Patterson from the first. Only Dona Ines, with her vivid face and her beautiful, empty, animal mind, seemed to him restful and gracious, like some handsome, well-behaved child, in this crazy world of sunshine and plenty and despair. For this reason she began to haunt him at night, so that he was unable to sleep, and he longed, not so much to make love to her as to rest his head against her and to feel her cool hand upon his forehead, soothing him, that he might forget for a few hours. But Dona Ines was watched so carefully that it seemed impossible to speak to her alone.

And then one day, when he had been on the island for more than three months and was in a mood of black depression, he encountered her in the woods.

He had wandered there in search of shade, aimless, solitary, and disconcerted. She was gathering moss, on her knees, her bright skirts kilted. Stars of sunlight, dripping through the green and matted tent of foliage, cast flickering, dappled shadows upon the amber of her neck and arms. When she heard his footsteps, she turned to look at him, smiling very wisely, her head turned to one side.

"May I speak to you," he asked her, "without being snarled at by the Captain?"

"But of course," she said. "Micah and Heywood went out an hour ago to fish on the other side of the island."

He sat down beside her on the green froth of the moss.

"Ines," he began, and he had never called her by her

name before, "I wonder if you will be patient and listen to me for a moment?"

She nodded, saying nothing; she was never very glib of words.

"It's this," he said, encouraged; "perhaps, being so much wiser, you can help me . . . It's a bad day with me; I've got the horrors. Today I believe all your crazy stories, and, try as I will, I can't escape from them . . . today I feel the island is shutting me in, and I want to run away from the island. What am I to do?"

"You must begin," she told him, "by making yourself more stupid than you are. Oh, it is easy for Heywood, more easy even for Judd. For you it is difficult. Can you not think only of today? Must you let your mind race on ahead?"

Her voice was murmurous and very soft. He said, after a pause:

"It would be easier, I think, if I might talk to you more often. Time, the time of the island, has touched you scarcely at all. With you one almost ceases to feel the horror."

"If it were not for Micah I would talk to you, yes, whenever you want. But you know how I am situated."

"Oh, don't think I'm trying to make love to you," he told her impatiently, "it's not that. It's only that you bring me peace — you're so beautiful, so restful."

Dona Ines looked away from him towards the green twilight.

"Perhaps that wasn't very polite of me. In fact, it was clumsily expressed. Let me try once more — listen, Ines, you're sanity, loveliness, a bright angel in a mad world. I respect you as I would respect a saint. But I want to be with you, I want to talk to you. I'm lonely when you're not there — I need your protection."

Dona Ines looked away from him towards the green twilight of the trees. His eyes devoured her dark clear-cut profile. She said at length, speaking very slowly in her grave, beautiful voice:

"*Mi querido,* I can't grant your request. I am too afraid

of Micah, and perhaps I am afraid of something else . . . listen, if I saw much of you I might forget that I should be a dead woman. I might forget that my heart is cold and my mind empty. I might wake up again, and I don't want to wake up. I am afraid of life, after so many years. And already you are making my sleep a little restless."

She turned her face towards him and he saw that the red flower of her mouth was trembling. A bright drop, that might have been a tear, save that she never wept, hung like a jewel upon the shadow of her lashes. Yet her face was radiant, transfigured, more sparkling than the sunshine.

Straightway, Patterson forgot about respect and saints and Captain Thunder, and kissed her on the lips.

For one enchanted moment she was acquiescent, then pushed him away, hiding her face in her hands. And he, realizing the horror that lay ahead for both, felt more like weeping than rejoicing.

"Go away," she whispered, "go away before you make me hate you for what you are doing. A moment ago you talked of peace: do you realize that you are stealing mine?"

He stammered, scarcely knowing what he said:

"There are better dreams."

"Not here," she told him; "here there are no dreams but bad ones, and so it is safer not to dream at all. Please, please, go away."

"Ines," he said eagerly, "I will go away — we'll both go away. If I build a boat, or a raft, and provision her, will you trust yourself to me? We'll escape — we may drown, but I promise you — "

He stopped. In her tired yet vivid eyes he had suddenly surprised, for the first time, the dead, haunted look that so much disconcerted him when he glimpsed it in the others' gaze. It was as if she retreated very far away, drawing down a blind.

She said, patiently, as one speaking to a child:

"Oh, my friend, please don't be so foolish . . .I have

tried, we have all tried, so many times. And it hurts, to fail so often."

"Then you won't come?"

She climbed slowly to her feet, brushing moss from her bright skirts. Then she shook her black, silken head twice, very emphatically.

"No. I will not come with you."

"Then," said Patterson, "since I can't stay here to watch you with the Captain, I shall escape alone. Won't you change your mind?"

She came near to him and put her hand for one moment upon his shoulder.

"No. I'll not change my mind."

And with a swishing of silk, that sounded strange enough in that tropical, emerald glade, she left him to his thoughts, and his thoughts were agony.

For weeks he slaved in secret to build a great rakish-looking solid raft that grew slowly into shape as it lay concealed amid the dusky green of overhanging branches. He had told no one save Dona Ines of his reso-lution to escape. The reason was simple; in his heart of hearts, he dreaded their bitter mockery, their cynical dis-belief in any possible salvation from the trap of the island. Yet he still had faith; once aboard his raft and he would be for ever borne away from those perilous and beckoning shores; he might find death, but this he did not really mind, although he much preferred the thought of human life, life with Ines. And then he had to remind himself that the Spanish woman was a thing of dust, to crumble away at the first contact with normal humanity, and that he would, in any event, be better without her, since she meant another mouth to feed.

But he still desired her, and it was as though the Cap-tain knew, for she was very seldom left alone. And so he toiled in secret, and in his spare time nursed Judd, who lay sick of a poisonous snake-bite that swelled his foot, and turned it black, and would have meant death in any other land.

Once, when his raft was nearly completed, he caught

Ines alone on the beach, where, against a background of golden rock, she fed a swirling silver mass of seagulls. The birds wheeled, crying harshly, and Dona Ines smiled. She wore a knot of scarlet passion-flowers in the dark satin of her hair. Patterson, determined not to miss a second alone with her, advanced triumphantly across the sands: the seagulls scattered.

"Look, you've frightened my birds," she complained indignantly.

"Never mind the birds — they can see you whenever they want. I can't. Ines, haven't you changed your mind about coming with me?"

She shook her head.

"Ines, please, *please* listen! Even if we drown out there together, wouldn't it be better than this?"

"Oh, yes, if we drowned. But we should not drown. We should come back here — to Micah — and then our lives would not be worth living."

"My life," he said, "isn't worth living now, not while I have to see you with that creature night and day."

"Be quiet," she warned in a low voice.

Patterson turned, following her eyes. Behind, only just out of earshot, stood the Captain, watching them sardonically. The breeze lifted the skirts of his green taffeta coat, ballooning them about his slender body. The green, too, seemed reflected in his face, so pale was it; paler, more waxen, even, than a corpse-candle.

"Are you also feeding the birds, Patterson?" inquired the Captain softly.

"No. I am looking for turtles' eggs."

"How many have you found?" the Captain wanted to know. Patterson felt rather foolish.

"None — yet."

"Then you had better make haste, unless you wish to fast for dinner. Come, my rose."

And Captain Thunder turned away indifferently, followed by Dona Ines, who walked behind him obediently, her head bent, with no backward look.

That night Patterson thought he heard weeping in the

hut that lay only a few hundred yards from his own, and he crouched, perspiring, sleepless, for many hours, until it was dark no longer, and bars of rose and lemon streaked the sky. Then he got up and went forth to the woods to complete his preparation for escape.

He had rigged up a sail upon his raft and had already floated her on a narrow lagoon that led towards the sea. He was taking with him three barrels of water, a barrel of bread, his fishing-tackle, a blanket, and a flint and tinder. He knew he would not starve, since fish were plentiful, but he was aware that he would, probably, unless he were fortunate enough to end in a shark's belly, die of a thirst that must endure for many days of torment in a pitiless and scorching heat. Yet he could not wait, he must start at once, before the sun was up, before the first sign of life from the hut nestling on the cliffs behind him. And so, at a moment's notice, he took his departure, nervous and weary and taut with anxiety, drifting with his raft like some dark bird against the misty violet-blue of the lagoon at dawn.

Everything was silent; trees and cliff and sky, the limpid reflection of these in the glassy waters of the lagoon; even the monkeys and the chattering parakeets, all were frozen into a breathless silence that seemed to watch, aghast, the reckless departure of this creature determined at all costs to break away from their sorrowful eternity.

Soon it was daylight, and the sun beat gilded wings, and Patterson drew near to the sea. A curve in the lagoon showed him the tawny cliff, and above it the huts. From the Captain's hut came a finger of blue smoke that climbed, very straight, into the bright clearness of the air.

"Goodbye, Ines."

And he was surprised to find how little pain there was for him in this parting. He reminded himself once more that she was a ghost, a creature of dust.

He passed the rocks and was soon outside, away from the island, on the sea itself. The ripples danced, white-crested, as though laced with silver. Patterson fished with success. He tried to fry his breakfast and, failing, devoured it half-raw, with a hunch of bread. It was very appetizing. After breakfast he lay watching, with ecstasy, a stiff breeze swell his sail.

Already the island seemed to have receded. Patterson gazed with exultation at the coral-whiteness of its strand, the radiant green foliage of the trees. An hour before, and these had been loathsome to him; now that they belonged to the past he grimaced at them and waved his hand.

The raft drifted on.

The sea was kind to him that day, he thought, so innocent and gay and tinted like forget-me-nots. Despite himself, despite his almost certain death, he found his mind flitting towards England, and his life there, as though he were fated to be saved.

He turned towards the island, gleaming in the distance. "Farewell!"

It was cry of defiance.

And, then, in a moment, like thunder splintering from the sky, came sudden and shattering catastrophe. He was never very clear as to what actually occurred. All he knew was that from peace and beauty there emerged swift chaos. A wall of water, all towering solid green and ribbed with foam, reared suddenly from the tranquil seas to bar his path like some great ogre's castle arisen by magic, huge, destructive, carven of emerald. Then there was darkness and a tremendous roaring sound, and the raft seemed to buck like a frightened horse. He heard the ripping of his sail and then he was pitched through the air and something seemed to split his head and he knew no more.

When he awoke, the sun beat hot upon his temples. He felt sick, his limbs ached, and he groaned. He lay still, his eyes closed, and tried to remember what had happened. And then he heard a sound that might have been some dirge sighed by the breeze, a soft murmuring music that seemed to him familiar. The song of the island. He knew, then, that he was back upon the island. He had no need to open his eyes.

"Oh, God," he sighed.

And the sweat trickled down his face.

And then, inevitably, sounding close to his ear, the sneering, hateful voice of Captain Thunder.

"Home so soon, my young friend? No, you would not believe, would you? You knew too much . . ."

Patterson made no sign of life. Back once more on the island. For all eternity . . . the island . . . and then the murmuring song swelled louder, louder, mocking him, laughing a little, as Ines had laughed when he told her he was going to escape. The song of the island! And he must hear it forever! He opened his eyes to find the Captain looking at him cynically.

"Now that you understand there is no escape," said the Captain, "perhaps you will not take it amiss if I venture to criticize your manner toward Madam Ines . . ."

But Patterson was not listening.

Anty Bligh

JOHN MASEFIELD

One night in the tropics I was "farmer" in the middle watch — that is, I had neither "wheel" nor "look-out" to stand during the four hours I stayed on deck. We were running down the Northeast Trades, and the ship was sailing herself, and the wind was gentle, and it was very still on board, the blocks whining as she rolled, and the waves talking, and the wheel-chains clanking, and a light noise aloft of pattering and tapping. The sea was all pale with moonlight, and from the lamp-room door, where the watch was mustered, I could see a red stain on the water from the port sidelight. The mate was walking the weather side of the poop, while the boatswain sat on the booby-hatch humming an old tune and making a sheath for his knife. The watch were lying on the deck, out of the moonlight, in the shadow of the break of the poop. Most of them were sleeping, propped against the bulkhead. One of them was singing a new chanty he had made, beating out the tune with his pipe-stem, in a quiet little voice that fitted the silence of the night.

Ha! Ha! Why don't you blow?
O ho!
Come, roll him over,

repeated over and over again, as though he could never tire of the beauty of the words and the tune.

Presently he got up from where he was and came over to me. He was one of the best men we had aboard — a young Dane who talked English like a native. We had had business dealings during the dog watch, some hours before, and he had bought a towel from me, and I had let him have it cheap, as I had one or two to spare. He sat down beside me, and began a conversation, discussing a number of sailor matters, such as the danger of sleeping in the moonlight, the poison supposed to lurk in cold boiled potatoes, and the folly of having a good time in port. From these we passed to the consideration of piracy, coloring our talk with anecdotes of pirates. "Ah, there was no pirate," said my friend, "like old Anty Bligh of Bristol. Dey hung old Anty Bligh on Fernando Noronha, where the prison is. And he walked after, Anty Bligh did. That shows how bad he was." "How did he walk?" I asked. "Let's hear about him." "Oh, they jest hung him," replied my friend, "like they'd hang anyone else, and they left him on the gallows after. Dey thought old Anty was too bad to bury, I guess. And there was a young Spanish Captain on the island in dem times. Frisco Baldo his name was. He was a terror. So the night dey hung old Anty, Frisco was getting gorgeous wid some other captains in a kind of drinking shanty. And de other captains say to Frisco, 'I bet you a month's pay you won't go out and put a rope round Anty's legs.' And 'I bet you a new suit of clothes you won't put a bowline around Anty's ankles.' And 'I bet you a cask of wine you won't put Anty's feet in a noose.' 'I bet you I will,' says Frisco Baldo. 'What's a dead man anyways,' he says, 'and why should I be feared of Anty Bligh? Give us a rope,' he says, 'and I'll lash him up with seven turns, like a sailor would a hammock.' So he drinks up his glass, and gets a stretch of rope, and out he

41

goes into the dark to where the gallows stood. It was a new moon dat time, and it was as dark as the end of a sea-boot and as blind as the toe. And the gallows was right down by the sea dat time because old Anty Bligh was a pirate. So he comes up under the gallows, and there was old Anty Bligh hanging. And 'Way-ho, Anty,' he says. 'Lash and carry, Anty,' he says. 'I'm going to lash you up like a hammock.' So he slips a bowline around Anty's feet." . . . Here my informant broke off his yarn to light his pipe. After a few puffs he went on.

"Now when a man's hanged in hemp," he said gravely, "you mustn't never touch him with what killed him, for fear he should come to life on you. You mark that. Don't you forget it. So soon as ever Frisco Baldo sets that bowline around Anty's feet, old Anty looks down from his noose, and though it was dark, Frisco Baldo could see him plain enough. 'Thank you, young man,' and Anty; 'just cast that turn off again. Burn my limbs,' he says, 'if you ain't got a neck! And now climb up here,' he says, 'and take my neck out of the noose. I'm as dry as a cask of split peas.' Now you may guess that Frisco Baldo feller he came out all over in a cold sweat. 'Git a gait on you,' says Anty. 'I ain't going to wait up here to please you.' So Frisco Baldo climbs up, and a sore job he had of it getting the noose off Anty. 'Get a gait on you,' says Anty, 'and go easy with them clumsy hands of yours. You'll give me a sore throat,' he says, 'the way you're carrying on. Now don't let me fall plop,' says Anty. 'Lower away handsomely,' he says, 'I'll make you a weary one if you let me fall plop,' he says. So Frisco lowers him away handsomely, and Anty comes to the ground, with the rope off him, only he still had his head to one side like he'd been hanged. 'Come here to me,' he says. So Frisco Baldo goes over to him. And Anty he jest put one arm round his neck, and gripped him tight and cold. 'Now march,' he says; 'march me down to the grog shop and get me a dram. None of your six-water dollops, neither,' he says; 'I'm as dry as a foul block,' he says. So Frisco and Anty they go to the grog shop, and all the while Anty's cold fingers was playing down Frisco's neck. And when they got to her grog shop der captains was all fell asleep. So Frisco takes a bottle of rum and Anty laps it down like he'd been used to it. 'Ah!' he says, 'thank ye,' he says, 'and now down to the Mole with ye,' he says, 'and we'll take a boat,' he says; 'I'm gone to England,' he says, 'to say good-bye to me mother.' So Frisco he come out all over in a cold sweat, for he was feared of the sea; but Anty's cold fingers was fiddling his neck, so he t'ink he better go. And when dey come to der Mole there was a boat there — one of those perry-acks, as they call them — and Anty he says, 'You take the oars,' he says. 'I'll steer,' he says, 'and every time you catch a crab,' he says, 'you'll get such a welt as you'll remember.' So Frisco shoves her off and rows out of the harbor, with old Anty Bligh at the tiller, telling him to put his beef on and to watch out he didn't catch no crabs. And he rowed, and he rowed, and he rowed, and every time he caught a crab — whack! he had it over the sconce with the tiller. And her perry-ack it went a great holy big skyoot, ninety knots in der quarter of an hour, so they soon sees the Bull Point Light and der Shutter Light, and then the lights of Bristol. 'Oars,' said Anty. 'Lie on yours oars,' he says; 'we got way enough.' Then dey make her fast to a dock-side and dey goes ashore, and Anty has his arm around Frisco's neck, and 'March,' he says; 'step lively,' he says; 'for Johnny comes marching home,' he says. By and by they come to a little house with a light in the window. 'Knock at the door,' says Anty. So Frisco knocks, and in they go. There was a fire burning in the room and some candles on the table, and there, by the fire, was a very ugly woman in a red flannel dress, and she'd a ring in her nose and a black cutty pipe between her lips. 'Good evening, mother,' says Anty. 'I come home,' he says. But the old woman she just looks at him but never says nothing. 'It's your son Anty that's come home to you,' he says again. So she looks at him again and, 'Aren't you ashamed of yourself, Anty,' she says, 'coming home the way you are? Don't you repent your goings-on?' she says. 'Dying disgraced,' she says, 'in a foreign land, with none to lay you out.' 'Mother,' he says, 'I repent in blood,' he says. 'You'll not deny me my rights?' he says. 'Not since you repent,' she says. 'Them as repents I got no quarrels with. You was always a bad one, Anty,' she says, 'but I hoped you'd come home in the end. Well, and now you're come,' she says. 'And I must bathe that throat of yours,' she says. 'It looks as though you been hit by something.' 'Be quick, mother,' he says; 'it's after midnight now,' he says.

"So she washed him in wine, the way you wash a corpse, and put him in a white linen shroud, with a wooden cross on his chest, and two silver pieces on his eyes, and a golden marigold between his lips. And together they carried him to the perry-ack and laid him in the stern sheets. 'Give way, young man,' she says; 'give way like glory. Pull, my heart of blood,' she says, 'or we'll have the dawn on us.' So he pulls, that Frisco Baldo does, and the perry-ack makes big southing — a degree a minute — and they comes ashore at the Mole just as the hens was settling to their second sleep. 'To the churchyard,' says the old woman; 'you take his legs.' So they carries him to the churchyard at the double. 'Get a gait on you,' says Anty. 'I feel the dawn in my bones,' he says. 'My wraith'll chase you if you ain't in time,' he says. And there was an empty grave, and they put him in, and shoveled in the clay, and the old woman poured out a bottle on the top of it. 'It's holy water,' she says, 'It's make his wraith rest easy.' Then she runs down to the sea's edge and gets into the perry-ack. And immediately she was hull down beyond the horizon, and the sun came up out of the sea, and the cocks cried cock-a-doodle in the henroost, and Frisco Baldo falls down into a swound. He was a changed man from that out."

"Lee for brace," said the mate above us. "Quit your chinning there, and go forward to the rope."

The Red Swimmer

ROBERT BLOCH

1

Luke Treach bowed and smirked in the Spanish sunlight as his distinguished passengers came up the gangplank. His curled and scented hair rippled most elegantly in the Caribbean breeze; a breeze that lifted the dainty ruffles at the wrists and throat of his rich velvet coat.

He made a fine figure of a Spanish gentleman, did English Luke Treach that merry morning, as he stood stroking his spade beard to hide the malicious smile which he had managed to erase from his lean, browned face, but which still persisted about his cruelly thin lips.

Captain Luke Treach bowed then, as the old grandee and his daughter ascended, bowed low a second time when the white-bearded gentleman addressed him as "Captain Obispo." Treach gazed covertly into the aged, aristocratic face of his passenger, then allowed his glance to embrace the figure of the woman. Abruptly he started, jerked erect.

Now Captain Treach had gazed on the fine ladies of old England, yes, and the plump, rosy-cheeked barmaids, too; he had seen the dusky Caribs that danced upon the beach; in Cuba and Barbados and the Antilles there were dark-eyed Spanish girls that lured with sly laughter, and mulatto or mestizo maidens savage in the charm of their delight. Captain Treach had known many women, but there was none to compare with the girl who now stood before him.

Her hair was ebony over ivory forehead, her eyes dark diamonds and lips warm ruby red. These comparisons came naturally to the Captain, for his covetous nature was ever ruling. But never had it ruled him as it did at this moment; he wanted this girl, with her maiden beauty of face and her slim, young, untaught body curved and lissome for delight. Young, dark, smiling — Body of Christ! The captain swore inwardly as his lips shaped their polite greeting.

Courteously he welcomed Señor Montelupe and his daughter to the ship. Yes, their cabins were in readiness, and he trusted that they would be comfortable. But certainly, they would cast off at once, and might the Blessed Savior speed them on a prosperous, untroubled voyage to Mother Spain.

Guns and men there? Yes, for there were pirates — cursed scoundrels, these buccaneers; and if they attacked, it was best to be ready — though Gracious God forbid!

Captain Treach escorted Señor Montelupe and his daughter to their cabins, then returned to watch his bullies bring up the chests and bags his passengers brought with them; chests and bags — silk, satin, gold, jewels.

It made Treach smile. He smiled again as he thought of pirates. This second smile made his wolfish face assume an almost beneficent aspect, for it was the charitable smile of one well pleased with himself. And Captain Luke Treach, now known as Captain Obispo, but more famous as "English Luke," had good reason to respect his cleverness.

First, he had taken the galleon. Few men had been lost, much wealth gained. After efficiently disposing of the crew and their captain, he had hit upon a brilliant idea. Instead of careening off some inlet and waiting until intermediaries reached him to buy and dispose of his loot, he would seek a regular port.

The galleon *Golden Crest* had been bound for Vera Cruz. Very well, he would sail for Vera Cruz, rig himself out in the captain's garb, and dress his men according to Spanish style. He and his mates spoke the tongue well — with a little careful disguise they would pass as Spaniards. On reaching port they could dispose of their cargo, cash in the booty, and sail away again swiftly with no one the wiser. Better still, the appearance of the ship would preclude any fuss such as might be occasioned by its disappearance; there would be no reprisal, no scouring of the seas by Spanish fleets in search of English Luke the buccaneer.

A noble idea, Luke Treach thought at the time. And it had worked. With the common seamen kept on shipboard against any betrayal, he and his lieutenants had entered town. Officials had even been permitted to land on the ship and inspect it. Trade had been accomplished without suspicion, and Luke was ready to sail.

Then Commandante Portiz had asked him to take passengers. At first Luke demurred, until he had learned that Señor Montelupe and his daughter were returning to Spain with all their wealth. They wanted to leave at once; he had been an official and there was some scandal.

Wealthy? Scandal meant money — it would be brought aboard ship. Luke Treach agreed, and the affair was settled.

Now they were ready to set sail, and more luck had befallen the clever captain. This daughter of Montelupe — she was a new treasure, another prize.

So Treach smiled indulgently when he thought of his cunning and what it had gained for him.

But ever business-like, his musing abruptly ceased and his thoughts turned to the exigencies of the moment. He gave the orders to lift anchor in the clarion voice for which he was justly famous.

A moment later he proved his English erudition in the matter of cursing, as he loosed a fine volley of oaths at the half-naked seamen straining at the ropes on deck.

Then Captain Treach sauntered below, gentleman-like, pausing merely to kick aside the sailor who chanced to stray across his path carrying a sparpiece. He rapped discreetly on the cabin door, surreptitiously spat out his plug of tobacco, and entered the Montelupe quarters.

The old man greeted him, but Captain Treach had eyes only for the appointments he found therein; for the piles of brocaded and jeweled cloth now removed from their wrappings and stacked against the wall; for the jewel caskets and the ingots in the rough seabags.

And then he stared at Ynez Montelupe, stared with the selfsame avidity. All the while he spoke graciously enough to the old fool, but his gaze burned a blush into the girl's cheeks, and he thought of the night — not to-night, but the next, when they would be past hail or chance of pursuit.

He chatted for perhaps an hour. Yes, he had an excellent voyage out. No, his passage had been free of storm or danger from freebooters, though that cursed Blackbeard was reputed to be in these waters. He fabricated news from Spain, glibly explained the death at sea of the ship's *padre*. He was forced to do most of the talking, for the dotish old man merely stared at him with his liquid, curiously youthful brown eyes. Treach didn't like that stare; it held a faint tinge of contempt or amusement; but then, he would not have to put up with it for long. On this thought he took his departure, after graciously asking their attendance at dinner in his own quarters.

Upstairs the gentlemanly mood left him, and he called for rum and his lieutenant, Roger Groat. Groat shambled into his cabin, mouthing oaths and damnations because the lace frippery at his wrists dangled into his tankard while he was drinking. The red-bearded lieutenant made it known that he was sick of wearing these thrice-damned Spanish spangles, and the men were tired of the masquerade as well. They grumbled because they weren't put ashore to amuse themselves with the proceeds of the plunder.

To this information Captain Treach listened with occasional frowns. Then he told Groat that they would sail on only another day, dispose of the old fool, and head in for the nearest island a few hours off their position at that time.

"Rich, isn't he?" muttered Groat. "Blackie and Tom swore he had bullion in those bags o' his."

He chuckled, then snickered as he brought a hairy paw down on the table at which they sat.

"And the girl's a beauty. A beauty, by God, and there'll be rare sport — "

Captain Treach raised his hand. A slight gesture, but the accompanying frown was enough to quell the big man into silence.

"The girl is mine," he snapped. "Mine alone. The swag we'll divide according to our articles, but the girl is mine.

"You and the others will have your fill of wenching when we put in, but she's mine."

Groat could not restrain a horse chuckle.

"I don't envy her, at that. Remember Lucy, on the English ship we took? When you finished with her and Salvatore tried to take her, you flayed the lass. And I warrant this one would prefer the crew's sport to the other end."

Captain Treach smiled. "Tell Salvatore I want wine for dinner. Amontillado. I want my guests to eat, drink, and be merry tonight."

They both laughed.

They both laughed. This Captain Obispo was certainly a witty man. And tonight he was outdoing himself. Señorita Ynez found her first instinctive dislike fading, though she still felt a tinge of strange panic whenever his beady eyes rested too intently upon her face or bosom.

As for Señor Montelupe, his taciturnity waned under the brandy and the mellow amontillado sherry. His reserve down, he proceeded to let his host guide the conversation into personal channels.

Captain Treach asked him about his duties in Vera Cruz; learned that the old man had held a secretarial post for years and owned several lucrative mines. There had been a scandal of sorts . . .

Money, the captain presumed. No, not exactly money. The old man's reticence held him silent for a moment, but the wine, the courtesy, the mood urged him on. His bright eyes grew shadowy as he spoke.

There was — was the captain a church-goer?

Something in the shadowed eyes cued Treach to ignore the natural lie and speak truly. No, he was not a son of the Mother Church.

That was well, said Señor Montelupe. For there was a charge against him, a charge of sorcery.

Yes, the Black Arts, as ignorant fools called them — the mantic arts. He had studied with the Moorish masters in Spain as a youth; not wizardry or witchcraft, but the true magics that lie in nature; aeromancy, the controlling of winds; hydromancy, divination and command of waters; pyromancy, the lore of fire. It was science, not sorcery, which he sought to rule, and the ancient Moors held secrets of natural wisdom known to seers before Solomon.

Here in this new world he had availed himself of his governmental position to study certain things; it would be wise for one so old to take heed of the Elixir Vitae, the Elixir of Life.

And native blood was cheap; slaves and peons died by

the dozens in the mines each day, perished by flogging and torture. He had meant no harm; he wanted to kill no one, but merely to study the blood of a few slaves, to experiment with revivification of the dead — that did no harm. And he *had* discovered things — marvelous secrets, gathered from the wisdom of Egyptis, the Orient, the Arab sages. In his hands he would use his knowledge for good, not evil.

But the natives complained, the people whispered, and the *alcalde* told the *padre*, who in turn brought tidings to the Commandante. And so Señor Montelupe had given up his post, taken his daughter — his wife was dead these many years, alas! — and departed for home.

Luke listened, with a polite show of interest. No need to antagonize the old duffer. He and his talk of magic — but then, what could one expect from a bloody Spaniard? — those fools were all alike with their Inquisition, and witch-burning, and alchemy.

Alchemy! The thought crossed his mind even as he nodded in polite assent to the grandee's words. Alchemy — the transmutation of base metals into gold, wasn't it? Perhaps this stupid Southern dog knew something. Best to draw him out.

Luke drew him out, aided by further drafts of wine. He politely hinted that a man of Señor Montelupe's wisdom must have uncovered secrets in his quest of baleful knowledge.

Señor Montelupe stroked his gray beard as he replied that he had uncovered secrets. His eyes flamed with a bright gleam of fanaticism as he leaned across the great cabin-table.

He, Montelupe, had succeeded in his experiments. Men had sought the Elixir of Life for centuries untold, without avail. Charm, incantation, invocation — all methods had failed. But he had come to a new world, and there his efforts had been crowned with triumphs. It was a great discovery; much toil and study had gone into it, and not a little blood. It was not generally known, but his wife had died from an injection of a spurious Elixir he had compounded in earlier studies. Since then the tragic failure had spurred him on, and many slaves had been sacrificed to the attainment of perfection. But he had done it — there was a vial filled with a golden liquid; not the mythical water of poor Ponce de Leon's Fountain of Youth, but the veritable *Elixir Vitae.* Its compoundment had cost Señor Montelupe many years of his life, but now when he returned to Spain with his wealth, he and his daughter would be insured eternity — eternity in which to study, to seek further wisdom.

Luke Treach frowned and swore damnation to himself. The blasted idiot was mad! No alchemical secrets here, no Philosopher's Stone, or anything real; only this demented gibberish about some crazy scheme of perpetual life. The Spanish dog bored him; for that he would pay on the morrow. And she would pay, too — Ynez, listening with a cryptic smile that implied belief in her father's words, and a covert glimmer in her eyes which proclaimed that she thought the captain an ignorant fool, incapable of understanding the magnitude of her sire's secrets.

Yes, he would pay, and she would pay — though in sweeter coinage.

With that thought hidden in his politely-phrased adieu, Luke Treach strode up on deck for a breath of fresh air; air untainted by this fool's talk of wizardry and enchantment.

He checked the position, oversaw the change of watch at the wheel, and retired to sleep against the morrow's sport.

Night clouds had scudded before the dawn, and the sun ruled azure southern heavens ere he awoke. The cabin window showed him the beauty of sea and sky, but his ears heard sounds most unlovely.

This was the day, and the men were drunk. Groat had evidently broken out the rum.

Cursing, Treach ran up on deck, and found shambles.

The *Golden Crest* drifted, unpiloted. Laughing, gleeful men overran the ship, moving about at will or clustering before the broached casks that stood upon the after-deck. The English sea-dogs had abandoned their Spanish costumes in favor of pirate regalia, or utter nakedness.

Treach saw his steward, Salvatore, slopping rum over his maroon coat with the white piping, then wiping his red mouth with the lacy sleeve that had once graced the arm of a Portuguese admiral of war. He saw Roger Groat slapping his naked, tattooed thighs with the flat of a cutlass as he danced about "One-Light" Samuel Slew, whose black eye-patch was the sole incongruous note in the ensemble he wore — the grotesque finery of some silken lady whose denuded body had long since passed to the mercies of the sharks. The rest roared and bellowed forth crude gibes, or shouted toasts over the swelling of their tankards.

Treach paused. The men had broken discipline, but they were in jovial mood and order could be restored. But what matter? Their drinking could have waited until night, as planned, but a few hours made no difference now. Let them have their sport. And he — now he could go below and seek Ynez.

He went, smiling.

Ynez and her father were staring out of the window, their eyes veiled with perplexity.

"What does this mean, Captain?" asked the old man, and Treach entered. Then his face betrayed that he knew the answer.

For Treach had entered without knocking, and he had entered not as Captain Obispo, but as English Luke — swaggering, his smile a sneer.

"What does this mean?" Ynez echoed, in a faint voice that trailed away beneath the intensity of Treach's stare.

Treach laughed.

"Mean? It means a lot, I fancy. Firstly, that you've made a mistake in taking passage with us. Ye see, we've changed our colors — we're an English crew, not Spanish, and we fly still a third flag today, I fancy. Have ye

53

heard of the Jolly Roger?"

He grinned. His bow was a mockery of previous courtliness.

"So it's English Luke Treach at yer service today, my friends."

"Buccaneer!" The old Spaniard scowled, then drew Ynez close to his side. She trembled in her father's arms, but her terror invested her with a weird enhancing of beauty; the beauty of a frightened fawn. Luke stared at the softness of her black eyes, at the trembling of her fear-taut body.

He stared so closely that he did not see the sudden gesture of the old man — did not observe his hand slip a tiny golden vial from his pocket to the bodice of his daughter.

He stared at the girl, and then he began to laugh. The laugh told all. It told Señor Montelupe that he need not waste words in threats or pleas. It told Ynez Montelupe that which made her crimson with shame.

Laughing, the pirate advanced. This time he saw the second movement of the old man — saw the silver dagger slid from the sleeve and raised on high. But his laughter did not cease as he tore the cutlass from its scabbard at his side. The blade slashed down upon the Spaniard's wrist. When it struck it seemed as though the steel had sent sparks flying, but it was only blood, spurting forth in tiny gouts as the hand fell severed to the cabin floor.

The old man cried out; then Luke was upon him, lifting the graybeard bodily and carrying him from the cabin. On deck he collared Roger Groat and kicked the form of the fainting grandee to indicate his prize.

"Amuse yourself," he instructed the lieutenant. "I go below again."

"Amuse *yourself*," parroted Groat, leering.

Treach good-naturedly pushed the man in the face with the flat of his wet blade, and went down the stairs again.

Once more he entered the cabin, and saw that Ynez stood there. She faced him now and she did not cringe. Her fea-

54

tures held no fear, for they were set in the immobility of death. Only her eyes were alive — so dreadfully, so intently alive that Luke Treach stood staring aghast into their black depths. His own face twisted as though seared by the black flame that leapt forth from her burning orbs. Then he mastered himself and advanced.

"Ye'd best pull no tricks with me, girl," he muttered.

Her dead face smiled a dead smile — the mirthless smile of a corpse that crawls to feed. And her voice spoke, muffled as though it came from the under-earth.

"I fear ye not," said Ynez. "I fear no man, and no thing. Ye had best fear *me*."

Her tone was leaden, and the words were heavy against Luke's ears. He grimaced, shrugged in a bravado he did not feel.

"Enough of this!" he growled. "Come, lass — "

"Wait."

Luke paused.

"Ye shall have will over me, if ye must. But dog though thou art, I warn thee still. My father gave me this."

She held up the little golden vial. It was empty.

"Ye heard what it contained — the precious distillation which insures eternal life. I drank of it. And so I warn thee. I cannot die, and the hatred within me cannot die. Use me as thou wilt; yea, cast me into the sea" — her eyes flamed — "but I shall return, Luke Treach. I shall return. And there will be reckoning."

For a moment the buccaneer trembled with instinctive horror. Then the wine mounted to his brain, and as the light faded from the girl's eyes he stepped across the cabin with a hoarse laugh. Ynez threw the empty vial in his face, but he only grinned.

3

Luke Treach stumbled from the cabin with a curse — stumbled with the body of the swooning girl across his shoulder. Lurching figures moved in the dusk, snarling and laughing in drunken animation.

Treach cursed savagely as he sought the deck and made for a group of huddling men that clustered about the mast.

He was rather surprised to see that old Señor Montelupe was still alive, considering what had been done to him.

The old grandee was nailed to the mast most painfully, by his remaining hand.

The men turned to Treach and regarded him with bleary eyes.

"What'll we do, Capt'n?" demanded Groat, moving to the pirate's side. "A tough old bird this vulture. He'll not die and he'll not be still. He hangs there and curses and prays in his Spanish, damme if he don't."

Treach smiled wolfishly.

"Perhaps I can devise a new diversion," he said.

There was snickering, for the buckos knew their captain. They watched as he threw the swooning Ynez to the deck, and the mangled head of Montelupe turned to follow Treach's movements.

The captain's knife flashed, and the anguished old man moaned aloud as he cast the terribly altered form over the vessel's side. Then Treach faced the father. The gray Spaniard stared from tortured eyes until Luke's face fell in shame.

"Fool!" The voice rang faint, but vibrant with hatred. "Fool!"

Luke wished to turn away, but those eyes, that voice, held him prisoner before the victim.

"There is vengeance for fools," hissed the old man. "I've prayed to the Powers while your dogs tormented me; prayed to Powers over wind and water. You and your currish crew are doomed, I swear — and your torment shall not end there."

Was this death-racked horror really smiling?

Luke shuddered. He stepped forward, blenching at the madman's eyes. For the old man was mumbling.

To the crew it appeared as if Montelupe were whispering in confidence to Treach, for the captain bent his head close to the ravaged face, and the Spaniard's lips moved. It was hard to hear what he was saying.

"Vengeance . . . my daughter . . . elixir . . . nothing can stop life that will flow eternally through veins . . . nothing can stop hate . . . vengeance for you . . . return."

In the gathering shadow it was difficult for the men to see the expression on their captain's face. Could it be fear at the dying man's whispers?

But a moment later everyone witnessed their captain's rage. For suddenly the horrid head writhed as the old Spaniard spat full in Treach's face.

Then a sword flashed out, and a red-daubed head rolled across the deck. At that moment the sky bled, and crimson waters bubbled against the sunset. When the maimed body went over the side, the waters stirred with a new turbulence, and a wind sprang up from the flaming western sky.

Treach shuddered even as he cursed, noting the silence of his companions, their furtive looks and gesturings. The imbecile had awed them with his curses — faith, but it was lucky they had not heard what the old devil had said there at the last! Still, his wizard babbling was working on these superstitious fools.

With an effort, Luke met the mood and mastered it. He shouted for fresh rum, roundly cuffed the nearest members of the crew, and swaggered forward.

After a time, his mates followed, and the warm bite of the liquor soon banished morbid melancholy.

They drank as sunset smoldered into dusk, drank as the dark clouds of night fled before the rise of wailing winds; drank even as the waters lashed the ship through trough and swell. For now white waves raced and reared, and the sea began to boil and bubble as though heated at some devil's cauldron from below.

Near midnight the storm broke, and the rain lashed the drunken roisterers from the deck. It was then that several awoke from their bemusement, but it was too late.

The *Golden Crest* whirled in an angry sea amidst a wind that shrieked and tore at sail and spar. Treach roared futile orders to the scant dozen of his crew that he could muster, but these did not avail. No one dared go aloft or brave the gale above the deck. Even when the mast fell, the panic-crazed men were helpless to forestall further disaster.

The black night hailed about them, and the sea surged over the decks as the ship heeled against the storm. Floundering figures were tossed screaming over the side as the waters retreated; cursing sailors blundered in the darkness as the yard-arms crashed about them to splinter the deck and cabins into a shambles.

Some there were who made a break for the boats. Five or six lifted one over the side and clambered in, just as a new wave struck. They dashed to death against the bows as the craft smashed to bits before the flooding impact of the water.

The ship lurched madly. It was leaking, foundering — that was a certainty. Treach collared Roger Groat, Salvatore, Samuel Slew, and as many others as he could shake into consciousness. His orders were curt, oath-weighted. They dashed below, returning with rations, water-jugs. A great combining wave crashed over the deck, then subsided as the men dashed for another boat.

They made it, lowered the ropes and floundered in, casting off just in time to escape the flooding fury that spent itself against the vessel's side.

Rowing was madness in the swirling waters, but they pushed away in time. Already the great vessel was rearing and plunging in the throes of final surrender. It rose and sank, and above the storm came the sound of faint shrieks as those left behind realized the imminence of their doom.

Then, with a geyser-burst, the waters boiled above the ship, poising against the ruined mast-stumps before they hurled down to smash the vessel to ruins.

With a rumble, they fell and claimed their own. The craft rose up, tilted at the bow, and fell into the gigantic trough as the wave crashed down upon it. There was a single mighty roar of triumph as the ship slid into the sea; then foaming waters closed about it, and the terrible circle spread and widened from the point of its disappearance.

Treach and the men met the shock, though two yammering forms disappeared under the drenching violence of the inundation and were sucked down by the hungry depths.

Then they tossed all alone in the black storm amidst the sound of gigantic laughter, and the booming wind mocked them through the night.

4

It was calm as death the next morning, and the waves purred against the side of the boat as though in satisfaction at the appeasement of their hunger.

The weary men slept as the sun rose; Treach huddled forward over the provisions, Roger Groat bent over his oar, Salvatore stretched across the seat, Sam Slew and Gorlac lying supine in the dampness at the bottom of the craft.

It was Gorlac who woke first; Gorlac, the gigantic Krooman. His brutal Negroid face wrinkled into a frown as he surveyed his sleeping companions and the empty sea in which they drifted. Then his eyes fell upon the two water-casks, the oiled sea-bag of provisions at the captain's side. He stretched black ape-arms forward, ate and drank noisily.

Treach chose this moment to awake, and for a second he stared at the giant Negro, who sat obliviously munching a slab of bully-beef. Then he snarled an oath and drew his knife. In a moment he had flung himself forward on the startled black and buried his blade in the gleaming ebon column of the corded neck.

Gorlac grunted in pain, and crushed the captain's body in a terrible embrace. His arms tightened as Treach tore the knife from the wound in the neck and stabbed again and again at the dark back.

The Negro, grimacing with mad pain, locked his great hands about the pirate's neck and squeezed — squeezed terribly, with sobs of agony as he sought to throttle his foe. Then Treach slid the knife around the ribs, arched upward in a silver slash, and disemboweled his antagonist. The ape-paws relaxed their grip, and the captain slid the twitching body over the side.

It fell with a splash, and disappeared. The captain crawled back to his place, feeling his throat experimentally to make sure that all was well: then polishing his knife carefully on his breeches. He looked up to face the stares of his awakened companions. The scuffle had taken place so quickly that the men were still rubbing their eyes and grumbling their bewilderment.

"Gorlac's gone," announced Treach, in a harsh voice. "And damn my lights and liver, the rest of ye curs will go too if I catch ye tampering with the provisions."

He took out a small stone from his blouse and began to sharpen his knife, gazing meaningly at his audience. They sat stolid, each man looking off into the empty sea and thinking his own thoughts.

Luke mused with the rest. His mind was teeming in turmoil. First thoughts were pangs of regret as he remembered the fine ship, the fine crew he had lost — and more tragic still, the stores of bullion and silver ingots; the money-chests gleaned from trading off loot for gold doubloons and pieces-of-eight. And there had been a small fortune in the silks and jewels and moneys left by his two passengers as well. It was all lost.

Further reflection was brought to bear on his own plight; adrift here in the boundless sea with three men, an open boat, and water and provisions for perhaps two days.

From these ponderings his thoughts strayed off into darker considerations. Luke Treach was a practical man and an all-round materialistic scoundrel to boot, but he could not help but remember the strange dying words of the Spaniard — he who claimed mantic powers. The wretch may have been raving, but he spoke of aeromancy, power over wind and water, and of conjuring up a storm. The storm had come. And the seer had cursed him with other things . . .

But enough! A little food, a little water, a few attempts at formulating a plan: these were the things he needed to drive such foolishness from his brain.

He apportioned a meager fare of beef and hard-tack to the three survivors of his crew, and snapped orders for rowing assignments and night watches. Dark grinning Salvatore, big dour Groat, and the leanly sinister "Dead-Light" Slew listened stolidly to his commands and set to.

But rowing is onerous, and the broiling sun of the mid-Caribbean no kindly overseer. The sea is a lonely place, and last night these men had glimpsed Death with jaws agape to swallow. Now they feared that those jaws would close about them again, not to engulf but to gnaw slowly with the sharp teeth of thirst and hunger.

The day passed in sullen, apprehensive silence; Groat and Slew, then Treach and Salvatore, taking the oars while the alternate pair rested and tried to shield their eyes from the eternal glare.

Row — but where? There was no compass, and until the stars shone, guidance was missing. Treach hoped to put south to the islands, and the sun's deceptive shimmer showed him the way none too truly.

Nevertheless the labor kept the men from thinking too much; kept them from remembering little things that now came to slyly torment Treach. There had been a little golden vial, and the wizard had sworn a vengeance. What was that about Eternal Life? Couldn't torture kill? What did it mean?

Sunset again — flaming sunset, like that in which Montelupe had died. He had died; the dead harm no one. She too could harm no one, now.

But it was night. Captain Treach apportioned the food in darkness, watched his companions at the water to insure that they were not over-greedy.

Treach snapped commands, set the course by the stars. The men hauled at the oars in silence, and the boat glided through black waters.

Groat and Slew labored. Salvatore dropped off to sleep, his swarthy face buried in his hands as he huddled up against the forward seat. Treach kept awake by sheer will, cursing mechanically at the oarsmen, so that the sound of his voice might break the sound of the Silence — the empty Silence of rolling waters. The very rustle and lap of the waves seemed to become a part of a maddening stillness that sapped the mind. The night sea was an entity that crawled about them. Treach felt this, although no concrete thought was formulated. But his instinct awakened him to fear; fear which the silent sea now personified. Here, drifting alone in the black infinitude, the Powers of which the dead wizard had spoken assumed a new reality. It was easy for the tired imagination to conceive of vast pulsing shapes, embodiments of the night and the wind and water.

Treach felt his burning forehead, drew the back of his hands over lips cracked with fever.

He fell asleep while the waters murmured. In his dreams the water was whispering. From far away it whispered — from behind the boat. The whispering grew louder. It was right behind the boat now. He could almost hear words floating up out of the water. The whispering was trying to tell him something — something about vengeance, and a curse — right under the boat now . . .

There was a scream of utter agony.

Treach wrenched himself from sleep, sat bolt-upright as the scream trailed off into a gurgling noise in the blackness.

"What's that?" he shouted to his companions.

For a moment there was no answer. Groat's face was buried in trembling hands.

Salvatore heard him, but when he opened his mouth it merely hung loosely, without moving in speech. And Slew was gone.

"Where's Sam?" shouted Treach.

Salvatore managed to regain partial control of his jaws.

"He — gone," the swarthy man spluttered. "It came over the side and took him and then it pulled him into the water — it took him — *santo Dios* — "

Then Treach was upon Salvatore, shaking his shoulders and shrieking into his very face.

"What took him, damme? Speak up, man, for the love of heaven!"

"I not know," whimpered the other. "I not know. We row here, and then Slew stop rowing. I take the oar. He just sit there at end of boat. All at once he say, 'Listen,' he say. 'I hear whisper.' I tell him he crazy. But he just sit and look at water and say, 'It getting louder.' All at once he lean down, and then — *sacramento!* — two arms come up out of water and go around his neck. He just scream once and then over side he go. No splash, no bubbles. He go, and I see arms — all red arms. All red!"

As the big man slumped down in the boat Treach peered wildly at the black waters about him. They were still, unruffled. No body, no rippling.

"You're daft, man," he whispered, but there was no conviction in his voice.

"Those red arms," Groat muttered, from behind. "I never believed in mermaids or sea-monsters, but — "

"Shut up, both of you! You're crazy! Slew fell overboard, that's all. Fever's got you. There's nothing in the water but sharks. And they have no arms."

"You threw something in the water with arms," Salvatore mumbled.

Treach struck the man across the mouth. "Shut up!" he screamed. "Let me alone."

Silently, he sat there until dawn arose, and when he saw its redness, he shuddered.

They were all mad now, food and water gone, Slew gone. And the sun, searing down, cooked the madness into their brains until thoughts writhed and twisted amidst flames.

Salvatore wouldn't row any more. He kept staring at the water behind the boat while Treach watched him.

Toward midday, Salvatore turned.

"There," he whispered. "I know. I know it come. I see it. There in the water. It following us. Swimming in water. Oh, Cap'n, look there."

"Shut up!" But Treach looked. It was only sunlight glinting on the waves behind.

"Look. It move again!"

Something was moving, way back.

"Sharks, you fool!"

"Sharks are not red."

"Shut up!"

They pulled the oars, but Salvatore gazed back as sunset dripped blood upon the waves. He was trembling and his face was soaking in perspiration not born of heat alone.

"Let us all stay awake tonight," he whispered. "Maybe we pray and it go away. Otherwise . . ."

"Quiet!" Treach snapped the command with his old authority.

But the authority was in his voice alone now. Inside, Luke Treach was afraid.

When the sun went down he heard the whispering at once. It welled out of the black waters, and he prayed that the moon might rise at once. Hearing that whispering in the blackness was too much. He turned toward the back of the boat. He'd talk to Salvatore, anything, just drown out that growing whisper. He turned — and saw.

The big man was on his knees. He was leaning over the gunwale. His arms were outstretched and he was staring down into the black water, his face icy with horror.

And two arms were rising out of the water — two long, red arms. They were pinkly phosphorescent in the darkness. They glowed like — like stripped flesh.

The arms reached out, twin serpents that embraced. Treach tried to call out, to motion to Groat. He was frozen, frozen in the arms that rose, embraced Salvatore. And silently, the big man toppled over the side. The splash broke the spell.

"Quick!" Treach screamed. Groat followed him on his

hands and knees as they thrashed their oars in the blackness of the waves. Nothing moved.

"Sharks move a lot," Groat muttered, in a hoarse voice. "Sharks move, and octopus move. But this — you saw?"

"I didn't see anything," Treach lied. "He was mad. Threw himself over."

"Drowning men move," Groat croaked.

Treach mastered himself. "Row," he commanded. "For God's sake, row, man! We must reach land before tomorrow night."

They rowed as though Death were at their heels. And in their hearts it was this they feared. They rowed past midnight; tired, feverish, aflame with thirst and hunger. But Fear called their strokes, and Fear drove the boat on through the inky, whispering waters.

Treach was nearly mad now. There was something out there! He could no longer keep from thinking of the curse — of what Inez had said about not being able to die. Yet he had killed her; what he did would kill anyone. She must be dead.

"What's that?" Groat had stopped rowing.

"Where?"

"Back there in the water — see, where the moonlight hits the wave."

"I don't see — " Treach stopped, eyes wide with dread.

"Yes, you do. You see it. That head, coming toward us."

They sat there while the bobbing thing approached. And the whispering rose about them in a great murmur as of winds rising from ocean depths, and the whispering was clear this time so that they heard.

"Where are you, Luke Treach? I come for you. You have taken my eyes, Luke Treach, and I cannot see. But you are there, and I come for you."

Groat began to laugh. A low chuckling rose from his throat until it drowned out the sound of the whispering. Groat raised his head to the moon and bayed his laughter. He sat there quaking with mirth.

And Treach watched him, then watched the bobbing head that circled the boat. It went around twice. It stopped for a moment on his side, and he saw a dark, seal-like outline that might or might not have been human. It hesitated in the water, and Treach drew his knife. Then it circled the boat again and came to rest on the side where Groat sat laughing. Two arms rose out of the water in the moonlight — two red arms, glistening and wet. And Groat went over, still laughing. His laughter rose, then bubbled away as the water dragged him down.

It was then that Treach himself began to laugh. All alone in the boat he sat, laughing up to the moon. He laughed because he knew he was mad, and yet he could not escape. Luke Treach seized an oar and began to row with demented fury.

The sun was high when he ceased. Madness passed, and the events of the night were a dream. Treach leaned back, rubbed his eyes, and looked around in amazement.

"Groat? Salvatore? Slew? Where are you?"

They were gone — but they couldn't be gone, or it would be true.

"Groat? Salvatore? Slew?"

And then the waves around the boat parted, and three heads appeared in the water. Sam Slew's one-eyed stare came from a blue, bloated face. Salvatore's eyes were closed and his mouth was sealed with seaweed. The drowned visage of Groat, smiling through a tangle of kelp, bobbed horridly on the waves. All three heads came to the side of the boat. They shimmered there through the haze of heat from the sun.

Treach had been screaming for a long time in a high shrill voice when they disappeared.

"Fever," he muttered. "Just one day more."

He clawed at the oars.

But now he couldn't keep his eyes off the water. And as noon approached, he could begin to see the swimmer behind — far off, crawling through the trough of waves. It was keeping distance; but a few strokes and it would be upon him.

The delirious pirate redoubled his efforts with every

ounce of remaining strength. And still the gap between boat and swimmer narrowed. Now Treach could see long red arms in the water. He could not quite make out a head or face, but he saw the arms. Remembering what he had done, he shuddered. *Red arms!*

He faced the sunset. A black bulk loomed from the water to his west. Dominica, he guessed. If he could make it before nightfall, he would be safe.

He rowed on, faster.

The swimmer was fast, too. The gap narrowed, just as the red band of sunset narrowed.

"How can she follow?" Treach muttered. "She's blind. I know that. She took the others, searching for me. How can she follow? Wizard tricks — that vial! Why didn't I believe it would keep her alive, even after *that!* I must row — harder."

Panting, the wrecked body of Luke Treach tugged at the oars. His bloodshot eyes stared now at the bobbing head just behind the boat. His ears buzzed, but he heard the whisperings.

"I swore it, Luke Treach. Now I come for you."

There was no use to row, but Treach rowed; no use to scream, but Treach screamed; screamed and rowed as the red thing swam around the boat. Then it was crawling over the side, and Luke Treach avoided the pinkish-red arms as they reached out. Laughing, he drew his knife. But then it crawled into the boat so that Treach saw it, drowned, yet livid all over. And he pointed the knife, but it came on, eyeless and groping. One hand grasped the knife and then both arms went around Luke Treach so that he fell back. The hand grasping the knife came down and a voice whispered:

"I came a long way — from death itself. And now I shall do to you what you did to me before you cast me over the side. You shall be as red as I am."

And the knife sang down as Luke Treach's knife had sung down when he killed Ynez before her father and cast her into the sea. It sang down, and when it ceased the red swimmer went over the side of the drifting boat and disappeared.

Night fell; and still the boat drifted. At dawn it bumped the shore.

Two men found it there some hours later.

They peered into it and shuddered at the sight of the figure lying on the bottom of the boat.

"Dead?" whispered one.

"Of course he's dead."

"Wrecked, doubtlessly, in an open boat."

"Yes." His voice was vibrant with horror. "But what could have done this to him?"

"Just what was done? — I cannot understand it yet."

The first man stared again at the red thing in the boat. "You fool," he said, "can't you see that this man was flayed alive?"

The Terrible Old Man

H.P. LOVECRAFT

It was the design of Angelo Ricci and Joe Czanek and Manuel Silva to call on the Terrible Old Man. This old man dwells all alone in a very ancient house in Water Street near the sea, and is reputed to be both exceedingly rich and exceedingly feeble; which forms a situation very attractive to men of the profession of Messrs. Ricci, Czanek, and Silva, for that profession was nothing less dignified than robbery.

The inhabitants of Kingsport say and think many things about the Terrible Old Man which generally keep him safe from the attentions of gentlemen like Mr. Ricci and his colleagues, despite the almost certain fact that he hides a fortune of indefinite magnitude somewhere about his musty and venerable abode. He is, in truth, a very strange person, believed to have been a captain of East India clipper ships in his day; so old that no one can remember when he was young, and so taciturn that few know his real name. Among the gnarled trees in the front yard of his aged and neglected place he maintains a strange collection of large stones, oddly grouped and painted so that they resemble the idols in some obscure Eastern temple. This collection frightens away most of the small boys who love to taunt the Terrible Old Man about his long white hair and beard, or to break the small-paned windows of his dwelling with wicked missiles; but there are other things which frighten the older and more curious folk who sometimes steal up to the house to peer in through the dusty panes. These folk say that on a table in a bare room on the ground floor are many peculiar bottles, in each a small piece of lead suspended pendulum-wise from a string. And they say that the Terrible Old Man talks to these bottles, addressing them by such names as Jack, Scar-Face, Long Tom, Spanish Joe, Peters, and Mate Ellis, and that whenever he speaks to a bottle the little lead pendulum within makes certain definite vibrations as if in answer. Those who have watched the tall, lean, Terrible Old Man in these peculiar conversations do not watch him again. But Angelo Ricci and Joe Czanek and Manuel Silva were not of Kingsport blood; they were of that new and heterogeneous alien stock which lies outside the charmed circle of New England life and traditions, and they saw in the Terrible Old Man merely a tottering, almost helpless greybeard, who could not walk without the aid of his knotted cane and whose thin, weak hands shook pitifully. They were really quite sorry in their way for the lonely, unpopular old fellow, whom everybody shunned, and at whom all the dogs barked singularly. But business is business, and to a robber whose soul is his profession, there is a lure and challenge about a very old and very feeble man who has no account at the bank, and who pays for his few necessities at the village store with Spanish gold and silver minted two centuries ago.

Messrs. Ricci, Czanek, and Silva selected the night of April eleventh for their call. Mr. Ricci and Mr. Silva were to interview the poor old gentleman, whilst Mr. Czanek waited for them and their presumably metallic burden with a covered motorcar in Ship Street, by the gate in the tall rear wall of their host's grounds. Desire to avoid needless explanations in the case of unexpected police intrusions prompted these plans for a quiet and unostentatious departure.

As prearranged, the three adventurers started out separately in order to prevent any evil-minded suspicions afterward. Messrs. Ricci and Silva met in Water Street by the old man's front gate, and although they did not like the way the moon shone down upon the painted stones through the budding branches of the gnarled trees, they had more important things to think about than mere idle superstition. They feared it might be unpleasant work making the Terrible Old Man loquacious concerning his hoarded gold and silver, for aged sea-captains are notably stubborn and perverse. Still, he was very old and very feeble, and there were two visitors. Messrs. Ricci and Silva were experienced in the art of making unwilling persons voluble, and the screams of a weak and exceptionally venerable man can easily be muffled. So they moved up to the one lighted window and heard the Terrible Old Man talking childishly to his bottles with pendulums. Then they donned masks and knocked politely at the weather-stained oaken door.

Waiting seemed very long to Mr. Czanek as he fidgeted restlessly in the covered motorcar by the Terrible Old Man's back gate in Ship Street. He was more than ordinarily tender-hearted, and he did not like the hideous screams he had heard in the ancient house just after the hour appointed for the deed. Had he not told his colleagues to be as gentle as possible with the pathetic old sea-captain? Very nervously he watched the narrow oaken gate in the high and ivy-clad stone wall. Frequently he consulted his watch, and wondered at the delay. Had the old man died before revealing where his treasure was hidden, and had a thorough search been necessary? Mr. Czanek did not like to wait so long in the dark in such a place. Then he sensed a soft tread or tapping on the walk inside the gate, heard a gentle fumbling at the rusty latch, and saw the narrow, heavy door swing inward. And in the pallid glow of the single dim street lamp he strained his eyes to see what his colleagues had brought out of that sinister house which loomed so close behind. But when he looked, he did not see what he had expected; for his colleagues were not there at all, but only the Terrible Old Man leaning quietly on his knotted cane and smiling hideously. Mr. Czanek had never noticed the color of that man's eyes; now he saw that they were yellow.

Little things make considerable excitement in little towns, which is the reason that Kingsport people talked all that spring and summer about the three unidentifiable bodies, horribly slashed as with many cutlasses, and horribly mangled as with the tread of many cruel boot-heels, which the tide washed in. And some people even spoke of things as trivial as the deserted motorcar found in Ship Street, or certain especially inhuman cries, probably of a stray animal or migratory bird, heard in the night by wakeful citizens. But in this idle village gossip the Terrible Old Man took no interest at all. He was by nature reserved, and when one is aged and feeble, one's reserve is doubly strong. Besides, so ancient a sea-captain must have witnessed scores of things much more stirring in the far-off days of his unremembered youth.

The Blue Spectacles

AUGUST DERLETH

When he reached Cartagena, Jesse Brennan knew that his traveling was done. He was old, he was tired, and his illness had finally become too burdensome; he could not go on. A doctor confirmed it: he had perhaps a month to live, perhaps not that. Cartagena was sunny and warm; the Atlantic shone cobalt from dawn to dusk; the ancient walls of the old Colombian city pleased him. He had done more than one man's share of exploring, of poking about in the old places and the odd corners of the earth; he had no one to mourn him but a few old friends scattered over the globe; he might as well die in Cartagena as anywhere. Back home in the United States it would be winter now, and he had no taste for winter — better the sun and the cloudless sky and the restless sea.

There remained the problem of disposing of those trifles he had collected — the things of value to fellow collectors. He set about this without delay, so that the burden of thinking about this final task might not cloud his last day. The stone clock of mysterious Indian origin

73

could go to Faulkner in Cairo. Stuart could have the old German book bound in human skin. Rawlings, a hermit in his Edinburgh garret, would enjoy the curious figure from Burma, and Vaclav would find Prague more interesting if he were the possessor of the Borgia ring. But to whom to send the blue spectacles? Ah, that was a problem! The old Chinese mandarin from whom he had got them had been convincingly solemn about the wonderful properties of the spectacles. Where, he wondered, could he find a man whose soul was "untouched" by sin, lest, by gazing through the blue glass, something should befall him?

He thought about the disposal of the blue spectacles for two days. After he had packed and shipped everything else, the spectacles remained. But then, in the night, under the guileless moon, it came to him: Alain Verneil, of course! Too honest for his own good, too sincere to recognize hypocrisy, faithful, dogged, moral — yes, the blue spectacles would be safe with him, if indeed they had any of the properties attributed to them. He did not remember Verneil's address, nor could he find it anywhere in his things, but Verneil had been curator of some sort of museum in New Orleans, and he would doubtless be in the directory; so he did up the spectacles in a compact box, wrote a letter to enclose with his gift — "I got these from an old Chinese in Tibet. How old they are I don't know; he didn't know, either. They are said to be magic, in a peculiar way. If anyone who is not wholly good looks through them something will happen to him — I gather that he will be given sight of himself in some previous incarnation or time or something of that sort, and that it will not be pleasant. Or a change of identity in which punishment shall fit his crimes — you know how these legends go. I am almost ashamed to confess that the old fellow was so convincing that I myself never wore them. I was never 'good,' much less 'wholly good,' and at this stage there is hardly any use lying about that, is there?" — addressed it to Alain Verneil, New Orleans, Louisiana, U.S.A., scrawled across one corner of the package, "Directory Service, Please," and dispatched it.

He put no return address on it, because Verneil would recognize the "Jesse" who had signed the letter. In any case, it did not matter; he was dead before the little package reached New Orleans.

It came into the city on the first day of the annual Mardi Gras, and, being marked for directory service, it was passed along to the proper quarters, where a much-harassed clerk, wishing her day over and her work done — though there were hours yet to pass — received it among other pieces of mail similarly marked. All in good time she came to the package from Cartagena, noticing the stamps first, and thinking of her niece's stamp collection. Being constantly subject to all kinds of script, she had developed some facility in reading the scrawls that passed beneath her eye. But Jesse Brennan's script, while superficially legible, tended toward carelessness, so that his *i*'s were dot-less, and many of his consonants run together, with the result that, shifting her eyes from the stamps to the address she must service, she read it at once: Alan Verneul — and why should she not, when one Alan Verneul's most spectacular divorce cases had been won that day, and his name was everywhere from the *Globe* to the *Picayune?* And who, but somebody in Colombia, would not know his address? She added it to Brennan's script, and sent the package on its way.

At the moment of its arrival, Alan Verneul was at the telephone. Where was the domino he had ordered? He knew it should be in his hands; indeed, it should have awaited him on his return from court, but, though his costume and everything else was in perfect readiness, there was no domino. And none other to be had, admitted his costumer reluctantly. Verneul's first thought, therefore, at the arrival of the package, was that the missing domino had turned up, though it was long since in the hands of a black roisterer, who had found it where it had been lost out of the package from the costumer's.

But the sight of the stamps disillusioned him. Nevertheless, he opened it, wondering whom he knew in Cartagena, where he had never been. He looked first at the signature. Perhaps Jesse Melanchton, who had gone to South America somewhere after his day in court. The letter puzzled him. He misread its salutation, which, characteristically, Brennan had written so that it might have been Alan, Alain, or Allen; he had no reason to feel that any error had been made. Still, Melanchton was likely to remember the address of his apartment.

He came at last to the spectacles.

Even he could recognize their age — it needed no explanation, such as was in the letter, for the glass in the spectacles was a strange cloudy blue, a kind of smoky blue the like of which he had never seen before; and their frame was evidently hand-wrought, of silver. He put them down on his dressing-table and read the letter once more. A curious thing, certainly. Whoever Jesse was, he was a superstitious man just as certainly.

He brushed the letter and the wrapping of the package to one side, and was about to lay the spectacles away when a thought struck him. He looked at the spectacles once again. They were large, square; they had but a narrow bridge, and were thickly framed. Awkward thing to wear, no doubt, but in the circumstances, quite proper. They were not out of character, since Verneul was about to join the maskers in the costume of a New Orleans dandy of more than a century ago, and the blue spectacles would do very well indeed in place of the missing domino.

He carried them to a mirror and put them on. He could not have devised a better concealment for his eyes, for he could see through them very well, but none could see his eyes behind them.

There were reasons why he would not like to be known behind his mask. There were irate husbands and equally irate fathers, some of whom had threatened him with various degrees of dire punishment. Moreover, as a divorce lawyer, he entertained many feminine clients, who, if they were not guilty of adultery when they came to him, were guilty at leaving, Verneul having a facility for exacting fees in coin other than money. His success in court bred envy and contempt; his successes with the ladies bred hatred and jealousy. But his boldness knew no end, and his self-assurance never faced retreat.

He got dressed, went outside, and took a cab to where the roistering crowds were gay along the streets. There he left the cab and mixed among them: tall, saturnine, handsome, still young at forty and attractive. Secure before his roving eyes, he wore the blue spectacles.

He had taken part in the Mardi Gras many times before. It was no novelty to him, and he had not come particularly to enjoy the celebrants or even to watch the parades and the floats; his role was predatory, and his eyes darted hither and yon in search of likely women who might be unable to resist his charms. He walked leisurely about; now that he was in the midst of the celebrants, he had ample time at his disposal, and there was no need to hasten. There were hours yet before he need make his choice among the masked women who danced all around him.

He had not gone far, however, before he reflected that he had never seen the crowds quite so riotous and gay, and, thinking thus, he chanced to look up to see where he was. After a moment of puzzled gazing, here and there, he had to admit to himself that he did not know; somehow, he had wandered into a section of the city completely strange to him, despite certain similarities in old gables and corners. Observing this, he stood quite still and scrutinized his surroundings with his practiced legal eye. During the interval of his examination, he saw surprising things abounding.

There were no street-lamps of any kind.

There was no modern vehicle in sight for as far as he could see, even such floats as were there being horse-drawn.

The hour being close to twilight, many of the roisterers carried crude, home-made torches, while others carried lanterns of a decidedly old-fashioned kind.

He noticed these facts with mounting amazement, but he had no time to speculate on them, for at the moment he felt the tap of a fan on his shoulder, and, turning, found himself looking into the eyes of a strikingly beautiful girl, momentarily raising her mask so that he might see her.

"I've been looking for you," she said, mysteriously.

"Have you?" he answered for lack of anything else to say.

"You're late."

"I came as soon as I could," he answered, determined to play her game.

How beautiful she was! Creole, he thought — certainly of mixed blood somewhere in her background. With black eyes like something alive and fathomless as a distant sea, soft, velvety skin, long, slender hands. Even in the ruffled and bustled costume she wore it was possible to recognize that her figure was superb. He forgot about the strangeness of the street on which they stood.

"Come," she said, and began to move swiftly away from him, darting in and out among the crowds.

His pulse quickened. "Wait for me," he called after her.

She turned her head briefly, and went on.

He started forward, determined to catch her. The old excitement of the chase filled him, and his only goal now was the pursuit, after which the conquest would surely be his. He did not stop to think who she might be; he had not recognized her face. He knew only that she was beautiful, far more than ordinarily so, that there was something haunting about her eyes and her mouth, that vaguely, deep, deep in his mind, there was a familiar echo, as if somehow, in a far past time, he had known the enchantment of loving a woman like her.

She wove in and out, fleetly, light and graceful.

But try as he might, somehow he could not catch up to her. She remained always just in sight, and once or twice she paused, mockingly, as if to wait for him; but always she was gone, just as he came within easy speaking distance. He smiled, and his smile held. In one way or another, in and out of Mardi Gras, he had done this a great many times — and almost always he had emerged the victor. There was no reason why he should not add this vixen to his list of conquests.

He redoubled his efforts.

Gradually, almost imperceptibly, the crowd thinned and was gone. They were alone in a side street, just the two of them, with her white dress six or seven doors ahead of him, and her mocking laughter drifting back in the warm air. Night had fallen, and no lights shone, but it did not matter; like a will-o-wisp she remained always just so far ahead of him, lighter and fleeter on her feet than he, and more sure of herself in the darkness, for once or twice he stumbled and almost fell.

He had no idea where he was; he did not care. His one thought was to catch up to the woman ahead of him; to find his way back would be a matter of moments, once the conquest had been accomplished.

Quite suddenly she paused. She waited until he was almost up to her; then she turned into a dark, bush-girt lawn, running swiftly to a wide verandah, up the steps to a door, and into the house that stood there. She left the door standing ajar, which was a patent invitation.

He followed.

Inside, despite the darkness, he saw her vanishing into a dimly lit room.

There, too, he followed.

Instantly, it seemed, the room was alight. The door was shut behind him; his quarry was over across the room. Before him and all around, even at his back, between him and the door, there were men — all in costume, the costume of pirates, clearly. But none was masked; and the domino was gone from the face of his quarry, also, as well as the smile.

For a moment the tableau held. Everyone looked at him with grim tenseness, as at an intruder whose intrusion must be punished. He felt a brief, thin pricking of fear, but, of course, it was Mardi Gras, and people would understand. Or would they? There was something ominous in the tense quiet of the room.

He looked quickly around, his eyes searching for a familiar face. He saw none.

The tableau broke.

The circle closed around him, save for one arc directly before him, in the center of which sat a roughly dandified man wearing a smart black beard and moustache. He was toying with a short-barreled pistol of some ancient manufacture. He gazed at Verneul with a mixture of indifference and contempt, which did not conceal his grimness.

"M. Verneul," he said, rather than asked.

"I am known," said Verneul, with a faint smile.

"Speak when you are spoken to," said his host curtly.

Verneul bridled. "Look here. I admit to entering the house, at the indirect invitation of the young lady, but . . ."

"M. Verneul has entered houses after young ladies before this, I think," drawled the seated gentleman. "And forced his attention with and without permission upon a good many of those young ladies." He nodded toward someone standing at his side. "Will you read the charges, Mr. Ariman?"

"Whom have I the honor of addressing?" asked Verneul peremptorily.

There was a ripple of laughter. The seated gentleman rose and made a mocking bow. "Pray forgive me, sir," he said with an edge of unmistakable contempt in his voice. "I an Jean Lafitte, at your service."

His acting, thought Verneul, was startlingly real. "I am sure you will excuse me, gentlemen," he said. "But it is Mardi Gras and . . ."

"Hold your tongue," said Lafitte, and waved a hand to Ariman. "Read."

"On the sixth of February of last year, he accomplished the seduction of Claire Pechon, sixteen, against her will," read Ariman in a clear voice. "On the second of March, Mlle. Julie Argenton, with child by him, took her own life by drowning. On the eighteenth of April, he seduced Mme. Thérèse Munon, wife of Léon, who, discovering himself a cuckold, shot his wife and then himself. On the tenth of May, he deflowered Janise Bourgereau, seventeen."

Verneul wanted to shout his denial of the ridiculous account, but there was something puzzling, something shockingly confusing inside him. For, though he knew none of the women whose names were being read out with such solemnity, it was undeniable that as each name was read, there rose from some unknown depth of memory the picture of a woman's face, successively — of a sixteen-year-old girl, and one slightly older, of a married woman, of another girl — pictures which, in some remote corner of his mind, were recognizable. Words struggled to his lips, but they were not of denial.

"The prosecutor has forgotten the year of his charge," he said, as if by rote.

"Since this is 1811, the year must be 1810," said Lafitte. "You are more particular in this than ever you were about your victims, M. Verneul."

The confusion inside him increased to chaos. Were there two of him, then, that he could remember things which he knew had never taken place? And what was this of 1810 and 1811 now in this twentieth century?

"M. Verneul does not seem to understand that he is standing trial," said Lafitte.

"Trial?" echoed Verneul. "Gentlemen, I am in a fog . . ."

"Indeed, indeed," murmured Lafitte. "A good ladies' man was never a good swordsman, and quicker to know fear than most men. You shall have justice, do not be alarmed. What have you to say in your defense?"

No words came. There were words deep inside him somewhere, but they could not find an outlet.

"Come, say — is it true that you have seduced young girls?"

He could not answer.

Lafitte turned to Ariman. "Put down that the prisoner has admitted it." And to Verneul once more. "And that you have persuaded silly married women to adultery?"

No answer.

"Once more, he assents. And now, M. Verneul, is it not true also that on the seventh of this month you attacked and ravaged Elise Gautier, my ward?" Lafitte fling his arm out to indicate the woman who, but so short a time gone by, had been his eagerly-desired quarry.

He want to say that he had never seen her before in his life; but he could not be sure. It seemed to him that memory of her lingered, but from what source? He could not say; he did not know. How had he come here? The woman, yes — but how had it happened? Part of him recalled the unlit streets and thought them natural; but part thought them wrong, knew them wrong. What was happening to him? What fantastic conspiracy was this?

Lafitte had stood up. "M. Paul Verneul, will you hear your sentence?"

He wanted to say, "My name is Alan, Alan Paul," but nothing came from his lips; and indeed, at the moment he could not be sure that anything at all came from any tongue or throat; for he had cast down his eyes, and seen not floor, but long grass, and an edge of stone, as of a stone box of some kind.

". . .To be shot," Lafitte was saying. "Now."

Instantly half a dozen of the old-fashioned pistols were leveled at him, cocked and ready.

"Aim," said Lafitte to the widening circle.

Verneul stood as if paralyzed. If only he could know! Which was the dream — this or that other? Which was the reality — that distant world in which he was a counselor, or this world of the dandy of New Orleans in 1811? Which, indeed?

"Fire!" said Lafitte.

There was a round of blasts. Briefly, the world of Alan Verneul was a turbulence of strange, smoky blue.

They found him in a long-abandoned cemetery in the outlying country south of New Orleans, though still within the city limits. Dead. By what means, none could say. There were some half a dozen bluish marks on his flesh, as if bullets had gone into him; but no skin was broken. In the course of the inquiry, it was discovered that Verneul had been seen rushing madly through the Mardi Gras crowds in pursuit of someone no one had been able to see; that he had been observed by a passer-by in the cemetery, standing quite alone, talking and gesticulating so that his observer thought him drunk and went on; that the cemetery stood on the site of an old house once the property of Désiré Gautier; that the house, according to legend, was the scene of the fatal shooting of an ancestor of Verneul's more than a century ago.

When he was found, Verneul still wore the blue spectacles.

Since Alain Verneil was curator of the city museum, he saw and recognized their value. And in good time, he got around to adding them to his collection, thus accomplishing Jesse Brennan's original intention.

Seven Turns in a Hangman's Rope

HENRY S. WHITEHEAD

1

I first became acutely aware of the dreadful tragedy of Saul Macartney one sunny morning early in the month of November of the year 1927. On that occasion, instead of walking across the hall from my bathroom after shaving and the early morning shower, I turned to the left upon emerging and, in my bathrobe and slippers, went along the upstairs hallway to my workroom on the northwest corner of the house into which I had just moved, in the west coast town of Frederiksted on the island of Santa Cruz.

This pleasant room gave a view through its several windows directly down from the hill on which the house was located, across the pretty town with its red roofs and varicolored houses, directly upon the indigo Caribbean. This workroom of mine had a north light from its two windows on that side and, as I used it only during the mornings, I thus escaped the terrific sun drenching to which, in the absence of any shade without, the room was subjected during the long West Indian afternoon.

The occasion for going in there was my desire to see, in the clear morning light, what that ancient oil painting looked like; the canvas which, without its frame, I had tacked up on the south wall the evening before.

This trophy, along with various other items of household flotsam and jetsam, had been taken the previous afternoon, which was a day after my arrival on the island, out of a kind of lumber room wherein the owners of the house had plainly been storing for the best part of a century the kinds of things which accumulate in a family. Of the considerable amount of material which my houseman, Stephen Penn, had taken out and stacked and piled in the upper hallway, there happened to be nothing of interest except this good-sized painting — which was about three feet by five in size. Stephen had paused to examine it curiously and it was this which drew my attention to it.

Under my first cursory examination, which was little more than a glance, I had supposed the thing to be one of those ubiquitous Victorian horrors of reproduction which fifty years ago might have been observed on the walls of most middle-class front parlors, and which were known as chromos. But later that evening, on picking it up and looking at it under the electric light, I found that it was honest paint, and I examined it more closely and with a constantly increasing interest.

The painting was obviously the work of a fairly clever amateur. The frame was very old and dry wood had been riddled through and through by wood-worms; it literally fell apart in my hands. I left it there on the floor for Stephen to brush up the next morning and took the canvas into my bedroom where there was a better light. The accumulation of many years' dust and grime had served to obscure its once crudely bright coloration. I carried it into my bathroom, made a lather of soap and warm water, and gave it a careful and much needed cleansing, after which the scene delineated before me assumed a surprising freshness and clarity.

After I had dried it off with a hand towel, using great care lest I crack the ancient pigment, I went over it with an oiled cloth. This process really brought it out, and although the canvas was something more than a century old, the long obscured and numerous figures with which it had been almost completely covered seemed once more as bright and clear — and quite as crude — as upon the long distant day when that rather clever amateur had laid down his (or perhaps her) brush after putting on the very last dab of vermilion paint.

The subject of this old painting, as I recognized quite soon, was an almost forgotten incident in the history of the old Danish West Indies. It had, quite obviously, been done from the viewpoint of a person on board a ship. Before me, as the setting of the scene, was the well-known harbor of St. Thomas with its dull red fort at my right — looking exactly as it does today. At the left-hand margin were the edges of various public buildings which have long since been replaced. In the midst, and occupying nearly the entire spread of the canvas, with Government Hill and its fine houses sketched in for background, was shown the execution of Fawcett, the pirate, with his two lieutenants; an occasion which had constituted a general holiday for the citizens of St. Thomas, and which had taken place, as I happened to be aware, on the eleventh of September, 1825. If the picture had been painted at that time, and it seemed apparent that such was the case, the canvas would be just one hundred and two years old.

My interest now thoroughly aroused, I bent over it and examined it with close attention. Then I went into my workroom and brought back my large magnifying glass.

My somewhat clever amateur artist had left nothing to the imagination. The picture contained no less than two hundred and three human figures. Of these, only those in the remoter backgrounds were sketched in roughly in the modern manner. The actual majority were very carefully depicted with a laborious infinitude of detail; and I suspected then, and since have found every reason to believe, that many, if not most of them, were portraits! There before my eyes were portly Danish worthies of a century ago, with their ladyfolk, all of whom had come out to see Captain Fawcett die. There were the officers of the garrison. There were the gendarmes of the period, in their stiff-looking uniforms after the manner of Frederick the Great.

There were Negroes, some with large gold rings hanging from one ear; Negresses in their bebustled gingham dresses and bare feet, their foulards or varicolored head handkerchiefs topped by the broad-brimmed plaited straw hats which are still to be seen along St. Thomas's concrete drives and sidewalks. There was the executioner, a huge, burly, fierce-looking black man; with the police-master standing beside and a little behind him, gorgeous in his glistening white drill uniform with its gilt decorations. The two stood on the central and largest of the three scaffolds.

The executioner was naked to the waist and had his woolly head bound up in a tight-fitting scarlet kerchief. He had only that moment sprung the drop, and there at the end of the manila rope (upon which the artist had carefully painted the seven turns of the traditional hangman's knot placed precisely under the left ear of the miscreant now receiving the just reward of his innumerable villainies) hung Captain Fawcett himself, the gruesome central figure of this holiday pageant — wearing top boots and a fine plum-colored laced coat.

On either side, and from the ropes of the two smaller gibbets, dangled those two lesser miscreants, Fawcett's mates. Obviously their several executions, like the preliminary bouts of a modern boxing program, had preceded the main event of the day.

The three gibbets had been erected well to the left of the central space which I have described. The main bulk of the spectators was consequentially to the right as one looked at the picture, on the fort side.

After more than a fascinating hour with my magnifying glass, it being then eleven o'clock and time to turn in, I carried the brittle old canvas into my workroom and by the rather dim light of the shaded reading lamp fastened it carefully at a convenient height against the south wall with thumbtacks. The last tack went through the arm of the hanging man nearest the picture's extreme left-hand margin. After accomplishing this, I went to bed.

The next morning, as I have mentioned, being curious to see how the thing looked in a suitable light, I walked into the workroom to look at it.

I received a devastating shock.

My eye settled after a moment or two upon that dangling mate whose body hung from its rope near the extreme left-hand margin of the picture. I found it difficult to believe my eyes. In this clear morning light the expression of the fellow's face had changed startlingly from what I remembered after looking at it closely through my magnifying glass. Last night it had been merely the face of a man just hanged; I had noted it particularly because, of all the more prominent figures, that face had been most obviously an attempt at exact portraiture.

Now it wore a new and unmistakable expression of acute agony.

And down the dangling arm, from the point which that last thumbtack had incontinently transfixed, there ran, and dripped off the fellow's fingers, a stream of bright, fresh, red blood . . .

2

Between the time when the clipper schooner, which had easily overhauled the Macartney trading vessel *Hope* — coming north across the Caribbean and heavily laden with sacked coffee from Barranquilla — had sent a challenging shot from its swivel-gun across the *Hope*'s bows, and his accomplishing the maneuver of coming about in obedience to that unmistakable summons, Captain Saul Macartney had definitely decided what policy he should follow.

He had made numerous voyages in the *Hope* among the bustling trade ports of the Caribbean and to and from his own home port of St. Thomas, and never before, by the grace of God and the Macartney luck, had any freetrader called upon him to stand and deliver on the high seas. But, like all seafaring men of Captain Macartney's generation, plying their trade in those latitudes in the early 1820s, he was well aware of what was now in store for him, his father's ship, and the members of his crew. The *Hope* would be looted; then probably scuttled, in accordance with the freetraders' well-nigh universal policy of destroying every scrap of evidence against them. As for himself and his men, they would be confronted with the formula —

"Join, or go over the side!"

A pirate's recruit was a pirate, at once involved in a status which was without the law. His evidence, even if he were attempting the dangerous double game of merely pretending to join his captor, was worthless.

There was one possible ray of hope, direct resistance being plainly out of the question. This might be one of the better established freebooters, a piratical captain and following whose notoriety was already so widespread, who was already so well known, that he would not take the trouble to destroy the *Hope;* or, beyond the usual offer made to all volunteers of a piratical crew — constantly in need of such replacements — to put the captured vessel, officers, and crew through the mill; once they were satisfied that there was nothing aboard this latest prize to repay them for the trouble and risk of capture and destruction.

The *Hope,* laden almost to her gunwales with sacked coffee, would provide lean pickings for a freetrader, despite the value of her bulk cargo in a legitimate port of trade like Savannah or Norfolk. There were cases, known to Captain Macartney, where a piratical outfit under the command of some notable such as Edward Thatch — often called Teach or Blackbeard — or England, or Fawcett, or Jacob Brenner, had merely sheered off and sailed away in search of more desirable game as soon as it was plain that the loot was neither easily portable nor of the type of value represented by bullion, silks, or the strongbox of some inter-island trading supercargo.

It was plain enough to Captain Saul Macartney, whose vessel had been stopped here about a day's sail southsouthwest of his home port of St. Thomas, capital of the Danish West Indies, and whose cargo was intended for delivery to several ship's brokerage houses in that clearinghouse port for the vast West Indian shipping trade, that his marauder of the high seas could do nothing with his coffee. These ideas were very prominent in his mind in the interval between his shouted orders and the subsequent period during which the *Hope,* her way slacking rapidly, hung in the wind, her jibs, booms, and loose rigging slapping angrily while the many boats from the freetrading vessel were slung outboard on a very brisk and workmanlike manner and dropped one after the other into the water alongside until every one — seven in all — had been launched.

These boats were so heavily manned as to leave them very low in the water. Now the oars moved with an almost delicate precision as though the rowers feared some mischance even in that placid sea. The *Hope*'s officers and crew — all of the latter Negroes — crowding along their vessel's starboard rail, the mates quiet and collected as men taking their cue from their superior officer; the crew goggle-eyed, chattering in low tones among themselves in groups and knots, motivated by the sudden looming terror which showed in a gray tinge upon their black skins.

Then, in a strident whisper from the first mate, a shrewd and experienced bucko, hailing originally from Portsmouth, New Hampshire, wise in the ways of these tropical latitudes from twenty years' continuous seafaring:

"God! It's Fawcett himself!"

Slowly, deliberately, as though extremely disdainful of any possible resistance, the seven boats drew toward the doomed *Hope.* The two foremost edged in close alongside her starboard quarter and threw small grapples handily from bow and stern and so hung in under the *Hope*'s lee.

Captain Saul Macartney, cupping his hands, addressed over the heads of the intervening six boatloads the man seated in the sternsheets of the outermost boat:

"Cargo of sacked Brazil coffee, Captain, and nothing else to make it worth your while to come aboard me — if you'll take my word for it. That's the facts, sir, so help me God!"

In silence from all hands in the boats and without any immediate reply from Fawcett, this piece of information was received. Captain Fawcett sat there at the sternsheets of his longboats, erect, silent, presumably pondering what Captain Saul Macartney had told him. He sat there calm and unruffled, a fine gold-laced tricorn hat on his head, which, together with the elegance of his wine-colored English broadcloth coat, threw into sharp relief his brutal, unshaven face with its sinister, shining white scar — the result of an old cutlass wound — which ran diagonally from the upper corner of his left ear forward down the cheek, across both lips, clear to the edge of his prominent chin.

Fawcett, the pirate, ended his reflective interval. He raised his head, rubbed a soiled hand through his beard's stubble and spat outboard.

"Any ship's biscuit left aboard ye?" he inquired, turning his eye along the *Hope*'s freeboard and thence contemplatively about her masts and rigging. "We're short."

"I have plenty, Captain. Will it answer if I have it passed over the side to ye?"

The two vessels and the seven heavily laden boats lay tossing silently in the gentle swell. Not a sound broke the tension while Captain Fawcett appeared to deliberate.

Then a second time he spat over the side of his longboat and rubbed his black stubbly chin with his hand, reflectively. Then he looked across his boats directly at Captain Saul Macartney. The ghost of a sour grin broke momentarily the grim straight line of his maimed and cruel mouth.

"I'll be comin' aboard ye, Captain," he said very slowly, "if ye have no objection to make."

A bellow of laughter at this sally of their captain's rose from the huddled pirate crew in the boats and broke the mounting tension. A Negro at the *Hope*'s rail cackled hysterically, and a chorus of jibes at this arose from the motley crews of the two boats grappled alongside.

In the silence which followed Captain Fawcett muttered a curt, monosyllabic order. The other five boats closed in without haste, two of them passing around the *Hope*'s stern and another around her bow. It was only a matter of a few seconds before the entire seven hung along the *Hope*'s sides like feasting wolves upon the flanks of a stricken deer. Then at a second brief order their crews came over the rails quietly and in good order, Fawcett himself arriving last upon the *Hope*'s deck. No resistance of any kind was offered. Captain Macartney had had the word passed quietly on that score while the pirates' boats were being slung into the water.

After the bustling scramble involved in nearly a hundred men climbing over the *Hope*'s rail from the seven boats and which was, despite the excellent order maintained, a maneuver involving considerable noisy activity, another and even a more ominous silence settled down upon the beleaguered *Hope*.

Supported by his two mates, one of whom was a small, neat, carefully dressed fellow, and the other an enormous German who sported a cavalry-man's moustache and walked truculently, Captain Fawcett proceeded directly aft, where he turned and faced forward, a mate on either side of him, and leaned against the superstructure of Captain Macartney's cabin.

Macartney's mates, taking pattern from this procedure, walked over from the rail and flanked him where he stood just aft of the *Hope*'s foremast. The rest of the freebooters, having apparently been left free by their officers to do as they pleased for the time being, strolled about the deck looking over the vessel's superficial equipment, and then gathered in little knots and groups about the eleven Negro members of the *Hope*'s crew.

Through this intermingling the comparative silence which had followed their coming aboard began to be dissipated with raillery, various low-voiced sallies of crude wit at the Negroes' expense, and an occasional burst of nervous or raucous laughter. All this, however, was carried on, as Captain Macartney took it in, in what was to him an unexpectedly restrained and quiet manner, utterly at variance with the reputed conduct of such a group of abandoned villains at sea, and to him, at least, convincing evidence that something sinister was in the wind.

This expectation had its fulfillment at a harsh blast from the whistle which, at Fawcett's nod, the huge German mate had taken from his pocket and blown.

Instantly the pirates closed in and seized those members of the *Hope*'s Negro crew who stood nearest them; several, sometimes five or six, men crowding in to overpower each individual. Five or six of the pirates who had been as though without purpose near the forward hatchway which led below decks began forthwith to knock out the wedges. The *Hope*'s Negroes, with a unanimity which bespoke the excellent discipline and strategy which Fawcett was generally understood to maintain, were hustled forward and thrust into the forecastle; the hatch of which, as soon as they were all inside, was forthwith closed tight and at once nailed fast by the undersized little Englishman who was Fawcett's ship's carpenter.

None of the *Hope*'s crew had been armed. None seemed to Captain Macartney to have been even slightly injured in the course of this rough and effective handling. Captain Macartney surmised, and rightly, that the pirates' intention was to preserve them alive either for ultimate sale into slavery, which was of course then extant throughout the West India Islands, or, perhaps, to convey them as shore servants to Fawcett's settlement which, it was generally believed, was well in the interior of the island of Andros in the Bahama group, where a network of interlacing creeks, rendering anything like pursuit and capture well-nigh out of the question, had made this private fastness a stronghold.

But Captain Macartney had little time to waste thinking over the fate of his crew. With perhaps a shade less of the roughness with which the Negroes had been seized he and his mates were almost simultaneously surrounded and marched aft to face their captors. It seemed plain that the usual choice was to be given only to the three of them.

Fawcett did not hesitate this time. He looked at the three men standing before him, lowered his head, relaxed his burly figure, and barked out —

"Ye'll join me or go over the side."

He pointed a dirty finger almost directly into the face of the older mate, who stood at his captain's right hand.

"You first," he barked again. "Name yer ch'ice, and name it now."

The hard-bitten New Hampshire Yankee stood true to the traditions of an honest sailorman.

"To hell with ye, ye damned scalawag," he drawled, and spat on the deck between Captain Fawcett's feet.

There could be but one reply on the part of a man of Fawcett's heady character to such an insult as this. With a speed that baffled the eye the great pistol which hung from the right side of his belt beneath the flap of his fine broadcloth coat was snatched free, and to the accompaniment of its tearing roar, its huge ounce ball smote through the luckless Yankee's forehead. As the acrid cloud of smoke from this detonation blew away Captain Macartney observed the huge German mate lifting the limp body which, as though it had been that of a child, he carried in great strides to the nearer rail and heaved overboard.

Fawcett pointed with his smoke weapon at Macartney's other mate, a small-built fellow, originally a British subject from the Island of Antigua. The mate merely nodded comprehendingly. Then —

"The same as Elias Perkins told ye, ye blasted swab,

94

and may ye rot deep in hell."

But Fawcett's surly humor appeared to have evaporated, to have discharged itself in the pistoling of the other man whose scattered brains had left an ugly smear on the *Hope*'s clean deck. He merely laughed and, with a comprehensive motion of his left hand, addressed the larger of his mates, who had resumed his position at his left.

"Take him, Franz," he ordered.

The huge mate launched himself upon the Antiguan like a ravening beast. With lightning-like rapidity his enormous left arm coiled crushingly about the doomed man's neck. Simultaneously, his open right hand against his victim's forehead, he pushed mightily. The little Antiguan's spine yielded with an audible crack and his limp body slithered loosely to the deck. Then with a sweeping, contemptuous motion, the huge mate grasped the limp form in one hand, lifting it by the front of the waistcoat and, whirling about, hurled it with a mighty pitch far outboard.

The German mate had not yet resumed his place beside Fawcett when Captain Saul Macartney addressed the pirate leader.

"I'm joining you, Captain," he said quietly.

And while the surprised Fawcett stared at him the newly enlisted freebooter, who had been Captain Saul Macartney of the schooner *Hope,* with a motion which did not suffer by comparison with Fawcett's for its swiftness, had produced a long dirk, taken the two lightning strides necessary for an effective stroke, and had plunged his weapon with a mighty upward thrust from under the ribs through the German mate's heart.

Withdrawing it instantly, he stooped over the sprawled body and wiped the dirk's blade in a nonchalant and leisurely manner on the dead ruffian's fine cambric shirt frill. As he proceeded to this task he turned his head upward and slightly to the left and looked squarely in the eye the stultified pirate captain who stood motionless and staring in his surprise at this totally unexpected feat of his newest recruit. From his crouching position Saul

95

Macartney spoke, quietly and without emphasis —

"Ye see, sir, I disliked this larrikin from the minute I clapped eyes on him; and I'll call your attention to the fact that I'm a sound navigator, and —" Saul Macartney smiled and showed his handsome teeth — "I'll ask your notice preliminary to my acting with you aft that it might equally well have been yourself that I scragged, and perhaps that'll serve to teach ye the manner of man that you're now taking on as an active lieutenant!"

Then Saul Macartney, his bantering smile gone now, his Macartney mouth set in a grim line, his cleansed dirk held ready in his sound right hand, stood menacingly before Captain Fawcett, their breasts almost touching, and in a quarter-deck voice inquired:

"And will ye be taking it or leaving it, Captain Fawcett?"

3

It was more than two months later when the *Hope,* her hull now painted a shining black, her topmasts lengthened all round by six feet, her spread of canvas vastly increased, eight carronade ports newly cut along her sides, and renamed the *Swallow,* entered the harbor of St. Thomas, dropped her anchor, and sent over her side a narrow longboat.

Into this boat, immediately after its crew of six oarsmen had settled down upon their thwarts and laid their six long sweeps out upon the harbor water, interested onlookers observed two officers descend over the *Swallow*'s side, where they occupied the sternsheets together. As the boat, rowed man-o'-war style, rapidly approached the wharves it was observed by those on shore that the two men seated astern were rather more than handsomely dressed.

The shorter and heavier man wore a fine sprigged long coat of English broadcloth with lapels, and a laced tricorn hat. His companion, whose appearance had about it something vaguely familiar, was arrayed in an equally rich and very well-tailored, though somewhat plainer, coat of a medium blue which set off his handsome figure admirably. This person wore no hat at all, nor any shade for his head against the glare of the eleven o'clock sun save a heavy crop of carefully arranged and naturally curly hair as black as a crow's wing.

So interesting, indeed, to the loungers along the wharves had been the entrance of this previously unknown vessel into the harbor and the subsequent coming ashore of these two fine gentlemen, that a considerable knot of sightseers was already assembled on the particular jetty toward which the longboat, smartly rowed, came steadily closer and closer. The hatless gentleman, who was by far the taller and handsomer of the two, appeared to be steering, the taut tiller ropes held firmly in his large and very shapely hands.

It was the Herr Rudolph Bernn, who had observed the crowd collecting on the jetty through the open windows of his airy shipping office close at hand, and who had clapped on his pith sun helmet and hastened to join the group, who was the first to recognize this taller officer.

"Gude Gott! If id iss nod Herr Captain Saul Macartney. Gude Gott, how they will be rejoiced — Oldt Macartney andt de Miss Camilla!"

Within five minutes the rapidly approaching longboat had been laid aside the pier head in navy style. Without any delay the two gentlemen, whose advent had so greatly interested the St. Thomas harbor watchers, stepped ashore with an air and mounted the jetty steps side by side. At once Saul Macartney, whose fine clothes so well became him, forged ahead of his well dressed, shaved, and curled companion. He wore the dazzling smile which revealed his magnificent teeth and which had served to disarm every woman upon whom it had been consciously turned since his eighth year or thereabouts.

Like a conquering hero this handsome young man — who had taken clearance from the South American port of Barranquilla nearly three months before and subsequently disappeared into thin air along with his vessel and all hands off the face of the waters — now stepped jauntily across the jetty toward the welcoming group whose numbers were, now that the news of his homecoming was beginning to trickle through the town, constantly increasing. He was instantaneously surrounded by these welcoming acquaintances who sought each to outdo his neighbor in the enthusiastic fervency of his congratulatory greetings.

During this demonstration the redoubtable and notorious Captain Fawcett stood quietly looking on throughout its milling course, a sardonic smile faintly relieving the crass repulsiveness of his maimed countenance. The pirate had been "shaved to the blood" that morning; dressed for the occasion with the greatest care. His carefully arranged locks were redolent of the oil of Bergamot, filched a week before out of the accessories of a lady passenger taken from the luckless vessel on which she had been coming out to the West Indies to join her planter husband. This lady had, after certain passing attentions from Saul Macartney, gone over the *Swallow*'s side in plain sight of the volcanic cone of Nevis, the island of her destination.

That Macartney had brought Captain Fawcett ashore with him here in St. Thomas was a piece of judgment so lamentably bad as to need no comment of any kind. His doing so initiated that swift course of events which brought down upon his handsome head that ruinous doom which stands, probably, as unique among the annals of retribution; that devastating doom which, for its horror and its strangeness, transcends and surpasses, in all human probability, even the direst fate, which, in this old world's long history, may have taken over any of the other sons of men.

But the sheer effrontery of that act was utterly characteristic of Saul Macartney.

In the course of the long, painstaking, and probably exhaustive research which I, Gerald Canevin, set in motion in order to secure the whole range of facts forming the basis of this narrative — an investigation which has extended through more than three years and has taken me down some very curious by-paths of antique West Indian history as well as into contact with various strange characters and around a few very alluring corners of research — one aspect of the whole affair stands out in my mind most prominently. This is the fact that — as those many who nowadays increasingly rely for guidance upon the once discredited but now reviving science of astrology would phrase it — Saul Macartney was in all ways "a typical Sagittarian"!

One of the more readily accessible facts which I looked up out of ancient, musty records in the course of this strange affair was the date of his birth. He had been born in the city of St. Thomas on the twenty-eighth of November, in the year 1795. He was thus twenty-nine — in his thirtieth year and the full vigor of his manhood — at the time when Captain Fawcett had captured the *Hope* and, having lightened that vessel by emptying her hold of her cargo which she consigned to the sea, and having scuttled his own disabled vessel, had sailed for his home base among the Andros creeks.

From there a month later the transformed *Swallow* had emerged to maraud upon the Spanish Main. He was not yet out of his twenties when he had chosen to tempt fate by coming ashore with Fawcett in St. Thomas. He was still short of thirty when a certain fateful day dawned in the month of September, 1825.

True to this hypothetical horoscope of his and to every sidereal circumstance accompanying it, Saul Macartney was an entirely self-centered person. With him the "main chance" had always been paramount. It was this addiction to the main chance which had caused him to join Fawcett. A similar motive had actuated him in the notable coup which had at once, because of its sheer directness and the courage involved in it, established him in the high esteem of the pirate captain. There had been no sentiment in his killing of the gigantic mate, Franz. He was not thinking of avenging his own faithful lieutenant whom that hulking beast had slain with his bare

99

hands before his eyes a moment before he had knifed the murderer.

His calculating sense of self-interest had been the whole motive behind that act. He could quite as easily have destroyed Fawcett, himself, as he characteristically pointed out to that ruffian. He would have done so with equal ruthlessness save for his knowledge of the fact that he would have been overwhelmed immediately thereafter by Fawcett's underlings.

There is very little question but what he would have before very long succeeded to the command of the *Swallow* and the control of the considerable commerce in slave trade and other similar illegitimate sources of revenue which went with the command of this piratical enterprise. He had already inaugurated the replacement of Captain Fawcett by himself in the esteem of that freebooter's numerous following well before the refurbished *Swallow* had sailed proudly out upon her current voyage. His unquestionable courage and enormous gift of personality had already been for some time combining actively to impress the pirate crew. Among them he was already a dominating figure.

Since well before he had attained manly maturity he had been irresistible to women. He was a natural fighter who loved conflict for its own sake. His skill with weapons was well-nigh phenomenal. In the prosecution of every affair which concerned his own benefit, he had always habituated himself to going straight to the mark. He was, in short, as it might be expressed, both with respect to women and the securing of his own advantage in general affairs, thoroughly spoiled by an unbroken course of getting precisely what he wanted.

This steady impact of continuous success and the sustained parallel effect of unceasing feminine admiration had entrenched in his character the fatal conviction that he could do as he pleased in every imaginable set of conditions.

The first reversal suffered in the unbroken course of selfish domination inaugurated itself not very long after he had stepped ashore with Captain Fawcett behind him. After ten minutes or so, Macartney gradually got himself free from the crowd of friends congratulating him there on the jetty.

Stimulated as he always was by such admiration, highly animated, his Irish blue eyes flashing, his smile unabated, his selfish heart full to repletion of his accustomed self-confidence, he disentangled himself from the still increasing crowd and, with several bows and various wavings of his left hand as he backed away from them, he rejoined Fawcett, linked his right arm through the crook of the pirate captain's left elbow, and proceeded to conduct him into town. Those fellows on the wharf were small fry! He would, as he smilingly mentioned in Fawcett's ear, prefer to introduce the captain at once into a gathering place where he would meet a group of gentlemen of great importance.

They walked up into the town and turned to the left through the bustling traffic of its chief thoroughfare and, proceeding to the westward for a couple of hundred feet or so, turned in through a wide arched doorway above which, on its bracket, perched guardian-like a small gilded rooster. This was Le Coq d'Or, rendezvous of the more prosperous merchants of the flourishing city of St. Thomas.

A considerable number of these prosperous worthies were already assembled at the time of their arrival in Le Coq d'Or. Several Negroes under the direction of the steward of this club-like clearing house were already bringing in and placing on the huge polished mahogany table the planter's punch, swizzles of brandy or rum, and sangaree such as always accompanied this late-morning assembly. It lacked only a minute or two of eleven, and the stroke of that hour was sacred at Le Coq d'Or and similar foregathering places as the swizzle hour. No less a personage than M. Daniell, some years before a refugee from the Haitian revolution and now a merchant prince here in the Danish colonial capital, was already twirling a carved swizzle stick in the fragrant iced interior of an enormous silver jug.

But this hospitable activity, as well as the innumerable conversations current about the board, ceased abruptly when these city burghers had recognized the tall, handsome gentleman in blue broadcloth who had just stepped in among them. It was, indeed, practically a repetition of what had occurred on the jetty, save that here, the corporate and individual greeting were, if anything, more intimate and more vociferous.

Here were the natural associates, the intimates, the social equals of the Macartneys themselves — a well-to-do clan of proud, self-respecting personages deriving from the class of Irish Protestant high gentry which had come into these islands three generations before upon the invitation of the Danish Colonial Government.

Among those who rose out of their chairs to surround Saul Macartney with hilarious greetings was Denis Macartney, his father. He had expected that the old man would be there. The two clasped each other in a long and affectionate embrace, Denis Macartney agitated and tearful, his son smiling with an unforced whimsicality throughout the intensive contact of this reunion. At last the Old Man, his tears of happiness still overflowing, held off and gazed fondly at his handsome, strapping son, a pair of still trembling hands upon the shoulders of the beautiful new broadcloth coat.

"An' where, in God's name, have ye been hidden' yourself away, me boy?" he asked solicitously.

The others grouped about, and now fallen silent, hovered about the edge of the demonstration, the universal West Indian courtesy only restraining their common enthusiasm to clasp the Macartney prodigal by his bronzed and shapely hands, to thump his back, to place kindly arms about his broad shoulders, later to thrust brimming goblets of cut crystal upon him that they might drink his health and generously toast his safe and unexpected return.

"I'll tell ye about that later, sir," said Saul Macartney, his dazzling smile lighting up his bronzed face. "Ye'll understand, sir, my anxiety to see Camilla; though, of course, I looked in upon ye first off."

And thereupon, in his sustained bravado, in the buoyancy of his fatal conviction that he, Saul Macartney, could get away with anything whatever he might choose to do, and taking full advantage of the disconcerting effect of his announcement that he must run off, he turned to Captain Fawcett, who had been standing close behind him, and, an arm about the captain's shoulders, presented him formally to his father, to M. Daniell, and, with a comprehensive wave of his disengaged arm, to the company at large; and, forthwith, well before the inevitable effect of this act could record itself upon the corporate mind of such a group, Saul Macartney had whirled about, reached the arched doorway almost at a run, and disappeared in the blinding glare, on his way to call upon his cousin, Camilla.

The group of gentlemen assembled in Le Coq d'Or that morning, intensely preoccupied as they had been with the unexpected restoration to their midst of the missing mariner, Macartney, had barely observed the person who had accompanied him. They were now rather abruptly left facing their new guest, and their immediate reaction after Macartney's hasty departure was to stage a greeting for this very evil-looking but highly dandified fellow whom they found in their midst. To this they proceeded forthwith, actuated primarily by the unfailing and highly developed courtesy which has always been the outstanding characteristic of the Lesser Antilles.

There was not a man present who had not winced at the name which Saul Macartney had so clearly pronounced in the course of his threefold introduction of Captain Fawcett. For this name, as that of one of the principal maritime scourges of the day, was indeed very familiar to these men, attuned as they were to seafaring matters. Several of them, in fact, vessel owners, had actually been sufferers at the hands of this man who now sat among them.

Courtesy, however — and to a guest in this central

sanctum — came first. Despite their initial suspicion, by no single overt act, nor by so much as a single glance, did any member of that polished company allow it to be suspected that he had at least given harborage to the idea the Saul Macartney had brought Fawcett the pirate here to Le Coq d'Or and left him among them as a guest.

Besides, doubtless, it occurred to each and every one of these excellent gentlemen, apart from the impossibility of such a situation being precipitated by anyone named Macartney — which was an additional loophole for them — the name of Fawcett was by no means an uncommon one; there might well be half a dozen Fawcetts on Lloyd's List who were or had been commanders of ships. It was, of course, possible that this over-dressed, tough-looking sea hawk had fooled the usually astute Saul.

As for Fawcett himself, the wolf among these domestic cattle, he was enjoying the situation vastly. The man was intelligent and shrewd, still capable of drawing about him the remnants of a genteel deportment; and, as the details of his projected coming ashore here had been quite fully discussed with Saul Macartney, he had anticipated and was quite well prepared to meet the reaction released at the first mention of that hated and dreaded name of his, and which he now plainly sensed all about him. There was probably even a touch of pride over what his nefarious reputation could evoke in a group like this to nerve him for the curious ordeal which had now begun for him.

It was, of course, his policy to play quietly a conservative — an almost negative — role. He busied now his always alert mind with this, returning courtesy for courtesy, and his hosts toasted him formally, assured him of their welcome, exchanged with him those general remarks which precede any real breaking of the ice between an established group and some unknown and untried newcomer.

It was Old Macartney who gave him his chief stimulation by inquiring:

"An' what of me dear son, Captain? Ye will have been

in his company for some time, it may be. It would be more than gracious of ye to relate to us — if so be ye're aware of it, perchance — what occurred to him on that last voyage of his from Sout' America."

At this really unexpected query the entire room fell silent. Every gentleman present restrained his own speech as though a signal had been given. Only the Negro servants, intent upon their duties, continued to speak to each other under their breaths and to move soft-footedly about the room.

Captain Fawcett recognized at once that Mr. Denis Macartney's question contained no challenge. He had even anticipated it, with a thin yarn of shipwreck, which he and Saul had concocted together. In a sudden access of whimsical bravado he abandoned this cooked-up tale. He would give them a story . . .

He turned with an elaborate show of courtesy to Old Macartney. He set down his half-empty goblet, paused, wiped his maimed mouth with a fine cambric handkerchief, and set himself, in the breathless silence all about him, to reply.

"The freetraders took him, sir," said Captain Fawcett. Then he nodded twice, deprecatingly; next he waved a hand, took up his goblet again, drank off its remaining contents in the sustained, pregnant silence, and again turned to Saul's father.

Settling himself somewhat more comfortably in his chair, he then proceeded to relate, with precise circumstantial detail, exactly what had actually taken place, only substituting for himself as the captor the name of the dreaded Jacob Brenner, who, like himself, had a place of refuge among the Andros creeks, and whom Captain Fawcett regarded with profound and bitter detestation as his principal rival.

He told his story through in the atmosphere of intense interest all about him. He made Captain Saul Macartney pretend to join the cutthroat Brenner and, the wish greatly father to the thought, brought his long yarn to a successful conclusion with the doughty Saul staging a desperate hand-to-hand encounter with his captor after going ashore with him on Andros Island, together with a really artistic sketching-in of his escape from the pirate settlement in a dinghy through the intricacies of the mosquito infested creeks; and his ultimate harborage — "well-nigh by chance, or trace of what he names 'the Macartney luck,' sir" — with himself.

"I've a very pleasant little spot there on Andros," added Captain Fawcett.

Then, satisfying another accession of his whimsicality:

"I'm certain any of you would be pleased with it, gentlemen. It's been good — very good and pleasurable, I do assure you — to have had Captain Macartney with me."

And Fawcett, the pirate, whose own longboat had fetched him ashore here from that very vessel whose capture by freetraders on the high seas he had just been so graphically recounting, with a concluding short bow and a flourish of his left hand, took up his recently replenished crystal goblet and, again facing the senior Macartney, toasted him roundly on this, the glad occasion of his seafaring son's prosperous return.

Saul Macartney walked rapidly across the crowded main thoroughfare so as to avoid being recognized and stopped. He turned up the precipitous, winding, and abruptly cornered street of varying width, and, following it between the many closely walled residences among which it wound, mounted at a rapid stride to a point two-thirds of the way up the hill. Here he paused to readjust his clothes and finally to wipe the sweat induced by his pace from his bronzed face with another fine cambric handkerchief like that being used by his colleague about this time down there at Le Coq d'Or. The two of them had divided evenly four dozen of these handkerchiefs not long before from the effects of a dandified French supercargo now feeding the fishes.

It was a very sultry day in the middle of the month of May, in that spring period when the *rata* drums of the Negroes may be heard booming nightly from the wooded hills in the interior of the islands; then the annual shift in the direction of the trade wind between the points east and west of north seems to hang a curtain of sultriness over St. Thomas on its three hillsides. It was one of those days when the burros' tongues hang out of dry mouths as they proceed along dusty roads; when centipedes leave their native dust and boldly cross the floors of houses; when ownerless dogs slink along the inner edges of the baking, narrow sidewalks in the slits of house shade away from the sun.

Saul Macartney had paused near the entrance to the spacious mansion of his uncle, Thomas Lanigan Macartney, which stood behind a stately grille of wrought iron eleven feet high, in its own grounds, and was approached through a wide gateway above which the cut stone arch supported a plaque on which had been carved the Macartney arms. Through this imposing entrance, his face now comfortably dry and his fine broadcloth coat readjusted to his entire satisfaction, Saul Macartney now entered and proceeded along the broad, shell-strewn path with its two borders of cemented pink conch shells toward the mansion.

Through the accident of being his father's first-born son and the rigid application of the principle of primogeniture which had always prevailed among the Macartney clan in the matter of inheritances, old T.L. Macartney possessed the bulk of the solid Macartney family fortune. He had married the only daughter of a retired Danish general who had been governor of the colony. Dying in office, the general had left behind him the memory of a sound administration and another substantial fortune which found its way through that connection into the Macartney coffers.   The only reason why Saul Macartney had not led his heavily endowed cousin, Camilla, to the altar long before, was merely because he knew he could marry her any time. Camilla's lips had parted and her blue eyes became mysterious, soft, and melting at every sight of him since about the time she was eight and he ten. As for Saul Macartney, he could not remember the time when it had not been his settled intention to marry his cousin Camilla when he got ready. He was as sure of her as of the rising and setting of the sun; as that failure was a word without meaning to him; as that the Santa Cruz rum was and always would be the natural drink of gentlemen and sailors.

Jens Sorensen, the black butler, who had witnessed his arrival, had the door open with a flourish when Saul was halfway between the gate and the gallery. His bow as this favored guest entered the house was profound enough to strain the seams of his green broadcloth livery coat.

But black Jens received no reward for his assiduousness from the returned prodigal, beyond a nod. This was not like Saul in the least, but black Jens understood perfectly why Captain Macartney had not quizzed him, paused to slap mightily his broad back under his green coat, or to tweak the lobe of his right ear ornamented with its heavy ring of virgin gold, all of which attentions black Jens could ordinarily expect from this fine gentleman of his family's close kinfolk. There had been no time for such persiflage.

For, hardly had black Jens's huge, soft right hand begun the motion of closing the great door, when Camilla Macartney, apprised by some subtlety of "the grapevine route" of her cousin's arrival, appeared on the threshold of the mansion's great drawing room, her lips parted, her eyes suffused with an inescapable emotion. Only momentarily she paused there. Then she was running toward him across the polished mahogany flooring of the wide hallway, and had melted into the firm clasp of Saul Macartney's brawny arms. Raising her head, she looked up into his face adoringly and Saul, responding, bent and kissed her long and tenderly. No sound save that occasioned by the soft-footed retirement of black Jens to his pantry broke the cool silence of the dignified hall. Then at last in a voice from Camilla Macartney that was a little above a whisper:

"Saul — Saul, my darling! I am so glad, so glad! You

will tell me all that transpired — later, Saul, my dear. Oh, it has been a dreadful time for me."

Withdrawing herself very gently from his embrace, she turned and, before the great Copenhagen mirror against the hallway's south wall, made a small readjustment in her coiffure — her hair was of the purest, cleanest Scandinavian gold, of a spun silk fineness. Beckoning her lover to follow, she then led the way into the mansion's drawing room.

As they entered, Camilla a step in advance of Macartney, there arose from a mahogany and rose-satin davenport the thickset figure of a handsome young man of about twenty-four, arrayed in the scarlet coat of his Brittanic Majesty's line regiments of infantry. This was Captain the Honorable William McMillin, who, as a freshly commissioned coronet-of-horse, had actually fought under Wellington at Waterloo ten years before. Recently he had attained his captaincy, and sold out to undertake here in the Danish West Indies the resident management of a group of Santa Crucian sugar estates, the property of his Scottish kinsfolk, the Comyns.

These two personable captains, one so-called because of his courtesy title, and the other with that honorable seafaring title really forfeited, were duty presented to each other by Camilla Macartney; and thereby was consummated another long stride forward in the rapid march of Saul Macartney's hovering doom.

The Scottish officer, sensing Saul's claim upon that household, retired ere long with precisely the correct degree of formality.

As soon as he was safely out of earshot Camilla Macartney rose and, seizing a small hassock, placed it near her cousin's feet. Seating herself upon this, she looked up adoringly into his face and, her whole soul in her eyes, begged him to tell her what had happened since the day when he had cleared the *Hope* from Barranquilla.

Again Saul Macartney rushed forward upon his fate.

He told her, with circumstantial detail, the cooked-up story of shipwreck, including a touching piece of invention about three days and nights on the *Hope*'s boats and his timely rescue by his new friend, Fawcett, master of the *Swallow* — a very charitable gentleman, proprietor of a kind of trading station on Andros in the Bahamas. Captain Fawcett, who had considerately brought the prodigal back to St. Thomas, was at the moment being entertained in Le Coq d'Or.

Camilla Macartney's eyes grew wide at the name of Saul's rescuer. The first intimation of her subsequent change of attitude began with her exclamation:

"Saul! Not — not Captain Fawcett, the pirate! Not that dreadful man! I had always understood that his lying-up place was in the Island of Andros, among the creeks!"

Saul Macartney lied easily, reassuringly. He turned upon his cousin — anxious, now, as he could see, and troubled — the full battery of his engaging personality. He showed those beautiful teeth of his in a smile that would have melted the heart of a Galatea.

Camilla dropped the subject, entered upon a long explication of her happiness, her delight at having him back. He must remain for breakfast. Was his friend and benefactor, Captain Fawcett, suitably housed? He might, of course, stay here — Father would be so delighted at having him . . .

It was as though she were attempting, subconsciously, to annihilate her first faint doubt of her cousin, Saul, in the enthusiasm for his rescuer. She rose and ran across the room, and jerked violently upon the ornamental bell rope. In almost immediate response to her ring black Jens entered the room softly, bowed before his mistress with a suggestion of prostrating himself.

"A place for Captain Macartney at the breakfast table. Champagne; two bottles — no, four — of the 1801 Chablis — Is Miranda well along with the shell-crustadas?"

Again Camilla Macartney was reassured. All these commands would be precisely carried out.

Thereafter for a space, indeed, until the noon breakfast was announced, conversation languished between the cousins. For the first time in his life, had Saul Macartney been to the slightest degree critically observant, he would have detected in Camilla's bearing a vague hint that her mind towards him was not wholly at rest; but of this he noticed nothing. As always, and especially now under the stimulation of this curious game of bravado he and Fawcett were playing here in St. Thomas, no warning, no sort of premonition, had penetrated the thick veneer of his selfishness, his fatuous conviction that any undertaking of his must necessarily proceed to a successful outcome.

He sat there thinking of how well he had managed things; of the chances of the *Swallow*'s next venture on the Main; of the ripe physical beauty of Camilla; of various women here in the town.

And Camilla Macartney, beautiful, strangely composed, exquisitely dressed, as always, sat straight upright across from him; and looked steadily at her cousin, Saul Macartney. It was as though she envisaged vaguely how he was to transform her love into black hatred. A thin shadow of pain lay across her own Irish-blue eyes.

Captain the Honorable William McMillin, like many other personable young gentlemen before him, had been very deeply impressed with the quality of Camilla Macartney. But it was not only that West Indian gentlewoman's social graces and cool blond beauty that were responsible for the favorable impression. The young captain, a thoroughly hard-headed Scot with very much more behind his handsome forehead than the necessary knowledge of military tactics possessed by the ordinary line regiment officer, had been even more deeply impressed by other qualities obviously possessed by his West Indian hostess. Among these was her intellect; unusual, he thought, in a colonial lady not yet quite twenty-eight. Nothing like Miss Macartney's control of the many servants of the household had ever seemed possible to the captain.

From black Jens, the butler, to the third scullery maid, all of them, as they came severally under the notice of this guest, appeared to accord her a reverence hardly dis-

111

tinguishable from acts of worship. In going about the town with her, either walking for early evening exercise or in her father's barouche to make or return formal calls, the trained and observant eye of the young Scotsman had not failed to notice her effect upon the swarming Negro population of the town.

Obeisances from these marked her passage among them. The gay stridency of their street conversations lulled itself and was still at her passing.

Doffed hats, bows, veritable obeisances in rows and by companies swayed these street loiterers as her moving about among them left them hushed and worshipful in her wake.

Captain McMillin noted the very general respectful attitude of these blacks toward their white overlords, but, his eyes told him plainly, they appeared to regard Camilla Macartney as a kind of divinity.

In the reasonable desire to satisfy his mounting curiosity Captain McMillin had broached the matter to his hostess. A canny Scot, he had approached this matter indirectly. His initial questions had had to do with native manners and customs, always a safe general topic in a colony.

Camilla's direct answers had at once surprised him with their clarity and the exactitude of their information. It was unusual and — as the subject broadened out between them and Camilla told him more about the Negroes, their beliefs, their manner of life, their customs and practices — it began to be plain to Captain McMillin that it was more than unusual; if someone entitled to do so had asked him his opinion on Camilla Macartney's grasp of this rather esoteric subject, and the captain had answered freely and frankly, he would have been obliged to admit that it seemed to him uncanny.

For behind those social graces of hers which made Camilla Macartney a notable figure in the polite society of this Danish Colonial capital, apart from the distinction of her family connection, her commanding position as the richest heiress in the colony, her acknowledged intellectual attainments, and the distinguished beauty of face and form which lent a pervading graciousness to her every act, Camilla Macartney was almost wholly occupied by two consuming interests.

Of these, the first, generally known by every man, woman, and child in St. Thomas, was her preoccupation with her cousin, Saul Macartney. The other, unsuspected by any white person in or out of Camilla Macartney's wide acquaintance, was her knowledge of the magic of the Negroes.

This subject had been virtually an obsession with her since childhood. Upon it she had centered her attention, concentrated her fine mind, and, using every possible opportunity which her independent position and the enormous amount of material at hand afforded, had mastered it in theory and practice throughout its almost innumerable ramifications.

There was, first, the *obeah*. This, deriving originally from the Ashantee slaves, had come into the West Indies through the gate of Jamaica. It was a combined system of magical formulas and the use of drugs. Through it, a skillful practitioner could obtain extraordinary results. It involved a very complete *materia medica,* and a background setting for the usage and practice thereof, which reached back through uncounted centuries into rituals that were the very heart of primitive savagery.

The much more greatly extended affair called Voodoo, an extraordinarily complex fabric of "black," "white," and revelatory occultism, had made its way through the islands chiefly through the Haitian doorway from its proximate source, Dahomey, whence the early French colonists of Hispaniola had brought their original quotas of black slaves.

Voodoo, an infinitely broader and more stratified system than the medieval *obeah,* involved much that appeared to the average white person mere superficial Negro "stupidness." But in its deeper and more basic aspects it included many very terrible things, which Camilla Macartney had encountered, succeeded in undertaking, and appropriated into this terrific fund of black learning which was hers as this fell subject took her through the dim backgrounds of its origin to the unspeakable snake worship of Africa's blackest and deadliest interior.

The considerable Negro population of the island, from the most fanatical *Hougan* presiding in the high hills over the dire periodic rites of the "baptism" and the slaughter of goats and bullocks and willingly offered human victims whose blood, mingled with red rum, made that unholy communion out of which grew the unnameable orgies of the deep interior heights, down to the lowliest pickaninny gathering fruits or stealing yams for the sustenance of his emaciated body — every one of these blacks was aware of this singular preoccupation; acknowledged the supremacy of this extraordinary white lady; paid her reverence; feared her acknowledged powers; would as soon have lopped off a foot as to cross her lightest wish.

Captain the Honorable William McMillin made up his mind that her grasp of these matters was extraordinary. His questionings and Camilla's informative replies had barely touched upon the edge of what she knew.

And the former captain, her cousin, Saul Macartney, did not know that his heiress cousin cherished any interest except that which she had always demonstrated so plainly in his own direction.

Going in to breakfast, Saul Macartney was nearly knocked off his feet by the physical impact of his uncle's greeting. Camilla's father had been spending the morning overlooking a property of his east of the town, in the direction of Smith's Bay. He had thus missed meeting Saul at Le Coq d'Or, but had learned of his nephew's arrival on his way home. The town, indeed, was agog with it.

So sustained was his enthusiasm, the more especially after imbibing his share of the unusually large provision of wine for a midday meal which his daughter's desire to honor the occasion had provided, that he monopolized most of his nephew's attention throughout breakfast and

114

later in the drawing room after the conclusion of the meal. It was perhaps because of this joviality on his uncle's part that Saul Macartney failed to observe the totally new expression which had rested like a very small cloud on Camilla Macartney's face ever since a short time before going into the dining room.

His uncle even insisted upon sending the prodigal home in the English barouche, and in this elegant equipage — with its sleek, Danish coach horse and the liveried Negroes on its box with cockades at the sides of their glistening silk toppers — he made the brief journey down one hill, a short distance through the town, and up another one to his father's house.

Here, it being well after two o'clock in the afternoon, and siesta hour, he found Fawcett, whom the Old Man had taken under his hospitable wing. The two had no private conversation together. Both were in high spirits and these Old Macartney fostered with his cordials, his French brandy, and a carafe of very ancient rum. The three men sat together over their liquor during the siesta hour, and during the session Old Macartney did most of the talking. He did not once refer to his son's capture by Brenner, the freebooter.

He confined himself in his desire to be entertaining to his son's benefactor, Captain Fawcett, to a joyous succession of merry tales and ripe, antique quips. Saul Macartney had therefore no reason to suspect, nor did it happen to occur to Fawcett to inform him, that the latter's account of Macartney's adventures since the time he had last been heard from until the present was in any wise different from the tale of shipwreck upon which they had agreed and which Macartney had told out in full to his cousin, Camilla.

The three had not finished their jovial session before various strange matters affecting them very nearly, odd rumors, now being discussed avidly in various offices, residences, and gathering places about St. Thomas, were gathering headway, taking on various characteristic exaggerations and, indeed, running like wildfire through the town.

In a place like St. Thomas, crossroads and clearing-house of the vast West Indian trade which came and went through that port and whose prosperity was dependent almost wholly upon shipping, even the town's riff-raff was accustomed to think and express itself in terms of ships.

It was an unimportant, loquacious Negro youth who started the ball a-rolling. This fellow, a professional diver, came up to one of the wharves in his slab-sided, home-made rowboat where he lounged aft, submitting to the propulsion of his coal-black younger brother, a scrawny lad of twelve. This wharf rat had had himself rowed out to the vessel from which the two notables he had observed had come ashore that morning. It was from the lips of this black ne'er-do-well that various other wharfside loiterers learned that the beautiful clipper vessel lying out there at anchor was provided with eight carronade ports.

Out of this idle curiosity thus initially aroused there proceeded various other harbor excursions in small boats. The black diver had somehow managed to miss the stanchion of the "long tom" which Fawcett, in an interval of prudence, had had dismounted the night before. The fact that the *Swallow* carried such an armament, how-ver, very soon trickled ashore.

This nucleus of interesting information was soon fol-lowed up and almost eclipsed in interest by the various discussions and arguments which were soon running rife among the shipping interests of the town over the extraordinary numbers of the *Swallow's* crew.

A round dozen, together with the usual pair of mates to supplement the captain, as all these experts on ships were well aware, would ordinarily suffice for a vessel of this tonnage. Accounts and the terms of the various argu-ments varied between estimates ranging from seventy-five to a hundred men on board the *Swallow*.

A side issue within this category was also warmly dis-cussed. Crews of vessels with home ports in the islands were commonly Negro crews. This unprecedented gath-

116

ering of men was a white group. Only two — certain of the debaters held out firmly that they had observed three — Negroes were to be perceived aboard the *Swallow,* and one of these, a gigantic brown man who wore nothing but earrings and a pair of faded dungaree trousers, was plainly the cook in charge of the *Swallow*'s galley, and the other, or others, were this fellow's assistants.

But the town got its real fillip from the quite definite statement of a small-fry worthy, one Jeems Pelman, who really gave them something to wrangle about when he came ashore after a visit of scrutiny and stated flatly that this rakish, shining, black-hulled clipper was none other vessel than the Macartney's *Hope,* upon both hull and rigging of which he had worked steadily for three months in his own shipyard when the *Hope* was built during the winter of 1819.

All these items of easily authenticated information bulked together and indicated to the comparatively unsophisticated, as well as to the wiseacres, only one possible conclusion. This was that the Macartney vessel, in command of which Captain Saul Macartney was known to have cleared from a South American port three months earlier, had as yet in some unexplained fashion been changed over into a freetrading ship and that the harsh-featured seadog in his fine clothes who had accompanied Captain Macartney ashore that morning could very well be none other than its commander.

A certain lapse of time is ordinarily requisite for the loquacious stage of drunkenness to overtake the average hard-headed seafaring man. The crew of Fawcett's longboat, after three weeks' continuous duty at sea, had bestowed the boat safely, engaged the services of an elderly Negro to watch it in their absence, and drifted into the low rum shop nearest their landing place; and there not long after their arrival Fawcett's boatswain, a Dutch island bruiser, had been recognized by several former acquaintances as a sailorman who had gone out of the harbor of St. Eustasia in a small trading schooner which had disappeared off the face of the wide Caribbean three years previously.

The rum-induced garrulity of this gentleman, as the report of it went forth and flared through the town, corroborated the as yet tentative conclusion that a fully manned pirate ship lay for the time being at anchor in the peaceful harbor of St. Thomas; and that its master, whose identity as a certain Captain Fawcett had spread downward through the social strata from Le Coq d'Or itself, was here ashore, hobnobbing with the town's high gentry, and actually a guest of the Macartneys.

By three o'clock in the afternoon the town was seething with the news. There had been no such choice morsel to roll on the tongue since Henry Morgan had sacked the city of Panama.

The first corroboration of that vague, distressing, but as yet unformed suspicion which had lodged itself in Camilla Macartney's mind came to her through Jens Sorensen, the butler. The "grapevine route," so-called — that curious door-to-door and mouth-to-ear method of communicating among the Negroes of the community — is very rapid as well as very mysterious. Black Jens had heard this devastating story relayed up to him from the lowest black riff-raff of the town's waterfront a matter of minutes after the name of their guest, seeping downward from Le Coq d'Or, had met, mingled with, and crowned the damnatory group of successive details from the wharves.

To anyone familiar with the effect of Voodoo upon the Negro mentality there would be nothing surprising in the fact that black Jens proceeded straight to his mistress to whisper the story without any delay. For fear is the dominant note of the Voodooist. The St. Thomas Negroes were actuated in their attitude toward Camilla Macartney by something infinitely deeper than that superficial respect which Captain McMillin had noted. They feared her and her proven powers as they feared the dreaded demigod Damballa, tutelary manifestation of the unnamed Guinea-Snake himself.

For it was not as one who only inquires and studies

118

that Camilla Macartney commanded awe and reverence of the St. Thomas Negroes. She had *practiced* this extraordinary art and it was her results as something quite tangible, definite, and unmistakable which formed the background of that vast respect, and which had brought black Jens cringing and trembling into her presence on this particular occasion.

And black Jens had not failed to include in his report the drunken sailorman's leering account of that captive lady's treatment by Saul Macartney — how an innocent young wife, off Nevis, had been outrageously forced into Saul's cabin, and when he had tired of her, how he had sent her back to the deck to go across the plank of death.

What desolation penetrated deep and lodged itself there in Camilla Macartney's soul can hardly be guessed at. From that moment she was convinced of the deep infamy of that entrancing lover-cousin of hers whom she had adored with her whole heart since remoteness of her early childhood.

But, however poignantly indescribable, however extremely devastating, may have been her private feelings, it is certain that she did not retire as the typical gentlewoman of the period would have done to eat out her heart in solitary desolation.

Within ten minutes, on the contrary, in response to her immediately issued orders, the English barouche with its sleek Danish horses, its cockaded servants on the box, was carrying her down the hill, rapidly along through the town, and then the heavy coach horses were sweating up the other hill toward her uncle's house. If the seed of hatred, planted by Saul's duplicity, were already sprouting, nevertheless she would warn him. She dreaded meeting him.

Saul Macartney, summoned away from the somewhat drowsy end of that afternoon's convivial session with Fawcett and the Old Man, found his cousin awaiting him near the drawing room door. She was standing, and her appearance was calm and collected. She addressed him directly, without preamble:

"Saul, it is known in the town. I came to warn you. It is running about the streets that this Captain Fawcett of yours is the pirate. One of his men has been recognized. He talked in one of the rum shops. They say that this ship is the *Hope*, altered into a different appearance. I advise you to go, Saul — go at once, while it is safe!"

Saul Macartney turned his old disarming smile upon his cousin. He could feel the liquor he had drunk warming him, but his hard Irish head was reasonably clear. He was not befuddled. He stepped toward her as though impulsively, his bronzed face flushed from his recent potations, his arms extended and spread in a carefree gesture as though he were about to take her in his embrace.

"Camilla, *allana,* ye should not sadden your sweet face over the likes of me. I know well what I'm about, me darling. And as for Fawcett — well, as ye're aware of his identity, ye'll know that he can care for himself. Very suitably, very suitably indeed."

He had advanced very close upon her now, but she stood unmoving, the serious expression of her face not changed. She only held up a hand in a slight gesture against him, as though to warn him to pause and think. Again, Saul Macartney stepped lightly toward his doom.

"And may I not be having a kiss, Camilla?" His smiling face was unperturbed, his self-confidence unimpaired even now. Then, fatally, he added, "And now that ye're here, *acushla,* why should ye not have me present my friend, the captain? 'Twas he, ye'll remember, that brought me back to ye. I could be fetching him within the moment."

But Camilla merely looked at him with a level gaze.

"I am going now," she said, ignoring his suggestion and the crass insult to her gentility involved in it, and which beneath her calm exterior had outraged her and seared her very soul. The seed was growing apace. "I have warned you, Saul."

She turned and walked out of the room and out of the house; then across the tiled gallery and down the black

120

marble steps, and out to her carriage.

Saul Macartney hastened back to his father and Fawcett. Despite his incurable bravado, motivated as always by his deep-seated selfishness, he had simply accepted the warning just given him at its face value. He addressed his drowsing father after a swift, meaningful glance at Fawcett:

"We shall be needing the carriage, sir, if so be it's agreeable to ye. We must be getting back on board, it appears, and I'll be hoping to look in on ye again in the morning, sir."

And without waiting for any permission, and ignoring his father's liquor-muffled protests against this abrupt departure, Saul Macartney rang the bell, ordered the family carriage to be waiting in the shortest possible time, and pressed a rix-dollar into the Negro butler's hand as an incentive to hasten the process.

Within a quarter of an hour, after hasty farewells to the tearful and now befuddled Old Man, these two precious scoundrels were well on their way through the town towards the jetty where they had landed, and where, upon arrival, they collected their boat's crew out of the rum shop with vigorous revilings and not a few hearty clouts, and were shortly speeding across the turquoise and indigo waters of St. Thomas harbor toward an anchored *Swallow*.

Inside half an hour from their going up over her side and the hoisting of the longboat, the *Swallow,* without reference to the harbormaster, clearance, or any other formality, was picking her lordly way daintily out past Colwell's Battery at the harbor mouth, and was soon lost to the sight of all curious watchers in the welcoming swell of the Caribbean.

This extraordinary visit of the supposedly long drowned Captain Macartney to his native town, and the circumstances accompanying it, was a nine-days' wonder in St. Thomas. The widespread discussion it provoked died down after a while, it being supplanted in current interest by the many occurrences in so busy a port-of-call.

It was not, of course, forgotten, although it dropped out of mind as a subject for acute debate.

Such opinion as remained after the arguments had been abandoned was divided opinion. Could the vessel possibly have been the Macartneys' *Hope?* Was this Captain Fawcett, the pirate? Had Captain Saul Macartney thrown in his lot with freetraders, or was such a course unthinkable on his part?

The yarn which Captain Fawcett had spun in Le Coq d'Or seemed the reasonable explanation — if it were true. In the face of the fact that no other counter-explanation had been definitely put forward by anybody, this version was tacitly accepted by St. Thomas society; but with the proviso, very generally made and very widely held, that this fellow must have been *the* Captain Fawcett after all. Saul Macartney had either been fooled by him, or else Saul's natural gratitude had served to cover, in his estimation of the fellow, any observed shortcomings on the part of this rescuer and friend-in-need.

Camilla Macartney made no allusion whatever, even within the family circle, to the story Saul had told *her.* She was not, of course, called upon to express any opinion outside. She was quite well aware that both versions were falsehoods.

She faced bravely, though with a sorely empty and broken heart, all her manifold social obligations in the town. Indeed, somewhat to distract her tortured mind, wherein that seed of hate was by now growing into a lusty plant, the heiress of the Macartney fortune engaged herself rather more fully than usual that summer season in the various current activities. She forced herself to a greater preoccupation than ever in her attention to her occult pursuits. She even took up afresh the oil painting, long ago abandoned by her, which had been one of her early "accomplishments."

It was during this period — a very dreadful one for her, succeeding as it did, abruptly upon her momentary happiness at her cousin Saul's restoration to the land of the living which had dissipated her acute and sustained grief over his presumptive loss at sea in the *Hope* — that she undertook, with what obscure premonitory motive derived from curious skill in the strange and terrible arts of the black people can only be darkly surmised — another and very definite task.

This was the painting of a panoramic view of the town as seen from the harbor. At this she toiled day after day from the awninged afterdeck of one of the smaller Macartney packet vessels. This boat had been anchored to serve her purpose at the point of vantage she had selected. She worked at her panorama in the clear, pure light of many early summer mornings. Before her on the rather large canvas she had chosen for this purpose there gradually grew into objectivity the wharves, the public buildings, the fort, the three hills with their red-roofed mansions, set amid decorative trees. Her almost incredible industry was, really, a symptom of the strange obsession now beginning to invade her reason. Camilla Macartney had suffered a definite mental lesion.

The scrupulous courtesy of the St. Thomians, that graceful mantle of manners which has never been allowed to wear thin, was unobtrusively interposed between the respected Macartneys and the dreadful scandal which had reached out and touched their impeccable family garment of respectability. By no word spoken, by no overt act, by not so much as a breath were they reminded of Captain Macartney's recent visit ashore or his hasty and irregular departure. Captain McMillin, therefore, as a guest of Camilla's father, heard nothing of it. He sensed, however, a certain indefinite undercurrent of family trouble and, yielding to this sure instinct, ended his visit with all the niceties of high breeding and departed from Santa Cruz.

Just before he left, on the morning after the farewell dinner which had been given as a final gesture in his honor, the captain managed to convey to Camilla the measure of his appreciation. He placed, as it were, his sword at her disposal! It was very nicely made — that gesture of gallantry. It was not to be mistaken for the preliminary to a possible later offer of marriage. It was anything but braggadocio. And it was somehow entirely appropriate to the situation. The handsome, upstanding captain left with his hostess precisely the impression he intended; that is, he left her the feeling that here was an adequate person to depend upon in a pinch, and that she had been invited to depend upon him should the pinch come.

A third of the way up one of the mountains northward and behind the three gentle hills on the southern slopes of which the ancient city of St. Thomas is built, there stood — and still stands — a small stone gentry residence originally built in the middle of the eighteenth century by an exiled French family which had taken refuge in this kindly Danish colony and played at raising vanilla up there on their airy little estate overlooking the town and sea.

This place was still known by its original name of Ma Folie — a title early bestowed upon it by Mme. la Marquise, who had looked up at it through a window in her temporary apartment in the Hotel du Commerce, in the town, while the roofing was being placed upon her new house, there and then assuring herself that only perched upon the back of one of those diminutive burros which cluttered up the town streets could anyone like herself possibly manage the ascent to such a site.

Ma Folie was now one of the many Macartney properties. It belonged to Camilla, having come to her as a portion of her maternal inheritance, and upon it she had reestablished the vanilla planting, helped out by several freshly cleared acres in cocoa. No donkey was required nowadays to convey a lady up the tortuous, steep little trail from the town of Ma Folie. A carriage road led past its unpretentious square entrance posts of whitewashed, cemented stone, and when Camilla Macartney visited her hillside estate the English barouche carried her there, the long climb causing the heavy coach horses to sweat mightily and helping, as the coal-black coachman said, to keep them in condition.

It was up here that she had long ago established what might be called her laboratory. It was at Ma Folie, whose village housed only Negroes selected by herself as her tenant-laborers, that she had, in the course of years, brought the practice of the "strange art" to its perfection. She had for some time now confined her practice to meeting what might be called charitable demands upon her.

Talismans to protect; amulets to attract or repel; potent ouangas — only such modest products of the fine art of Voodoo as these went out from that occult workshop of hers at Ma Folie — went out into the eager, outstretched hands of the afflicted whose manifold plights had engaged Camilla Macartney's sympathy; to the relief of those abject ones who called upon her, in fear and trembling, as their last resort against who knows what obscure devilish attacks, what outrageous charmings, wrought by the inimical ruthlessness of one to another.

No vanilla pod, no single cocoa bean had been stolen from Ma Folie estate since Camilla Macartney had planted it afresh nine years before . . .

It was about ten o'clock in the morning of a day near the middle of August that a kind of tremor of emotion ran through the town of St. Thomas, a matter of minutes after a report of the official watcher and the many other persons in the town and along the wharves whose sustained interest in shipping matters caused their eyes to turn ever and anon toward the wide harbor mouth. The *Swallow,* which three months before had literally run away, ignoring all the niceties of a ship's departure from any port and even the official leavetaking, was coming in brazenly, lilting daintily along under the stiff trade, her decks visibly swarming with the many members of her efficient and numerous crew.

She came up into the wind like a little man-o'-war, jauntily, her sails coming down simultaneously with a precision to warm the hearts of those ship-wise watchers, her rigging slatting with reports like musket shots, the furling and stowing of canvas a truly marvelous demonstration of the efficiency which now reigned aft.

These details of rapid-fire seamanship, swiftly as they were being handled, were as yet incomplete when the longboat went straight down from its davits into the water and Saul Macartney followed his boat's crew over the side and picked up his tiller ropes.

The *Swallow*'s anchorage this time was closer in, and it seemed no time at all to the thronging, gaping watchers on the jetty before he sprang ashore and was up the steps. There was no rum shop for the boat's crew this time. Without their officer's even looking back at them over his shoulder the oarsmen pushed off, turned about, and rowed back to the *Swallow*.

Saul Macartney was, if possible, even more debonair than ever. His self-confident smile adorned his even more heavily bronzed face. He was hatless, as usual, and his handsome figure was mightily set off by a gaily sprigged waistcoat and a ruffled shirt of fine cambric which showed between the silver-braided lapels of the maroon-colored coat of French cloth with a deep velvet collar, the pantaloons of which, matching the coat's cloth, were strapped under a pair of low boots of very shining black leather.

The throng on the jetty was plainly in a different mood as compared to the vociferous, welcoming mob of three months before. They stayed close together in a little phalanx this time and from them came fewer welcoming smiles.

Plainly sensing this, Saul Macartney bestowed on this riff-raff of the wharves no more than a passing glance of smiling raillery. He passed them and entered the town with rapid, purposeful strides as though intent on some very definite business and, utterly ignoring the hum of released though muted conversation which rose behind him as though from an aroused swarm of bees, entered the main thoroughfare, turned sharply to his left along it, proceeded in this direction some forty feet, and turned into the small office of one Axel Petersen, a purveyor of ships' stores.

Blond, stout, genial Axel Petersen stared from his broad, comfortable desk at this entrance and allowed his lower jaw to sag. Then he rose uncertainly to his feet and his four neatly garbed mulatto clerks rose from their four respective high stools with him and, in precise conformity with their employer's facial reaction, their four pairs of mottled-iris eyes rounded out altogether like saucers, and their four lower jaws sagged in unison.

Saul Macartney threw back his head and laughed aloud. Then, addressing Petersen:

"Axel, Axel! I wouldn't have thought it of ye! 'Tis but stores I'm after, man — vast stores, the likes of which ye might be selling in the course of a week to five vessels, if so be ye had the fortune to get that many all in one week!" Then, a shade more seriously, "'Tis pork I want; beans, coffee in sacks, limes by the gunny sack — a hundred and one things, all of them written down to save ye trouble, ye great, feckless porker! And here — beside the list which I'm handing ye now — is the reassurance —"

And Saul Macartney, thrusting his list of ship's supplies neatly printed on a long slip of paper under the nose of the stultified Petersen, slapped down upon the desk top beside it the bulging purse which he had hauled out of the tail pocket of his beautiful, maroon-colored French coat.

"There's two hundred and fifty English sovereigns there forninst ye, Axel. Ye can have it counted out or do it yourself, and if that does not suffice to cover the list, why, there's another shot in this locker behind it, ye *omadhoun* — ye fat robber of pettifogging ship's stewards!"

And before the protruding, bemused blue eyes of portly Axel Petersen, Saul Macartney shook banteringly a thick sheaf of Bank of England ten-pound notes. By the time he had returned these to the same capacious pocket, he was at the door, had paused, turned, and, leaning for an instant nonchalantly against the door jamb, remarked —

"Ye're to have the stores piled up on your wharf not an instant later than two o'clock this day." Then, the bantering smile again to the fore, and shaking a long, shapely

127

forefinger toward the goggling dealer in ship's stores, he added, "Ye'll observe, Axel, I'm not taking your store by force and arms. I'm not sacking this town — this time!"

Then Saul Macartney was gone, and Axel Petersen, muttering unintelligibly as he assembled his scattered wits and those of his four clerks, the heavy purse clutched tightly by its middle in one pudgy hand, and the long list of the *Swallow*'s required stores held a little unsteadily before his nearsighted blue eyes, methodically began the process of getting this enormous order assembled.

It was with a perfectly calm exterior that Camilla Macartney received her cousin Saul a quarter of an hour later. The turmoil beneath this prideful reserve might, perhaps, be guessed at; but as the art of guessing had never formed any part of Saul Macartney's mental equipment, he made no effort in that direction.

He began at once with his usual self-confident directness upon what he had come to say.

"Camilla, *acushla,* I've come to ye in haste, 'tis true, and I'm asking your indulgence for that. 'Twas gracious of ye, as always, to be here at home when I chanced to arrive.

"I'll go straight to the point, if so be ye have no objections to make, and say in plain words what I well know to have been in the hearts of the two of us this many a year. I'm asking ye now, Camilla — I'm begging ye with my whole soul to say that ye'll drive down with me now, Camilla, to the English Church, and the two of us be married, and then sail with me for the truly magnificent home I've been establishing for ye over on Andros."

Camilla Macartney continued to sit, outwardly unmoved, where she had received him when black Jens had shown him into the drawing room. She had not been looking at her cousin during this characteristically confident and even impulsive declaration of his. Her eyes were upon her hands which lay, lightly clasped, in her lap, and she did not raise them to reply. She did not, however, keep him waiting. She said, in a perfectly level voice in which there was apparently no single trace or indication of the tearing, internal emotion which surged through her outraged heart at this last and unforgivable insult —

"I shall not become your wife, Saul — now or ever."

Then, as he stood before her, his buoyant self-confidence for once checked, his face suddenly configured into something like the momentary grotesqueness of Axel Petersen's, she added, in that same level tone, which had about it now, however, the smallest suggestion of rising inflection:

"Do not come to me again. Go now — at once."

This final interview with her cousin Saul was unquestionably the element which served to crystallize into an active and sustained hatred the successive emotional crises and their consequent abnormal states of mind which the events here recorded had stirred up within this woman so terribly equipped for vengeance. The seed of hatred was now a full-grown plant.

Upon a woman of Camilla Macartney's depth and emotional capacity the felonious behavior of Saul Macartney had had a very terrible, and a very deep-reaching, mental effect. She had adored and worshipped him for as long as she could remember. He had torn down and riven apart and left lying about her in brutally shattered fragments the whole structure of her life. He had smashed the solid pride of her family into shreds. He had disgraced himself blatantly, deliberately, with a ruthless abandon. He had piled insult to her upon insult. He had taken her pure love for him, crushed and defiled it.

And now these irresistible blows had had the terrible effect of breaking down the serene composure of this gentlewoman. All her love for her cousin and all her pride in him were transformed into one definite, flaming, and consuming purpose: She must wipe out those dreadful stains!

Arrived in the empty library, Camilla Macartney went straight to the great rosewood desk, and without any delay wrote a letter. The black footman who hurried with this missive down the hill actually passed Saul Macartney, likewise descending it. Within a very short time

after its reception, the captain of the little packet-vessel
— upon which, anchored quite close to shore, Camilla
Macartney had been painting her nearly finished panorama of the town — had gone ashore to round out his full
crew. The packet itself, with Camilla Macartney on
board, sailed out of St. Thomas harbor that afternoon in
plain sight of the restocked *Swallow,* whose great spread
of gleaming white canvas showed gloriously under the
afternoon's sun as she laid her course due southwest. The
packet, laying hers to the southward, rolled and tossed at
a steady eight-knot clip under the spanking trade,
straight for the Island of Santa Cruz.

Captain the Honorable William McMillin was
summoned from his seven o'clock dinner in his estate
house up in the gentle hills of the island's north side, and
only his phlegmatic Scottish temperament, working together with his aristocratic self-control, prevented *his*
shapely jaw from sagging and his blue eyes from becoming saucer-like when they had recorded for him the identity of this wholly unexpected visitor. Camilla Macartney wasted none of the captain's time, nor was her arrival cause for any cooling of the excellent repast from
which he had arisen to receive her.

"I have not," said she downrightly in response to the
astounded captain's initial inquiry at to whether she had
dined. "And," she added, "I should be glad to sit down
with you at once, if that meets your convenience, sir. It is,
as you may very well have surmised, a very deep and
pressing matter upon which I have ventured to come to
you. That, I should imagine, would best be discussed
while we sit at table, and so without delay."

Again the captain demonstrated his admirable
manners. He merely bowed and led the way to the door of
his dining room.

Once seated opposite Captain McMillin, Camilla
Macartney again went straight to her point. The captain
quite definitely forgot to eat in the amazing and immediate interest of what she proceeded to say.

"I am offering the reward of a thousand English

130

sovereigns for the apprehension at sea and the bringing to St. Thomas for their trials of the freetrader, Fawcett, and his mates. It may very well be no secret to you, sir, that a member of our family is one of these men. I think that any comment between us upon that subject will be superfluity. You will take note, if you please, that it is I, a member of our family, who offer the reward I have named for his apprehension. You will understand — everything that is involved.

"Earlier this day it was proposed to me that I should sail away upon a ship without very much notice. I have come here to you, sir, on one of my father's vessels — Captain Stewart, her commander, a trusted man in our employ, has accompanied me all the way to your door. He is here now, waiting in the hired *calèche* which I secured in Frederiksted for the drive here to your house. Perhaps you will be good enough to have some food taken to him.

"I have come, Captain McMillin, in all this haste, actually to request you to do the same thing that I mentioned — you made me see when you were our guest, that I could wholly rely on you, sir. I am here to ask you, as a military man, to command the expedition which I am sending out. I am asking you to sail back with Captain Stewart and me for St. Thomas — tonight."

Captain McMillin looked at Camilla Macartney across the length of his glistening mahogany dining table. He had been listening very carefully to her speech. He rang his table bell now that he was sure she was finished, and when his serving man answered this summons, ordered him to prepare a repast for the waiting ship's captain, and to send in to him his groom. Then, with a bow to his guest, and pushing back his chair and rising, he said:

"You will excuse me, Miss Macartney, I trust, for the little time I shall require to pack. It will not occupy me very long."

The story of how the *Hyperion,* newest and swiftest of all the Macartney vessels, was outfitted and armed for the pursuit and capture of Captain Fawcett is a little epic in itself. It would include among the many details extant to the intensive search among the shipping resources of St. Thomas, for the swivelgun which, two days after Captain McMillin's arrival on the scene, was being securely bolted through the oak timbers of the *Hyperion's* afterdeck.

A surprisingly complete record of this extraordinary piece of activity survives among the ancient colonial archives. Perhaps the recording clerk of the period, in his Government House office, was, like everyone else in St. Thomas, fascinated by the ruthless swiftness with which that job, under the impact of Camilla Macartney's eye, was pushed through to a successful conclusion in precisely forty-eight hours. Nothing like this rate of speed had ever been heard of, even in St. Thomas. The many men engaged in this herculean task at Pelman's Shipyard worked day and night continuously in three eight-hour shifts.

It is significant that these shipwrights and other skilled artisans were all Negroes. They had assembled in their scores and dozens from every quarter of the widespread town, irrespective of age or exactions of their current employment from the instant that the grapevine route spread through the black population of the town the summons to this task which Camilla Macartney had quietly uttered in the ear of her butler, Jens Sorensen.

The *Hyperion,* under the command of her own officers but with the understanding that Captain McMillin was in sole charge of the expedition, came up with the *Swallow* a little under four days from the hour of her sailing out of St. Thomas harbor.

Captain McMillin caught Fawcett at a vast disadvantage. The *Swallow,* very lightly manned at the moment, hung in stays, her riding sails flapping with reports like pistol shots as her graceful head was held into the wind.

She lay some ten shiplengths away to the leeward of an American merchant vessel about which the *Swallow*'s boats — now nine in number — were grouped, a single member of the crew in each. Fawcett and his two lieutenants, and nine-tenths of his crew cutthroats, were ransacking their prize, whose officers, crew, and passengers had been disposed of under nailed hatches. They appeared, indeed, to be so thoroughly occupied in this nefarious work as to have ignored entirely any preparations for meeting the *Hyperion*'s attack — a circumstance sufficiently strange to have impressed Captain McMillin profoundly.

The *Hyperion*'s officers, unable to account for this singular quiescence on the part of the pirates, attributed it to their probably failing to suspect that the *Hyperion* was anything but another trading vessel which had happened to blunder along on her course into this proximity. With a strange, quick gripping at the heart, quite new in his experience, Captain McMillin permitted himself to suspect, though for a brief instant only, that something of the strange power which he had glimpsed in his contacts with Camilla Macartney, might in some extraordinary fashion be somehow responsible for this phenomenon.

But this thought, as too utterly ridiculous for harborage in normal man's mind, he put away from him instanter.

The strategy of this situation appeared to be simple. And Captain McMillin ordered a dozen men in charge of the *Hyperion*'s second mate over the side in the largest of the boats. The maneuver of dropping an already manned boat from the davits — a risky undertaking in any event — was handled successfully, an exceptionally quiet sea contributing to the management of this piece of seamanship.

This boat's crew, all Negroes and all armed with the pistols and cutlasses which had been hastily served out to them, had no difficulty whatever in getting over the *Swallow*'s side and making themselves masters of the pirate vessel. The dozen Negroes had butchered the seven members of the pirate crew left on board the *Swallow* within forty seconds of their landing upon her deck, and Mr. Matthews, the officer in charge of them, hauled down with his own hand the Jolly Roger which, true to the freetrading traditions of the Main, flaunted at the *Swallow*'s main peak.

The magnificent cooperation of the fifteen Negroes constituting the *Hyperion*'s deck crew made possible the next daring piece of seamanship which the *Hyperion*'s captain had agreed to attempt. This was Captain McMillin's plan.

The *Hyperion* should lay alongside the American vessel, grapple to her and board — with all hands — from deck to deck. This idea, almost unheard of in modern sea warfare, had suggested itself as practicable in this instance to Captain McMillin, from his reading. Such had been the tactics of the antique Mediterranean galleys.

For the purpose of retaining the outward appearance of a simple trader, Captain McMillin had concealed the thirty-three additional members of his heavily armed crew, and these had not been brought on deck until he was almost ready to have the grapples thrown. These reserves now swarmed upon the *Hyperion*'s deck in the midst of bedlam of shouts, yells, and curses, punctuated by pistol shots, from the pirate crew on board their prize.

These were taken at a vast disadvantage. Their prize vessel was immobile. They had for what appeared to Captain McMillin some inexplicable reason, apparently failed until the very last moment to realize the *Hyperion*'s intentions. Most of them were busily engaged in looting their prize. Under this process five of the *Swallow*'s nine boats had already been laden gunwale deep with the miscellaneous plunder already taken out of the American ship. Two of these laden small boats and two others of the *Swallow*'s nine were crushed like eggshells as the *Hyperion* closed in and threw her grappling hooks.

Then, in a silence new and strange in Captain McMillin's previous experience in hand-to-hand fighting, his forty-eight black fighting men followed him over the rails and fell upon the pirates.

Within three minutes the American vessel's deck was a shambles. Camilla Macartney's black myrmidons, like militant fiends from some strange hell of their own, their eyeballs rolling, their white teeth flashing as they bared their lips in the ecstasy of this mission of wholesale slaughter, spread irresistibly with grunts and low mutterings and strange cries about that deck.

Not a member of the pirate crew escaped their ruthless onslaught. Hard skulls were split asunder and lopped arms strewed the deck, though bodies were transfixed, and the gasping wounded men were trampled lifeless in the terrible energy of these black fighting men.

Then abruptly, save for a harsh sobbing sound from laboring, panting lungs after their terrific exertion, a strange silence fell, and toward Captain McMillin, who stood well-nigh aghast over the utter strangeness of this unprecedented carnage which had just taken place under his eye and under his command, there came a huge, black, diffidently smiling Negro, his feet scarlet as he slouched along that moist and slippery deck, a crimson cutlass dangling loosely now from the red hand at the end of a red arm. This one, addressing the captain in a low, humble, and deprecating voice, said —

"Come, now, please, me Marster — come, please sar, see de t'ree gentlemahn you is tell us to sabe alive!"

And Captain McMillin, bemused, followed this guide along the deck slushed and scarlet with the lifeblood of those pulped heads which had been Captain Fawcett's pirate crew, stepped aft to where, behind the main deck house, three trussed and helpless white men lay upon a cleaner section of that vessel's deck, under the baleful eye of another strapping black man with red feet and a naked red cutlass brandished in a red hand.

The *Swallow,* her own somewhat blood-soiled deck now shining spotless under the mighty holystonings it had received at the hands of its prize crew of twelve under the command of the *Hyperion*'s second mate, the Danish flag now flying gaily from her masthead, followed the *Hyperion* into St. Thomas harbor on the second day of

September, 1825. The two vessels came up to their designated anchorages smartly, and shortly thereafter, and for the last time, Saul Macartney, accompanied by his crony, Captain Fawcett, and his colleague, the other pirate mate, was rowed ashore in the familiar longboat.

But during this short and rapid trip these three gentlemen did not, for once, occupy the sternsheets. They sat forward, their hands and feet in irons, the six oarsmen between them and Mr. Matthews, the *Hyperion's* mate, who held the tiller rope, and Captain the Honorable William McMillin, who sat erect beside him.

5

I have already recorded my first horrified reaction to the appearance of the handsome black-haired piratical mate whose painted arm my innocent thumbtack had penetrated. My next reaction, rather curiously, was the pressing insistent, sudden impulse to withdraw that tack. I did so forthwith — with trembling fingers, I here openly confess.

My third and final reaction, which came to me not long afterward and when I had somewhat succeeded in pulling myself together, was once more to get out my magnifying glass and take another good look through it. After all, I told myself, I was here confronted with nothing more in the way of material facts than a large-sized, somewhat crudely done, and very old oil painting.

I got the glass and reassured myself. The "blood" was, of course — as now critically examined, magnified by sixteen diameters — merely a few spattered drops of the very same vermilion pigment which my somewhat clever amateur artist had used for the red roofs of the houses, the foulards of the Negresses, and those many glorious flaming flower blossoms.

Quite obviously these particular spatters of red had not been in the liquid state for more than a century. Having ascertained these facts beyond the shadow of any lingering doubt in the field of everyday material fact, my one remaining bit of surviving wonderment settled itself about the minor puzzle of just why I had failed to observe these spots of ancient, dry, and brittle paint during the long and careful scrutiny to which I had subjected the picture the evening before. A curious coincidence, this — that the tiny red spots should happen to be precisely in the place where blood would be showing if it had flowed from my tack wound in that dangled painted arm.

I looked next, curiously, through my glass at the fellow's face. I could perceive now none of that acutely agonized expression which had accentuated my first startled horror at the sight of the blood.

And so, pretty well reassured, I went back to my bedroom and finished dressing. And thereafter, as the course of affairs proceeded, I could not get the thing out of my mind. I will pass over any attempt at describing the psychological processes involved and say here merely that by the end of a couple of weeks or so I was in that state of obsession which made it impossible for me to do my regular work, or, indeed, to think of anything else. And then, chiefly to relieve my mind of this vastly annoying preoccupation, I began upon that course of investigatory research to which I have already alluded.

When I had finished this, had gone down to the end of the last bypath which it involved, it was well on in the year 1930. It had taken three years, and — it was worth it.

I was in St. Thomas that season and St. Thomas was still operating under the regime which had prevailed since the spring of 1917, at which time the United States had purchased the old Danish West Indies from Denmark as a war treasure, during the presidency of Woodrow Wilson.

In 1930 our naval forces had not yet withdrawn from our Virgin Island Colony. The administration was still actively under the direction of his Excellency Captain Waldo Evans, U.S.N. Retired, and the heads of the major departments were still the efficient and personable gentlemen assigned to those duties by the Secretary of the Navy.

My intimate friend, Dr. Pelletier, the pride of the

U.S.N. Medical Corps, was still in active charge of the Naval Hospital, and I could rely upon Dr. Pelletier, whose interest in and knowledge of the strange and *outré* beliefs, customs and practices of numerous strange corners of this partly civilized world of ours were both deep and, as it seemed to me, virtually exhaustive.

To this good friend of mine, this walking encyclopedia of strange knowledge, I took, naturally, my findings in this very strange and utterly fascinating story of old St. Thomas. We spent several long evenings together over it, and when I had imparted all the facts while my surgeon friend listened, as is his custom, for hours on end without a single interruption, we proceeded to spend many more evenings discussing it, sometimes at the hospitable doctor's bachelor dinner table and afterward far into those tropic nights of spice and balm, and sometimes at my house which is quite near the old T.L. Macartney mansion on Denmark Hill.

In the course of these many evenings I added to the account of the affair which had emerged out of my long investigation two additional phases of this matter which I have not included in my account as written out here because, in the form in which these took my mind, they were almost totally conjectural.

Of these, the first took its point of departure from the depiction of the rope, as shown in the painting, with which Saul Macartney had been hanged. I have mentioned the painstaking particularity with which the artist had put in the minor details of the composition. I have illustrated this by stating that the seven traditional turns of the hangman's knot were to be seen showing plainly under Captain Fawcett's left ear. The same type of knot, I may add here, was also painted laboriously upon the noose which had done to death Fawcett's other mate.

But Saul Macartney's rope did not show such a knot. In fact, it showed virtually no knot at all. Even under the magnifying glass a knot expert would have been unable to name in any category of knots the inconspicuous slight enlargement at the place where Saul Macartney's noose was joined. Another point about this rope which might or might not have any significance, was the fact that it was of a color slightly but yet distinctly different from the hemp color of the other two. Saul Macartney's rope was of a faint greenish blue color.

Upon this rather slight basis for conjecture I hazarded the following enlargement:

That Camilla Macartney, just after the verdict of the Danish Colonial High Court had become known to her — and I ventured to express the belief that she had known it before any other white person — said in her quiet voice to her black butler, Jens Sorensen:

"I am going to Ma Folie. Tonight, at nine o'clock precisely, Ajax Mendoza is to come to me there."

And — this is merely my imaginative supplement, it will be remembered, based on my own knowledge of the dark ways of Voodoo — burly black Ajax Mendoza, capital executioner in the honorable employ of the Danish Colonial Administration, whose father, Jupiter Mendoza, had held that office before him, and whose grandfather, Achilles Mendoza (whose most notable performance had been the racking of the insurrectionist leader, Black Tancrède, who had been brought back to the capital in chains after the perpetration of his many atrocities in the St. Jan Uprising of the slaves in 1733), had been the first of the line; that Ajax Mendoza, not fierce and truculent as he looked standing there beside the police-master on Captain Fawcett's gallow platform, but trembling and cringing, had kept the appointment to which he had been summoned.

Having received his orders, he had then hastened to bring to Camilla Macartney the particular length of thin manila rope which was later to be strung from the arm of Saul Macartney's gallows and had left it with her until she returned it to him before the hour of the execution; and that he had received it back and reeved it through its pulley with even more fear and trembling and cringings at being obliged to handle this transmuted thing whose very color was a terror and a distress to him, now that it had passed through that fearsome laboratory of "white missy who knew the snake" . . .

And my second conjectural hypothesis I based upon the fact which my research had revealed to me that all the members of the honorable clan of Macartney resident in St. Thomas had, with obvious propriety, kept to their closely shuttered several residences during the entire day of that public execution. That is, all of the Macartneys expect the heiress of the Macartney fortune, Camilla.

Half an hour before high noon on that public holiday the English barouche had deposited Camilla Macartney at one of the wharves a little away from the center of the town where that great throng had gathered to see the pirates hanged, and from there she had been rowed out to the small vessel which had that morning gone back to its old anchorage near the shore.

There, in her old place under the awning of the after-deck, she had very calmly and deliberately set up her easel and placed before her the all but finished panorama upon which she had been working, and had thereupon began to paint, and so had continued quietly painting until the three bodies of those pirates which had been left dangling "for the space of a whole hour," according to the sentence, "as a salutary example," and had then ended her work and gone back to the wharf carrying carefully the now finished panorama to where the English barouche awaited her.

By conjecture, on the basis of these facts, I managed somehow to convey to Dr. Pelletier, a man whose mind is attuned to such matters, the tentative, uncertain idea — I should not dare to name it a conviction — that Camilla Macartney, by some application of that uncanny skill of hers in the arts of darkness, had as it were, caught the life principle of her cousin, Saul Macartney, as it escaped from his splendid body there at the end of that slightly discolored and curious knotted rope, and fastened it down upon her canvas within the simulacrum of that little painted figure through the arm of which I had thrust a thumbtack!

These two queer ideas of mine, which had been knocking about inside my head, strangely enough did not provoke the retort "Outrageous!" from Dr. Pelletier, a man of the highest scientific attainments. I had hesitated to put such thoughts into words, and I confess that I was surprised that his response in the form of a series of nods of the head did not seem to indicate the indulgence of a normal mind toward the drivelings of some imbecile.

Dr. Pelletier deferred any verbal reply to this imaginative climax of mine, placed as it was at the very end of our discussion. When he did shift his mighty bulk where it reclined in my Chinese rattan lounge chair on my airy west gallery — a sure preliminary to any remarks from him — his first words surprised me a little.

"Is there any doubt, Canevin, in your mind about the identity of this painted portrait figure of the mate with Saul Macartney himself?"

"No," said I. "I was able to secure two faded old ambrotypes of Saul Macartney — at least, I was given a good look at them. There can, I think, be no question on that score."

For the space of several minutes Pelletier remained silent. Then he slightly shifted his leonine head to look at me.

"Canevin," said he, "people like you and me who have seen this kind of thing working under our very eyes, all around us, among people like these West Indian blacks, well — we know."

Then, more animatedly, and sitting up a little in his chair, the doctor said:

"On that basis, Canevin — on the pragmatic basis, if you will, and that, God knows, is scientific, based on observation — the only thing that we can do is to give this queer, devilish thing the benefit of the doubt. Our doubt, to say nothing of what the general public would think of such ideas!"

"Should you say that there is anything that can be done about it?" I inquired. "I have the picture, you know, and you have heard the — well, the facts as they have come under my observation. Is there any — what shall I say? — any responsibility involved on the basis of those facts and any conjectural additions that you and I may choose to make?"

"That," said Pelletier, "is what I meant by the benefit of the doubt. Thinking about this for the moment in terms of the limitations, the incompleteness, of human knowledge and the short distance we have managed to travel along the road of civilization, I should say that there is — a responsibility."

"What shall I do — if anything?" said I, a little taken aback at this downrightness.

Again Dr. Pelletier looked at me for a long moment, and nodded his head several times. Then:

"Burn the thing, Canevin. Fire — the solvent. Do you comprehend me? Have I said enough?"

I thought over this through the space of several silent minutes. Then, a trifle hesitantly because I was not at all sure that I had grasped the implications which lay below this very simple suggestion —

"You mean — ?"

"That if there is anything in it, Canevin — that benefit of the doubt again, you see — if, to put such an outrageous hypothesis in the sane phrase, the life, the soul, the personality remains unreleased, and that because of Camilla Macartney's use of a pragmatic 'magical' skill such as is operative today over there in the hills of Haiti; to name only one focus of this particular cultus — well, then . . ."

This time it was I who nodded; slowly, several times. After that I sat quietly in my chair for long minutes in the little silence which lay between us. We had said, it seemed to me, everything that was to be said. I — we — had gone as far as human limitations permitted in the long investigation of this strange affair. Then I summoned my houseman, Stephen Penn.

"Stephen," said I, "go and find out if the charcoal pots in the kitchen have burned out since breakfast. I imagine that about this time there would be a little charcoal left to burn out in each of them. If so, put all the charcoal into one pot and bring it out here on the gallery. If not, fix me a new charcoal fire in the largest pot. Fill it about half full."

"Yes, sar," said Stephen, and departed on this errand.

Within three minutes the excellent Stephen was back. He set down on the tile floor beside my chair the largest of my four kitchen charcoal pots. It was half full of brightly glowing embers. I sent him away before I went into the house to fetch the painting. It was a curious fact that this faithful suitor of mine, a *zambo* or medium brown Negro, and a native of St. Thomas, had manifested an increasing aversion to anything like contact with or even sight of the old picture, an aversion dating from that afternoon when he had discovered it, three years before, in the lumber room of my Santa Crucian hired residence.

Then I brought it out and laid it flat, after clearing a place for it, on the large plain table which stands against the wall of the house on my gallery. Pelletier came over and stood beside me, and in silence we looked long and searchingly at Camilla Macartney's panorama for the last time.

Then, with the sharp, small blade of my pocketknife, I cut it cleanly through again and again until it was in seven or eight strips. A little of the old brittle paint cracked and flaked off in this process. Having piled the strips one on top of another, I picked up the topmost of the three or four spread newspapers which I had placed under the canvas to save the table top from my knife point, and these flakes and chips I poured first off the newspaper's edge upon the glowing embers. These bits of dry, ancient pigment hissed, flared up, and then quickly melted away. Then I burned the strips very carefully until all but one were consumed.

This, perhaps because of some latent dramatic instinct whose existence until that moment I had never really suspected, was the one containing the figure of Saul Macartney. I paused, the strip in my hand, and looked at Pelletier. His face was inscrutable. He nodded his head at me, however, as though to encourage me to proceed and finish my task.

With perhaps a trifle of extra care I inserted the end of this last strip into the charcoal pot.

It caught fire and began to burn through precisely as its predecessors had caught and burned, and finally disintegrated into a light grayish ash. Then a very strange thing happened —

There was no slightest breath of air moving in that sheltered corner of the gallery. The entire solid bulk of the house sheltered it from the steady northeast trade — now at three in the afternoon at its lowest daily ebb, a mere wavering, tenuous pulsing.

And yet, at the precise instant when the solid material of that last strip had been transmuted by the power of the fire into the whitish, wavering ghost of material objects which we name ash — from the very center of the still brightly glowing charcoal embers there arose a thin, delicate wisp of greenish blue smoke which spiraled before our eyes under the impact of some obscure pulsation in the quiet air about us, then stiffened, as yet unbroken, into a taut vertical line, the upper end of which abruptly turned, curving down upon itself, completing the representation of the hangman's noose; and then, instantly, this contour wavered and broke and ceased to be, and all that remained there before our fascinated eyes was a kitchen charcoal pot containing a now rapidly dulling mass of rose-colored embers.

Guests from Gibbet Island

WASHINGTON IRVING

Whoever has visited the ancient and renowned village of
Communipaw may have noticed an old stone building, of
most ruinous and sinister appearance. The doors and
window-shutters are ready to drop from their hinges; old
clothes are stuffed in the broken panes of glass, while
legions of half-starved dogs prowl about the premises,
and rush out to bark at every passer-by, for your beggarly
house in a village is most apt to swarm with profligate
and ill-conditioned dogs. What adds to the sinister appearance of this mansion is a tall frame in front, not a
little resembling a gallows, and which looks as if waiting
to accommodate some of the inhabitants with a well-
merited airing. It is not a gallows, however, but an ancient sign-post; for this dwelling in the golden days of
Communipaw was one of the most orderly and peaceful of
village taverns, where public affairs were talked and
smoked over. In fact, it was in this very building that
Oloffe the Dreamer and his companions concerted that
great voyage of discovery and colonization in which they

explored Buttermilk Channel, were nearly shipwrecked in the strait of Hell Gate, and finally landed on the island of Manhattan, and founded the great city of New Amsterdam.

Even after the province had been cruelly wrested from the sway of their High Mightinesses by the combined forces of the British and the Yankees, this tavern continued its ancient loyalty. It is true, the head of the Prince of Orange disappeared from the sign, a strange bird being painted over it, with the explanatory legend of "Die Wilde Gans," or, The Wild Goose; but this all the world knew to be a sly riddle of the landlord, the worthy Teunis Van Gieson, a knowing man, in a small way, who laid his finger beside his nose and winked, when anyone studied the significance of his sign, and observed that his goose was hatching, but would join the flock whenever they flew over the water; an enigma which was the perpetual recreation and delight of the loyal but fat-headed burghers of Communipaw.

Under the sway of this patriotic, though discreet and quiet publican, the tavern continued to flourish in primeval tranquility, and was the resort of true-hearted Nederlanders, from all parts of Pavonia; who met here quietly and secretly, to smoke and drink the downfall of Briton and Yankee, and success to Admiral Van Tromp.

The only drawback on the comfort of the establishment was a nephew of mine host, a sister's son, Yan Yost Vanderscamp by name, and a real scamp by nature. This unlucky whipster showed an early propensity to mischief, which he gratified in a small way by playing tricks upon the frequenters of the Wild Goose — putting gunpowder in their pipes, or squibs in their pockets, and astonishing them with an explosion, while they sat nodding around the fire-place in the bar-room; and if perchance a worthy burgher from some distant part of Pavonia lingered until dark over his potation, it was odds but young Vanderscamp would slip a brier under his horse's tail, as he mounted, and send him chattering along the road, in neck-or-nothing style, to the infinite

146

astonishment and discomfort of the rider.

It may be wondered at, that mine host of the Wild Goose did not turn such a graceless varlet out of doors; but Teunis Van Gieson was an easy-tempered man, and, having no child of his own, looked upon his nephew with almost parental indulgence. His patience and good-nature were doomed to be tried by another inmate of his mansion. This was a cross-grained curmudgeon of a Negro, named Pluto, who was a kind of enigma in Communipaw. Where he came from, nobody knew. He was found one morning, after a storm, cast like a sea-monster on the strand, in front of the Wild Goose, and lay there, more dead than alive. The neighbors gathered round, and speculated on this production of the deep; whether it were fish or flesh, or a compound of both, commonly yclept a merman. The kind-hearted Teunis Van Gieson, seeing that he wore the human form, took him into his house, and warmed him into life. By degrees, he showed signs of intelligence, and even uttered sounds very much like language, but which no one in Communipaw could understand. Some thought him a Negro just from Guinea, who had either fallen overboard, or escaped from a slave-ship. Nothing, however, could ever draw from him any account of his origin. When questioned on the subject, he merely pointed to Gibbet Island, a small rocky islet which lies in the open bay, just opposite Communipaw, as if that were his native place, though everybody knew it had never been inhabited.

In the process of time, he acquired something of the Dutch language; that is to say, he learnt all its vocabulary of oaths and maledictions, with just words sufficient to string them together. *"Donder en blicksem!"* (thunder and lightening) was the gentlest of his ejaculations. For years he kept about the Wild Goose, more like one of those familiar spirits, or household goblins, we read of, than like a human being. He acknowledged allegiance to no one, but performed various domestic offices, when it suited his humor; waiting occasionally on the guests, grooming the horses, cutting wood, drawing water; and

147

all this without being ordered. Lay any command on him, and the stubborn sea-urchin was sure to rebel. He was never so much at home, however, as when on the water, plying about in skiff or canoe, entirely alone, fishing, crabbing, or grabbing for oysters, and would bring home quantities for the larder of the Wild Goose, which he would throw down at the kitchen door, with a growl. No wind or weather deterred him from launching forth on his favorite element; indeed, the wilder the weather, the more he seemed to enjoy it. If a storm was brewing, he was sure to put off from shore; and would be seen far out in the bay, his light skiff dancing like a feather on the waves, when sea and sky were in turmoil, and the stoutest ships were fain to lower their sails. Sometimes on such occasions he would be absent for days together. How he weathered the tempest, and how and where he subsided, no one could divine, nor did anyone venture to ask, for all had an almost superstitious awe of him. Some of the Communipaw oystermen declared they had more than once seen him suddenly disappear, canoe and all, as if plunged beneath the waves, and after a while come up again, in quite a different part of the bay; whence they concluded that he could live under water like that notable species of wild-duck commonly called the hell-diver. All began to consider him in the light of a foul-weather bird, like the Mother Carey's chicken, or stormy petrel; and whenever they saw him putting far out in his skiff, in cloudy weather, made up their minds for a storm.

The only being for whom he seemed to have any liking was Yan Yost Vanderscamp, and him he liked for his very wickedness. He in a manner took the boy under his tutelage, prompted him to all kinds of mischief, aided him in every wild harum-scarum freak, until the lad became the complete scapegrace of the village, a pest to his uncle and to every one else. Nor were his pranks confined to the land; he soon learned to accompany old Pluto on the water. Together these worthies would cruise about the broad bay, and all the neighboring straits and rivers; poking around in skiffs and canoes; robbing the set nets of the fisherman; landing in remote coasts, and laying waste orchards and watermelon patches; in short, carrying on a complete system of piracy, on a small scale. Piloted by Pluto, the youthful Vanderscamp soon became acquainted with all the bays, rivers, creeks, and inlets of the watery world around him; could navigate from the Hook to Spiting Devil on the darkest night, and learned to set even the terrors of Hell Gate at defiance.

At length Negro and boy suddenly disappeared, and days and weeks elapsed, but without tidings of them. Some said they must have run away and gone to sea; others jocosely hinted that old Pluto, being no other than his namesake in disguise, had spirited away the boy to the nether regions. All, however, agreed to one thing, that the village was well rid of them.

In the process of time, the good Teunis Van Gieson slept with his fathers, and the tavern remained shut up, waiting for a claimant, for the next heir was Yan Yost Vanderscamp, and he had not been heard of for years. At length, one day, a boat was seen pulling for shore, from a long, black, rakish-looking schooner, that lay at anchor in the bay. The boat's crew seemed worthy of the craft from which they debarked. Never had such a set of noisy, roistering, swaggering varlets landed in peaceful Communipaw. They were outlandish in garb and demeanor, and were headed by a rough, burly ruffian, with fiery whiskers, a copper nose, a scar across his face, and a great Flaunderish beaver slouched on one side of his head, in whom, to their dismay, the quiet inhabitants were made to recognize their early pest, Yan Yost Vanderscamp. The rear of this hopeful gang was brought up by old Pluto, who had lost an eye, grown grizzly-headed, and looked more like a devil than ever. Vanderscamp renewed his acquaintance with the old burghers, much against their will, and in a manner not at all to their taste. He slapped them familiarly on the back, gave them an iron grip of the hand, and was hail-fellow-well-met. According to his own account, he had been the world over, and made money by bags full, had ships in every sea, and now meant to turn the Wild Goose into a country-seat, where he and his comrades, all rich merchants from foreign parts, might enjoy themselves in the interval of their voyages.

Sure enough, in a little while there was a complete metamorphose of the Wild Goose. From being a quiet, peaceful Dutch public-house, it became a riotous, uproarious private dwelling; a complete rendezvous for boisterous men of the seas, who came here to have what they called a "blow-out" on dry land, and might be seen at all hours, lounging about the door, or lolling out of the windows, swearing among themselves and cracking rough jokes on every passer-by. The house was fitted up, too, in so strange a manner: hammocks slung to the walls, instead of bedsteads; odd kinds of furniture, of foreign fashion; bamboo couches, Spanish chairs; pistols, cutlasses, and blunderbusses, suspended on every peg; silver crucifixes on the mantel-pieces, silver candlesticks and porringers on the tables, contrasting oddly with the pewter and Delf ware of the original establishment. And then the strange amusements of these seamonsters! Pitching Spanish dollars, instead of quoits; firing blunderbusses out of the window; shooting at a mark, or at any unhappy dog, or cat, or pig, or barn-door fowl, that might happen to come within reach.

The only being who seemed to relish their rough waggery was old Pluto; and yet he led but a dog's life of it, for they practiced all kinds of manual jokes upon him, kicked him about like a foot-ball, shook him by his grizzly mop of wool, and never spoke to him without coupling a curse by way of adjective, to his name, and consigning him to the infernal regions. The old fellow, however, seemed to like them the better the more they cursed him, though his utmost expression of pleasure never amounted to more than the growl of a petted bear, when his ears are rubbed.

Old Pluto was the ministering spirit at the orgies of the Wild Goose; and such orgies as took place there! Such drinking, singing, whooping, swearing; with an occasional interlude of quarreling and fighting. The noisier grew the revel, the more old Pluto plied the potations, until the guests would become frantic in their merriment, smashing everything to pieces, and throwing the house out of the windows. Sometimes, after a drinking bout, they sallied forth and scourged the village, to the dismay of the worthy burghers, who gathered their women within doors, and would have shut up the house. Vanderscamp, however, was not to be rebuffed. He insisted on renewing acquaintance with his old neighbors, and on introducing his friends, the merchants, to their families; swore he was on the lookout for a wife, and meant, before he stopped, to find husbands for all their daughters. So, will-ye, nill-ye, sociable he was; swaggered about their best parlors, with his hat to one side of his head; sat on the good-wife's nicely waxed mahogany table, kicking his heels against the carved and polished leg; kissed and tousled the young *vrows;* and, if they frowned and pouted, gave them a gold rosary, or a sparkling cross, to put them in good humor again.

Sometimes nothing would satisfy him, but he must have some of his old neighbors to dinner at the Wild Goose. There was no refusing him, for he had the complete upper hand of the community, and the peaceful burghers all stood in awe of him. But what a time would the quiet, worthy men have, among these rake-hells, who would delight to astound them with the most extravagant gunpowder tales, embroidered with all kinds of foreign oaths, clink the can with them, pledge them in deep potations, bawl drinking-songs in their ears, and occasionally fire pistols over their heads, or under the table, and then laugh in their faces, and ask them how they liked the smell of gunpowder.

Thus was the little village of Communipaw for a time like the unfortunate wight possessed with devils; until Vanderscamp and his brother merchants would sail on another trading voyage, when the Wild Goose would be shut up and everything relapse into quiet, only to be disturbed by his next visitation.

151

The mystery of all these proceedings gradually dawned upon the tardy intellects of Communipaw. These were the times of the notorious Captain Kidd, when the American harbors were the resorts of piratical adventurers of all kinds, who, under pretext of mercantile voyages, scoured the West Indies, made plundering descents upon the Spanish Main, visited even the remote Indian Seas, and then came to dispose of their booty, have their revels, and fit out new expeditions in the English colonies.

Vanderscamp had served in this hopeful school, and, having risen to importance among the buccaneers, had pitched upon his native village and early home, as a quiet, out-of-the-way, unsuspected place, where he and his comrades, while anchored at New York, might have their feasts, and concert their plans, without molestation.

At length the attention of the British government was called to these piratical enterprises, that were becoming so frequent and outrageous. Vigorous measures were taken to check and punish them. Several of the most noted freebooters were caught and executed, and three of Vanderscamp's chosen comrades, the most riotous swash-bucklers of the Wild Goose, were hanged in chains in Gibbet Island, in full sight of their favorite resort. As to Vanderscamp himself, he and his man Pluto again disappeared, and it was hoped by the people of Communipaw that he had fallen in some foreign brawl, or been swung on some foreign gallows.

For a time, therefore, the tranquility of the village was restored; the worthy Dutchmen once more smoked their pipes in peace, eyeing with peculiar complacency their old pests and terrors, the pirates, dangling and drying in the sun, on Gibbet Island.

This perfect calm was doomed at length to be ruffled. The fiery persecution of the pirates gradually subsided. Justice was satisfied with the examples that had been made, and there was no more talk of Kidd, and the other heroes of like kidney. On a calm summer evening, a boat, somewhat heavily laden, was seen pulling into Communipaw. What was the surprise and disquiet of the inhabitants to see Yan Yost Vanderscamp seated at the helm, and his man Pluto tugging at the oar! Vanderscamp, however, was apparently an altered man. He brought home with him a wife, who seemed to be a shrew, and to have the upper hand of him. He no longer was the swaggering, bully ruffian, but affected the regular merchant, and talked of retiring from business, and settling down quietly, to pass the rest of his days in his native place.

The Wild Goose mansion was again opened, but with diminished splendor, and no riot. It is true, Vanderscamp had frequent nautical visitors, and the sound of revelry was occasionally overheard in his house; but everything seemed to be done under the rose, and old Pluto was the only servant that officiated at these orgies. The visitors, indeed, were by no means of the turbulent stamp of their predecessors; but quiet mysterious traders; full of nods, and winks, and hieroglyphic signs, with whom, to use their cant phrase, "everything was smug." Their ships came to anchor at night, in the lower bay; and, on a private signal, Vanderscamp would launch his boat, and, accompanied solely by his man Pluto, would make them mysterious visits. Sometimes boats pulled in at night, in front of the Wild Goose, and various articles of merchandise were landed in the dark, and spirited away, nobody knew whither. One of the more curious of the inhabitants kept watch, and caught a glimpse of the feature of some of these night visitors, by the casual glance of a lantern, and declared that he recognized more than one of the freebooting frequenters of the Wild Goose, in former times; whence he concluded that Vanderscamp was at his old game, and that this mysterious merchandise was nothing more nor less than piratical plunder. The more charitable opinion, however, was, that Vanderscamp and his comrades, having been driven from their old line of business by the "oppressions of government," had resorted to smuggling to make both ends meet.

Be that as it may, I come now to the extraordinary fact which is the butt-end of this story. It happened, late one night, that Yan Yost Vanderscamp was returning across the broad bay, in his light skiff, rowed by his man Pluto. He had been carousing on board of a vessel, newly arrived, and was somewhat obfuscated in intellect, by the liquor he had imbibed. It was a still, sultry night; a heavy mass of lurid clouds was rising in the west, with the low muttering of distant thunder. Vanderscamp called on Pluto to pull lustily, that they might get home before the gathering storm. The old Negro made no reply, but shaped his course so as to skirt the rocky shores of Gibbet Island. A faint creaking overhead caused Vanderscamp to cast up his eyes, when, to his horror, he beheld the bodies of his three pot companions and brothers in iniquity dangling in the moonlight, their rags fluttering, and their chains creaking, as they were slowly swung backward and forward by the rising breeze.

"What do you mean, you blockhead!" cried Vanderscamp, "by pulling so close to the island?"

"I thought you'd be glad to see your old friends once more," growled the Negro; "you were never afraid of a living man, what do you fear from the dead?"

"Who's afraid?" hiccoughed Vanderscamp, partly heated by liquor, partly nettled by the jeer of the Negro; "who's afraid? Hang me, but I would be glad to see them once more, alive or dead, at the Wild Goose. Come, my lads in the wind!" continued he, taking a draught and flourishing the bottle over his head, "here's fair weather to you in the other world; and if you should be walking the rounds tonight, odds fish! but I'll be happy if you will drop in to supper."

A dismal creaking was the only reply. The wind blew loud and shrill, and as it whistled round the gallows, and among the bones, sounded as if they were laughing and gibbering in the air. Old Pluto chuckled to himself, and now pulled for home. The storm burst over the voyagers, while they were yet far from shore. The rain fell in torrents, and thunder crashed and pealed, and the lightning kept up an incessant blaze. It was stark midnight before they landed at Communipaw.

Dripping and shivering, Vanderscamp crawled homeward. He was completely sobered by the storm, the water soaked from without having diluted and cooled the liquor within. Arrived at the Wild Goose, he knocked timidly and dubiously at the door; for he dreaded the reception he was to experience from his wife. He had reason to do so. She met him at the threshold, in a precious ill-humor.

"Is this a time," said she, "to keep people out of their beds, and to bring home company, to turn the house upside down?"

"Company?" said Vanderscamp, meekly; "I have brought no company with me, wife?"

"No, indeed! they have got here before you, but by your invitation; and blessed-looking company they are, truly!"

Vanderscamp's knees smote together. "For the love of heaven, where are they, wife?"

"Where? — why in the blue room, upstairs, making themselves as much at home as if the house were their own."

Vanderscamp made a desperate effort, scrambled up to the room, and threw open the door. Sure enough, there at a table, on which burned a light as blue as brimstone, sat the three guests from Gibbet Island, with halters round their necks, and bobbing their cups together, as if they were hob-or-nobbing, and trolling the old Dutch freebooter's glee, since translated into English:

> *"For three merry lads be we,*
> *And three merry lads be we;*
> *I on the land, and thou on the sand,*
> *And Jack on the gallows-tree."*

Vanderscamp saw and heard no more. Starting back with horror, he missed his footing on the landing-place, and fell from the top of the stairs to the bottom. He was taken up speechless, either from the fall or the fright, and was buried in the yard of the little Dutch church at

Bergen, on the following Sunday.

From that day forward the fate of the Wild Goose was sealed. It was pronounced a haunted house, and avoided accordingly. No one inhabited it but Vanderscamp's shrew of a widow and old Pluto, and they were considered little better than its hobgoblin visitors. Pluto grew more and more haggard and morose, and looked more like an imp of darkness than a human being. He spoke to no one, but went about muttering to himself; or, as some hinted, talking with the devil, who, though unseen, was ever at his elbow. Now and then he was seen pulling about the bay alone in his skiff, in dark weather, or at the approach of nightfall; nobody could tell why, unless, on an errand to invite more guests from the gallows. Indeed, it was affirmed that the Wild Goose still continued to be a house of entertainment for such guests, and that on stormy nights the blue chamber was occasionally illuminated, and sounds of diabolical merriment were overheard, mingling with the howling of the tempest. Some treated these as idle stories, until on one such night, it was about the time of the equinox, there was a horrible uproar in the Wild Goose, that could not be mistaken. It was not so much the sound of revelry, however, as strife, with two or three piercing shrieks, that pervaded every part of the village. Nevertheless, no one thought of hastening to the spot. On the contrary, the honest burghers of Communipaw drew their nightcaps over their ears, and buried their heads under their bedclothes, at the thoughts of Vanderscamp and his gallows companions.

The next morning some of the bolder and more curious undertook to reconnoiter. All was quiet and lifeless at the Wild Goose. The door yawned wide open, and had evidently been open all night, for the storm had beaten into the house. Gathering more courage from the silence and apparent desertion, they gradually ventured over the threshold. The house had indeed the air of having been possessed by devils. Everything was topsy-turvy; trunks had been broken open, and chests of drawers and corner cupboards turned inside out, as in a time of general sack and pillage; but the most woeful sight was the widow of Yan Yost Vanderscamp, extended a corpse on the floor of the blue chamber, with the marks of a deadly gripe on the windpipe.

All now was conjecture and dismay at Communipaw; and the disappearance of old Pluto, who was nowhere to be found, gave rise to all kinds of surmises. Some suggested that the Negro had betrayed the house to some of Vanderscamp's buccaneering associates, and that they had decamped together with the booty; others surmised that the Negro was nothing more nor less than the devil incarnate, who had now accomplished his ends, and made off with his dues.

Events, however, vindicated the Negro from this last implication. His skiff was picked up, drifting about the bay, bottom upward, as if wrecked in a tempest; and his body was found, shortly afterward, by some Communipaw fishermen, stranded among the rocks of Gibbet Island, near the foot of the pirate gallows. The fishermen shook their heads and observed that old Pluto had ventured once too often to invite guests from Gibbet Island.

A Vintage from Atlantis

CLARK ASHTON SMITH

I thank you, friend, but I am no drinker of wine, not even
if it be the rarest Canary or the oldest Amontillado. Wine
is a mocker, strong drink is raging . . . and more than
others, I have reason to know the truth that was writ by
Solomon the Jewish king. Give ear, if ye will, and I shall
tell you a story such as would halt the half-drained cup
on the lips of the hardiest bibber.

We were seven-and-thirty buccaneers, who raked the
Spanish Main under Barnaby Dwale, he that was called
Red Barnaby for the spilling of blood that attended him
everywhere. Our ship, the *Black Falcon*, could outfly and
outstrike all other craft that flew the Jolly Roger. Full
often, Captain Dwale was wont to seek a remote isle on
the eastward verge of the West Indies, and lighten the
vessel of its weight of ingots and doubloons.

The isle was far from the common course of maritime
traffic, and was not known to maps or other mariners; so
it suited our purpose well. It was a place of palms and
sand and cliffs, with a small harbor sheltered by the curv-

158

ing outstretched arms of rugged reefs, on which the dark ocean climbed and gnashed its fangs of white foam without troubling the tranquil waters beyond. I know not how many times we had visited the isle; but the soil beneath many a coco-tree was heavy with our hidden trove. There we had stored the loot of bullion-laden ships, the massy plate and jewels of cathedral towns.

Even as to all mortal things, an ending came at last to our visits. We had gathered a goodly cargo, but might have stayed longer on the open main where the Spaniards passed, if a tempest had not impended. We were near the secret isle, as it chanced, when the skies began to blacken; and wallowing heavily in the rising seas we fled to placid harbor, reaching it by nightfall. Before dawn the hurricane had blown by; and the sun came up in cloudless amber and blue. We proceeded with the landing and burying of our chests of coin and gems and ingots, which was a task of some length; and afterward we refilled our water-casks at a cool sweet spring that ran from beneath the palmy hill not far inland.

It was now midafternoon. Captain Dwale was planning to weigh anchor shortly and follow the westering sun toward the Caribbees. There were nine of us, loading the last barrels into the boats, with Red Barnaby looking on and cursing us for being slower than mud-turtles; and we were bending knee-deep in the tepid, lazy water, when suddenly the captain ceased to swear, and we saw that he was no longer watching us. He had turned his back and was stooping over a strange object that must have drifted in with the tide, after the storm: a huge and barnacle-laden thing that lay on the sand, half in and half out of the shoaling water. Somehow, none of us had perceived it heretofore.

Red Barnaby was not silent long.

"Come here, ye chancre-eaten coistrels," he called to us. We obeyed willingly enough, and gathered around the beached object, which our captain was examining with much perplexity. We too were greatly bewondered when we saw the thing more closely; and none of us

159

could name it offhand or with certainty.

The object had the form of a great jar, with a tapering neck and a deep, round, abdominous body. It was wholly encrusted with shells and corals that had gathered upon it as if through many ages in the ocean deeps, and was festooned with weeds and sea-flowers such as we had never before beheld; so that we could not determine the substance of which it was made.

At the order of Captain Dwale, we rolled it out of the water and beyond reach of the tide, into the shade of nearby palms; though it required the efforts of four men to move the unwieldy thing, which was strangely ponderous. We found that it would stand easily on end, with its top reaching almost to the shoulders of a tall man. While we were handling the great jar, we heard a swishing noise from within, as if it were filled with some sort of liquor.

Our captain, as it chanced, was a learned man.

"By the communion cup of Satan!" he swore. "If this thing is not an antique wine-jar, then I am a Bedlamite. Such vessels — though mayhap they were not so huge — were employed by the Romans to store the goodly vintages of Falernus and Cecuba. Indeed, there is today a Spanish wine — that Valdepeñas — which is kept in earthen jars. But this, if I mistake not, is neither from Spain nor olden Rome. It is ancient enough, by its look, to have come from that long-sunken isle, the Atlantis whereof Plato speaks. Truly, there should be a rare vintage within, a wine that was mellowed in the youth of the world, before the founding of Rome and Athens; and which, perchance, has gathered fire and strength with the centuries. Ho! my rascal sea-bullies! We sail not from this harbor till the jar is broached. And if the liquor within be sound and potable, we shall make holiday this evening on the sands."

"Belike, 'tis a funeral urn, full of plaguey cinders and ashes," said the mate, Roger Aglone, who had a gloomy turn of thought.

Red Barnaby had drawn his cutlass and was busily prying away the crust of barnacles and quaint fantastic coral-growths from the top of the jar. Layer on layer of them he removed, and swore mightily at this increment of forgotten years. At last a great stopper of earthenware, sealed with a clear wax that had grown harder than amber, was revealed by his prying. The stopper was graven with queer letters of an unknown language, plainly to be seen; but the wax refused the cutlass-point. So, losing all patience, the captain seized a mighty fragment of stone, which a lesser man could scarce have lifted, and broke therewith the neck of the jar.

Now even in those days, I, Stephen Magbane, the one Puritan amid that Christless crew, was no bibber of wine or spirituous liquors, but a staunch Rechabite on all occasions. Therefore I held back, feeling little concern other than that of reprobation, while the others pressed about the jar and sniffed greedily at the contents. But, almost immediately with its opening, my nostrils were assailed by an odor of heathen spices, heavy and strange; and the very inhalation thereof cause me to feel a sort of giddiness, so that I thought it well to retreat still further. But the others were eager as midges around a fermenting-vat in autumn.

"'Sblood! 'Tis a royal vintage!" roared the captain, after he had dipped a forefinger in the jar and sucked the purple drops that dripped from it. "Avast, ye slumgullions! Stow the water-casks on board, and summon all hands ashore, leaving only a watch there to ward the vessel. We'll have a gala night before we sack any more Spaniards."

We obeyed his order; and there was much rejoicing amid the crew of the *Black Falcon* at the news of our find and the postponement of the voyage. Three men, grumbling sorely at their absence from the revels, were left on board; though, in that tranquil harbor, such vigilance was virtually needless. We others returned to the shore, bringing a supply of pannikins in which to serve the wine, and provision for a feast. Then we gathered pieces of drift with which to build a great fire, and caught several tortoises along the sands, and unearthed their hidden eggs, so that we might have an abundance and variety of victuals.

In these preparations I took part with no special ardor. Knowing my habit of abstention, and being of a somewhat malicious and tormenting humor, Captain Dwale had expressly commanded my presence at the feast. However, I anticipated nothing more than a little ribaldry at my expense, as was customary at such times; and being partial to fresh tortoise-meat, I was not wholly unresigned to my lot as a witness of the Babylonian inebrieties of the others.

At nightfall, the feasting and drinking began; and the fire of driftwood, with eerie witch-colors of blue and green and white amid the flame, leapt high in the dusk while the sunset died to a handful of red embers far on purpling seas.

It was a strange wine that the crew and captain swilled from their pannikins. I saw that the stuff was thick and dark, as if it had been mingled with blood; and the air was filled with the reek of those pagan spices, hot and rich and unholy, that might have poured from a broken tomb of antique emperors. And stranger still was the intoxication of that wine; for those who drank it became still and thoughtful and sullen; and there was no singing of lewd songs, no playing of apish antics.

Red Barnaby had been drinking longer than the others, having begun to sample the vintage while the crew were making ready for their revel. To our wonderment, he ceased to swear at us after the first cupful, and no longer ordered us about or paid us any heed, but sat peering into the sunset with eyes that held the dazzlement of unknown dreams. And one by one, as they began to drink, the others were likewise affected, so that I marveled much at the unwonted power of the wine. I had never before beheld an intoxication of such nature; for they spoke not nor ate, and moved only to refill their cups from the mighty jar.

The night had grown dark as indigo beyond the flickering fire, and there was no moon; and the firelight blinded the stars. But one by one, after an interval, the drinkers rose from their places and stood staring into the darkness toward the sea. Unquietly they stood, and strained forward, peering intently as men who behold some marvelous thing; and queerly they muttered to one another, with unintelligible words. I knew not why they stared and muttered thus, unless it were because of some madness that had come upon them from the wine; for naught was visible in the dark, and I heard nothing, save the low murmur of wavelets lapping on the sand.

Louder grew the muttering; and some raised their hands and pointed seaward, babbling wildly as if in delirium. Noting their demeanor, and doubtful as to what further turn their madness might take, I bethought me to withdraw along the shore. But when I began to move away, those who were nearest me appeared to waken from their dream, and restrained me with rough hands. Then, with drunken, gibbering words, of which I could make no sense, they held me helpless while one of their number forced me to drink from a pannikin filled with the purple wine.

I fought against them, doubly unwilling to quaff that nameless vintage, and much of it was spilled. The stuff was sweet as liquid honey to the taste, but burned like hell-fire in my throat. I turned giddy; and a sort of dark confusion possessed my senses by degrees; and I seemed to hear and see and feel as in the mounting fever of calenture.

The air about me seemed to brighten, with a redness of ghostly blood that was everywhere; a light that came not from the fire nor from the nocturnal heavens. I beheld the faces and forms of the drinkers, standing without shadow, as if mantled with a rosy phosphorescence. And beyond them, where they stared in troubled and restless wonder, the darkness was illumed with the strange light.

Mad and unholy was the vision that I saw; for the harbor waves no longer lapped on the sand, and the sea had wholly vanished. The *Black Falcon* was gone, and where the reefs had been, great marble walls ascended, flushed as if with the ruby of lost sunsets. Above them were haughty domes of heathen temples, and spires of pagan palaces; and beneath were mighty streets and causeys where people passed in a neverending throng. I thought that I had gazed upon some immemorial city, such as had flourished in Earth's prime; and I saw the trees of its terraced gardens, fairer than the palms of Eden. Listening, I heard the sound of dulcimers that were sweet as the moaning of women; and the cry of horns that told forgotten glorious things; and the wild sweet singing of people who passed to some hidden, sacred festival within the walls.

I saw that the light poured upward from the city, and was born of its streets and buildings. It blinded the heavens above; and the horizon beyond was lost in a shining mist. One building there was, a high fane above the rest, from which the light streamed in a ruddier flood; and from its open portals music came, sorcerous and beguiling as the far voices of bygone years. And the revellers passed gaily into its portals, but none came forth. The weird music seemed to call me and entice me; and I longed to tread the streets of the alien city, and a deep desire was upon me to mingle with its people and pass into the flowing fane.

Verily I knew why the drinkers had stared at the darkness and had muttered among themselves in wonder. I knew that they also longed to descend into the city. And I saw that a great causey, built of marble and gleaming with the red luster, ran downward from their very feet over meadows of unknown blossoms to the foremost buildings.

Then, as I watched and listened, the singing grew sweeter, the music stranger, and the rosy luster brightened. Then, with no backward glance, no word or gesture of injunction to his men, Captain Dwale went slowly forward, treading the marble causey like a dreamer who walks in his dream. And after him, one by one, Roger Aglone and the crew followed in the same manner, going toward the city.

Haply I too should have followed, drawn by the witching music. For truly it seemed that I had trod the ways of that city in former time, and had known the things whereof the music told and the voices sang. Well did I remember why the people passed eternally into the fane, and why they came not forth; and there, it seemed, I should meet familiar and beloved faces, and take part in mysteries recalled from the foundered years.

All this, which the wine had remembered through its sleep in the ocean depths, was mine to behold and conceive for a moment. And well it was that I had drunk less of that evil and pagan vintage than the others, and was less besotted than they with its luring vision. For, even as Captain Dwale and his crew went toward the city, it appeared to me that rosy glow began to fade a little. The walls took on a wavering thinness, and the domes grew insubstantial. The rose departed, the light was pale as a phosphor of the tomb; and the people went to and fro like phantoms, with a thin crying of ghostly horns and a ghostly singing. Dimly above the sunken causey the harbor waves returned; and Red Barnaby and his men walked down beneath them. Slowly the waters darkened above the fading spires and walls; and the midnight blackened upon the sea; and the city was lost like the vanished bubbles of wine.

A terror came upon me, knowing the fate of those others. I fled swiftly, stumbling in darkness toward the palmy hill that crowned the isle. No vestige remained of the rosy light; and the sky was filled with returning stars. And looking oceanward as I climbed the hill, I saw a lantern that burned on the *Black Falcon* — in the harbor, and discerned the embers of our fire that smoldered on the sands. Then, praying with a fearful fervor, I waited for dawn.

The Digging at Pistol Key

CARL JACOBI

Although he had lived in Trinidad for more than fifteen years, Jason Cunard might as well have remained in Devonshire, his original home, for all the local background he had absorbed. He read only British newspapers, the *Times* and the *Daily Mail,* which he received by weekly post, and he even had his tea sent him from a shop in Southhampton, unmindful of the fact that he could have obtained the same brand, minus the heavy tax, at the local importer in Port-of-Spain.

Of course, Cunard got into town only once a month, and then his time was pretty well occupied with business matters concerning his sugar plantation. He had a house on a rather barren promontory midway between Port-of-Spain and San Fernando which was known as Pistol Key. But his plantation sprawled over a large tract in the center of the island.

Cunard frankly admitted there was nothing about Trinidad he liked. He thought the climate insufferable, the people — the Britishers, that is — provincial, and the

166

rest of the population, a polyglot of races that could be grouped collectively as "natives and foreigners." He dreamed constantly of Devonshire, though he knew of course he would never go back.

Whether it was due to this brooding or his savage temper, the fact remained that he had the greatest difficulty in keeping house-servants. Since his wife had died two years ago, he had had no less than seven; Caribs, quadroons, and Creoles of one sort or another. His latest, a lean, gangly black boy, went by the name of Christopher, and was undoubtedly the worst of the lot.

As Cunard entered the house now, he was in a distinctly bad frame of mind. Coming down the coast highway, he had had the misfortune to have a flat tire and had damaged his clothes considerably in changing it. He rang the antiquated bell-pull savagely.

Presently Christopher shambled through the connecting doorway.

"Put the car in the garage," Cunard said tersely. "And after dinner repair the spare tire. Some fool left a broken bottle on the road."

The Negro remained standing where he was, and Cunard saw then that he was trembling with fear.

"Well, what the devil's the matter?"

Christopher ran his tongue over his upper lip. "Can't go out dere, sar," he said.

"Can't . . . Why not?"

"De holes in de yard. Der dere again."

For the first time in more than an hour Cunard permitted himself to smile. While he was totally without sympathy for the superstitions of these blacks, he found the intermittent recurrence of these holes in his property amusing. For he knew quite well that superstition had nothing to do with them.

It all went back to that most diabolical of buccaneers, Francis L'Ollonais, and his voyage to the Gulf of Venezuela in the middle of the seventeenth century. After sacking Maracaibo, L'Ollonais sailed with his murderous crew for Tortuga. He ran into heavy storms and was forced to put back in here at Trinidad.

Three or four years ago some idiot by the idiotic name of Arlanpeel had written and published a pamphlet entitled *Fifty Thousand Pieces of Eight* in which he sought to prove by various references that L'Ollonais had buried a portion of his pirate booty on Pistol Key. The pamphlet had sold out its small edition, and Cunard was aware that copies had now become a collector's item. As a result, Pistol Key had come into considerable fame. Tourists stopping off at Port-of-Spain frequently telephoned Cunard, asking permission to visit his property, a request which of course he always refused.

And the holes! From time to time during the night Cunard would be awakened by the sound of a spade grating against gravel, and looking out his bedroom window, he would see a carefully shielded lantern down among the cabbage palms. In the morning there would be a shallow excavation several feet across with the dirt heaped hastily on all four sides.

The thought of persons less fortunate than himself making clandestine efforts to capture a mythical fortune dating to the seventeenth century touched Cunard's sense of humor. "You heard me, Christopher," he snapped to the houseboy, "put the car in the garage." But the black remained cowering by the door until Cunard, his patience exhausted, dealt him a sharp slap across the face with the flat of his hand. The boy's eyes kindled, and he went out silently.

Cunard went up to his bathroom and washed the road grime from his hands. Then he proceeded to dress for his solitary dinner, a custom which he never neglected. Downstairs, he got to thinking again about those holes in his yard and decided to have a look at them. He took a flashlight and went out the rear entrance and under the cabbage palms. Fireflies flashed in the darkness in the darkness and a belated qu'est-ce-qu'il-dit bird asked its eternal question.

Forty yards from the house he came upon the diggings Christopher had reported. That they were the work of some ambitious fortune-hunter was made doubly apparent by the discarded tape-measure and the cheap compass which lay beside the newly turned earth. Again Cunard smiled. It would be "forty paces from this point to the north end of a shadow cast by a man fifteen hands high," or some fiddlefaddle. Even if L'Ollonais had ever buried money here — and there was no direct evidence that he had — it had probably been carted away long years ago.

He saw Christopher returning from the garage then. The houseboy was walking swiftly, mumbling a low litany to himself. In his right hand he held a small cross fashioned of two bent twigs. Back in the house, Cunard told himself irritably that Christopher was a fool. After all, he had seen his mother come into plenty of trouble because of her insistence on practicing *obeah*. She had professed to be an *obeah*-woman and was forever speaking incantations over broken eggshells, bones, tufts of hair, and other disagreeable objects. Employed as a laundress by Cunard, he had discovered her one day dropping a white powder into his tea cup, and unmindful of her plea that it was merely a good-health charm designed to cure his recurrent spells of malaria, he had turned her over to the constabulary. He had pressed charges too, testifying that the woman had attempted to poison him. Largely because of his influence, she had been convicted and sent to the convict Depot at Tobago. Christopher had stayed on because he had no other place to go.

The meal over, Cunard went into the library with the intention of reading for several hours. Although the *Times* and the *Daily Mail* reached him in bundles of six copies a fortnight or so after they were published, he made it a practice to read only Monday's copy on Monday and so on through the week, thus preserving the impression that he was still in England.

But this night as he strode across to his favorite chair, he drew up short with a grasp. The complete week's bundle of newspapers had been torn open and their contents scattered about in a wild disorganized pile. To add to this sacrilege, one of the sheets had a ragged hole in it where an entire column had been torn out. For an instant Cunard was speechless. Then he wheeled on Christopher.

"Come here, you black devil," he roared. "Did you do this?"

The houseboy looked puzzled.

"No, sar," he said.

"Don't lie to me. How dare you open my papers?"

But Christopher insisted he knew nothing of the matter. He had placed the papers on their arrival in the library and had not touched them since.

Cunard's rage was mounting steadily. A mistake he might have excused, but an out-and-out lie . . .

"Come with me," he said in a cold voice.

Deliberately he led the way into the kitchen, looked about him carefully. Nothing there. He went back across the little corridor of the houseboy's small room under the stairway. While Christopher stood protesting in the doorway, Cunard matched across to the table and silently picked up a torn section of a newspaper.

"So you did lie!" he snarled.

The sight of the houseboy with his perpetual grin there in the doorway was too much for the planter. His rage beyond control, he seized the first object within reach — a heavy length of wood resting on a little bracket mounted on the wall — and threw it with all his strength.

The missile struck Christopher squarely on the temple. He uttered no cry, but remained motionless a moment, the grin frozen on his face. Then his legs buckled and he slumped slowly to the floor.

Cunard's fists clenched. "That'll teach you to respect other people's property," he said. His anger, swift to come, was receding as quickly, and noting that the houseboy lay utterly still, he stepped forward and stirred him with his foot.

Christopher's head rolled horribly.

Quickly Cunard stooped and felt for a pulse. None was discernible. With trembling fingers he drew out a pocket mirror and placed it by the boy's lips. For a long moment he held it there, but there was no resultant cloud of moisture. Christopher was dead!

Cunard staggered across to a chair and sat down. Christopher's death was one thing and one thing only — murder! The fact that he was a man of color and Cunard an influential planter would mean nothing in a Crown court of law. He could see the bewigged magistrate now; he could hear the evidence of island witnesses, testifying as to his uncontrollable temper, his savage treatment of servants.

Even if there were not actual danger of incarceration — and he knew there was — it would mean the loss of his social position and prestige.

And then Cunard happened to think of the holes in his yard. A new one — a grave for the dead houseboy — would never be noticed, and he could always improvise some sort of story that the boy had run off. As far as Cunard knew, other than the old crone who was his mother, Christopher had no other kin, having come originally from Jamaica.

The planter was quite calm now. He went to his room, changed to a suit of old clothes and a pair of rubber-soled shoes. Then returning to the little room under the stairs, he rolled the body of the houseboy into a piece of sailcloth and carried it out into the yard.

He chose a spot near the far corner of his property where a clump of bamboo grew wild and would effectually shield him from eyes, and half an hour later Cunard returned to the house. There he carefully cleaned the clinging loam from the garden spade, washed his shoes, and brushed his trousers.

It was when he went again to the room under the stairs to gather together Christopher's few possessions that he saw the piece of wood that had served as the death missile. Cunard picked it up and frowned. The thing was a *obeah* fetish apparently, an ugly little carving with a crude likeness of an animal head and a squat human body. The lower half of the image ended in a flat panel, the surface of which was covered with wavy lines, so that the prostrate figure looked as if it were partially immersed in water. Out of that carved water two arms extended upward, as in supplication, and they were arms that were strangely reminiscent for Cunard. Christopher's mother had had arms like that, smooth and strangely youthful for a person of her age. There was even a chip of white coral on one of the fingers like the coral ring the old woman always wore.

Cunard threw the thing onto the pile of other objects he had gathered — spare clothes, several bright-colored scarves, a sack of cheap tobacco — made a bundle of them and burned them in the old-fashioned cookstove with which the kitchen was equipped.

The last object to go into the fire was the newspaper clipping, and the planter saw then with a kind of grim horror that Christopher had not lied at all, that the top of the paper in fact bore a date-line several months old and was one of a lot he had given to the houseboy "to look at de pictures."

For several days after that Cunard did not leave his house. He felt nervous and ill at ease, and he caught himself looking out the window toward the bamboo thicket on more than one occasion. Curiously too, there was an odd murmuring in his ears like the sound of distant water flowing.

On the third day, however, he was sufficiently himself to make a trip to town. He drove the car at a fast clip to Port-of-Spain, parked on Marine Square, and went about his business. He was walking down Frederick Street half an hour later when he suddenly became aware that an aged Negro woman with head tied in a red kerchief was following him.

Cunard didn't have a direct view of her until just as he turned a corner, and then only a glance, but his heart stopped dead still for an instant. Surely that black woman was Christopher's mother whom he had sent to prison. True, her face was almost hidden by the folds of the loosely-draped kerchief, but he had seen her hand, and there was the coral ring on it. Wild thoughts rushed to Cunard's head. Had the woman been released then? Had she missed her son, and did she suspect what had happened?

Cunard drew up in a doorway, but the old crone did not pass him, and when he looked back down the street, she was nowhere in sight.

Nevertheless the incident unnerved him. When, later in the day, he met Inspector Bainley of the Constabulary, he seized the opportunity to ask several questions that would ease his mind.

"Where have you been keeping yourself?" Bainley asked. "I haven't seen much of you lately."

Cunard lit a cigar with what he hoped was a certain amount of casualness.

"I've been pretty busy," he replied. "My houseboy skipped, you know. The blighter packed off without warning."

"So?" said Bainley. "I thought Christopher was a pretty steady chap."

"In a way," said Cunard. "And in a way he wasn't." And then: "By the way, do you remember his mother? I was wondering whether she had been released. I thought I saw her a moment ago on the street."

The Inspector smiled a thin smile. "Then you were seeing things," he said. "She committed suicide over at the Convict Depot at Tobago two months ago."

Cunard stared.

"At least we called it suicide," Inspector Bainley went on. "She took some sort of an *obeah* potion when she found we weren't going to let her go, and simply lay back and died. It was rather odd that the medico couldn't find any trace of poison though."

Cunard was rather vague about the rest of the day's events. He recalled making some trifling purchases, but his mind was wandering and twice he had to be reminded to pick up his change. At four o'clock he abruptly found himself thinking of his old friend, Hugh Donay, and the fact that Donay had employed Christopher's mother a

173

year or so before she had entered Cunard's services. Donay had a villa just outside of town, and it would take only a few moments to see him. Of course there was no reason to see him. If Bainley said the old woman had committed suicide, that settled it. Yet Cunard told himself the inspector might have been mistaken or perhaps joking. He himself was a strong believer in the powers of observation, and it bothered him to have doubts cast upon them.

The planter drove through the St. Clair district and turned into a driveway before a sprawling house with a roof of red tile. Donay, a thin waspish man, was lounging in a hammock and greeted Cunard effusively. "Tried to get you by phone the other day," he said, "but you weren't at home. Had something to tell you. About that L'Ollonais treasure that's supposed to be buried on your property."

Cunard frowned. "Have you started believing that too?"

"This was an article in the *Daily Mail,* and it had some new angles that were rather interesting. I get my paper here in town before you do out there on Pistol Key, you know."

Cunard attempted to swing the conversation into other channels, but Donay was persistent.

"Funny thing about that article," he said. "I read it the same day the burglar was here."

"Burglar?" Cunard lifted his eyes.

"Well," Donay said, "Jim Barrett was over here, and I showed him the paper. Barrett said it was the first description he had read that sounded logical and that the directions given for locating the treasure were very clear and concise. Just at that moment there was a sound in the corridor and Barrett leaped up and made a dash for the kitchen.

"I might tell you that for several days I thought prowlers were about. The lock on the cellar door was found broken, and several times I'd heard footsteps in the laundry-room. Several things were out of place in the laundry-room too, though what anyone would want there is more than I can see.

"Anyway, Barrett shouted that someone was in the house. We followed the sounds down into the cellar, and just as we entered the door into the laundry-room, there was a crash and the sound of glass breaking." Donay smiled sheepishly as if to excuse all these details.

"It was only a bottle of bluing," he went on, "but what I can't figure out is how the prowler got in and out of that room without our seeing anyone pass. There's only one door, you know, and the windows are all high up."

"Was anything stolen?" Cunard asked.

"Nothing that I'm aware of. That bluing though was running across the floor toward a hamper of clean linen, and without thinking I used the first thing handy to wipe it up. It happened to be the newspaper with that treasure article in it. So I'm afraid . . ."

"It doesn't matter. I can read it in my copy," Cunard said. But even as he spoke, a vision of his own torn paper flashed to him. "That isn't quite all," Donay said. "The next day I found every blessed wastebasket in the house turned upside down and their contents scattered about. Queer, isn't it?"

The conversation changed after that, and they talked of idle things. But just before he left Cunard said casually: "By the way, my houseboy Christopher's run off. Didn't his mother work for you as a laundress or something?"

"That's right," Donay said, "I turned her over to you when I took a trip to the States. Don't you remember?"

Cunard drove through town again, heading for the highway to Pistol Key. He had just turned off Marine Square when he suddenly slammed down hard on the brakes. The woman darted from the curb directly into his path, and with the lowering sun in his eyes, he did not see her until it was too late. Cunard got out of the car, shaking like a leaf, fully expecting to find a crumpled body on the bumper.

But there was no one there, and a group of Portuguese street laborers eyed him curiously as he peered around

175

and under the car. He was almost overcome with relief, but at the same time he was disturbed. For in that flash he had seen of the woman against the sun, he was almost sure had seen the youthful dark-skinned arms of Christopher's mother.

Back at Pistol Key Cunard spent an uneasy night. The sensation of distant running water was stronger in his ears now. "Too much quinine," he told himself. "I'll have to cut down on the stuff."

He lay awake for some time, thinking of the day's events. But as he went over the major details in retrospection, he found himself supplying the missing minor details and so fell into a haze of peaceful drowsiness.

At two o'clock by the radium clock on the chiffonier, he awoke abruptly. The house was utterly still, but through the open window came an intermittent metallic sound. It died away, returned after an interval of several minutes. Cunard got out of bed, put on his brocaded dressing robe, and strode to the window. A full moon illuminated the grounds save where the palmistes cast their darker shadow, and there was no living person in evidence.

Below him and slightly to the left there was a freshly dug hole. But it was not that that caused Cunard to pass his hands before his eyes as if he had been dreaming. It was the sight of a spade alternately disappearing in the hole and reappearing to pile the loosened soil on the growing mound. A spade that moved slowly, controlled by aged yet youthful-appearing arms and hands — *but arms unattached to any human body!*

In the morning Cunard called the Port-of-Spain *Journal,* instructing them to run an advertisement for a houseboy, a task which he had neglected the day before. Then he went out to his post box to get the mail.

The morning mist had not yet cleared. It hung over the hibiscus hedges like an endless line of white shrouds. As he reached the end of the lane, Cunard thought he saw a figure turn from the post box and move quickly toward a grove of ceiba trees. He thought nothing of it at first, for those trees flanked the main road which was traveled by residents of the little native settlement at the far end of Pistol Key. But then he realized that the figure had moved away from the road, in a direction leading obliquely toward his own house.

Still the matter did not concern him particularly until he opened the post box. There was a single letter there, and it had not come by regular mail; the dirty brown envelope bore neither stamp nor cancellation mark. Inside was a torn piece of newspaper.

Cunard realized at once that it was the missing piece from his *Daily Mail*. But who besides Christopher could have had access to the house and who would steal a newspaper column and return it in the post box?

The first part was a commonplace enough account of the opening of new auction parlors in Southwick Street, London, and a description of some of the more unusual articles that had been placed for sale there. Cunard, reading swiftly, found his eye attracted to the following:

Among the afternoon offerings was the library of the late Sir Adrian Fell of Queen Anne's Court, which included an authentic first edition of McNair's *Bottle of Heliotrope* and a rare quarto volume of *Lucri Causa*. There was also a curious volume which purported to be the diary of the Caribbean buccaneer, Francis L'Ollonais, written while under the protection of the French West Indies Company at Tortuga.

This correspondent had opportunity to examine the latter book and found some interesting passages. According to the executors of the estate, it had been obtained by Sir Adrian on his trip to Kingston in 1904, and so far as is known, is the only copy in existence.

Under the heading "The Maracaibo voyage," L'Ollonais describes his destruction of that town, of his escape with an enormous booty, and of the storms which beset him on his return trip to Tortuga. It is here that the diary ceases to be a chronological datebook and becomes instead a romantic narrative.

L'Ollonais, driven southward, managed to land on

Trinidad, on a promontory known as Pistol Key. There "By a greate pile of stone whiche looked fair like two horses running," he buried the equivalent of fifty thousand pieces of eight. His directions for locating the treasure are worth quoting:

"Sixty paces from the south forward angle of the horse rock to the crossing of a line west by south west by the compass from a black painted stone shaped like a broken needle near the shore. At this point if a man will stand in the light of a full moon at the eleventh hour, the shadow of his head will fall upon the place."

How many persons, he wondered, had seen that newspaper story. There were Hugh Donay and Jim Barrett, of course, but they didn't count. Few others here subscribed to the *Daily Mail*. Of those that did, the odds were against any of them wading through such a dull account. The fact remained, however, that someone had read it in his own copy and had been sufficiently interested to tear it from the sheet. Who was that person? And why had he seen fit to return it by way of his post box?

The landmarks he knew only too well. He had often remarked that that stone near the end of his property resembled two galloping horses. And the black stone "like a broken needle" was still there, a rod or two from the shore.

Suddenly fear struck Cunard — fear that he might already be too late. He leaped from his chair and ran out into the grounds.

There were four holes and the beginning of a fifth in evidence. But, moving from one to another, the planter saw with relief that all were shallow and showed no traces of any object having been taken from them.

Cunard hastened back to the house where he procured a small but accurate compass and a ball of twine. Then he went into the tool-house and brought out a pair of oars for the dory that was moored at the water's edge on a little spit of sand.

An hour later his work was finished. He had rowed the

dory out to the needle point of rock and fastened one end of the twine to it. The other end he stretched across to the horse rock in the corner of his property. Then he counted off the required sixty paces and planted a stick in the ground to mark the spot. After that there was nothing he could do until night. He hoped there would be no clouds to obstruct the moon.

During the war Cunard had made a superficial study of electricity and wireless as part of what he considered his patriotic duties, and he now proceeded to wire a crude but efficient alarm system around the general area where he conceived the treasure to be. Back in the house he settled himself to wait until the moon-rise. In the quiet of inactivity he was conscious again of that sound of distant water flowing. He made a round of all taps in the house, but none was leaking.

During his solitary dinner he caught himself glancing out the window into the grounds, and once he thought he saw a shadow move across the lawn and into the trees. But it must have been a passing cloud for he didn't see it again.

At 2:00 p.m. a knock sounded on the door. Cunard was surprised and somewhat disconcerted to see Inspector Bainley standing on the veranda.

"Just passing by," Bainley said, smiling genially. "Had a sudden call from the native village out on the key. Seems a black boy got into some trouble out there. Thought it might be your Christopher."

"But that's imposs — " Cunard checked himself. "I hardly think it likely," he amended. "Christopher would probably go as far as he could, once he started."

They drank rum. The inspector seemed in no hurry to leave, and Cunard was torn between two desires, not to be alone and to be free from Bainley's gimlet eyes which always seemed to be moving about restlessly.

Finally he did go, however. The throb of his car was just dying off down the road when Cunard heard a new sound which electrified him to attention. The alarm bell!

Yet there was no one in the grounds. The wires were

undisturbed, and the makeshift switch he had fashioned was still open. The bell was silent when he reached it.

With the moon high over his shoulder Cunard wielded his spade rapidly. The spot where the shadow of his head fell was disagreeably close to the bamboo thicket where he had buried Christopher, but as a matter of fact, he wasn't quite sure where that grave was, so cleverly had he hidden all traces of his work.

The hole had now been dug to a depth of four feet, but there was no indication anything had been buried there. Cunard toiled strenuously another half hour. And then quite suddenly his spade struck something hard and metallic. A wave of excitement swept over him. He switched on his flashlight and turned it in the hole. Yes, there it was, the rusted top of a large iron chest — the treasure of L'Ollonais.

He resumed digging, but as he dug he became aware that the sand, at first dry and hard, had grown moist and soggy. The spade became increasingly heavy with each scoop, and presently water was running off it, glistening in the moonlight. Water began to fill the bottom of the hole too, making it difficult for Cunard to work.

But it was not until ten minutes later he saw something protruding from the water. In the moonlight two slender dark objects were reaching outward, a pair of Negro feminine arms gently weaving to and fro.

Cunard stiffened while a wave of horror swept over him. They were dark-skinned arms of an aged Negress, yet somehow they were smooth and youthful. The middle finger of the left hand bore a ring of white coral. Cunard screamed and lunged backward, too late. One of those grasping hands encircled his ankle and jerked him forward. And as he fell across the hole, those hands wrapped themselves about his throat and drew his head slowly but deliberately downward . . .

"Yes, it's a queer case," Bainley said, tamping tobacco into his pipe. "But then, of course, no more queer than a lot of things that happen here in the islands."

"You say this fellow, Cunard, murdered his houseboy,

180

Christopher?" the Warrant Officer said.

Bainley nodded. "I knew his savage temper would get the better of him some day. He buried the body in the yard and apparently rigged up that alarm arrangement to warn him of any trespassers. Then he contrived that story which he told me, that Christopher had run off.

"Of course we know now that Cunard was trying to find that buried treasure by following the directions given in that newspaper clipping. But that doesn't explain why he disregarded those directions and attempted to dig open the houseboy's grave again. Or why, before he had finished, he thrust his head into the shallow hole and lay in the pool of seepage water until he drowned."

Before I Wake . . .

HENRY KUTTNER

This is the story of a boy named Pete Coutinho, who had a spell put on him. Some people might have called it a curse. I don't know. It depends on a lot of things, on whether you've got gypsy blood, like old Beatriz Sousa, who learned a lot about magic from the wild *gitana* tribe in the mountains beyond Lisbon, and whether you're satisfied with a fisherman's life in Cabrillo.

Not that a fisherman's life is a bad one, far from it. By day you go out in the boats that rock smoothly across the blue Gulf waters, and at night you can listen to music and drink wine at the Shore Haven or the Castle or any of the other taverns on Front Street. What more do you want? What more is there?

And what does any sensible man, or any sensible boy, want with that sorcerous sort of glamor that can make everything incredibly bright and shining, deepening colors till they hurt, while wild music swings down from stars that have turned strange and alive? Pete shouldn't have wanted that, I suppose, but he did, and probably that's why there happened to him — what did happen. And the trouble began long before the actual magic started working.

Pedro Ignacio da Silva Coutinho, with a name far too long for his thin, wiry, fourteen-year-old body, used to sit on the wharf, looking out at the bright blue-green Gulf water and thinking about what lay beyond that turquoise plain. He heard the men talking about Tampico and the Isle of Pines and such, and those names always held magic for him. Later on, when he got his growth, he intended to go to those places, and he knew what they'd look like.

The Isle of Pines was Circe's isle, with white marble columns here and there in the dark green, and pirates would be dueling with a flash of clashing swords and a flash of recklessly smiling white teeth. The Gulf, like the Caribbean, is haunted by the ghosts of the old buccaneers. Tampico, to Pete, wasn't the industrial shipping port his father knew. It had palaces and parrots of many colors, and winding white roads. It was an Arabian Nights city, with robed magicians wandering the streets, benign most of the time, but with gnarled hands like tree-roots that could weave spells.

Manoel, his father, could have told him a different story, for Manoel had shipped once under sail, in the old days, before he settled down to a fisherman's life in Cabrillo. But Manoel didn't talk a great deal. Men talk to men, not to boys, and that was why Pete didn't learn as much as he might have from the sun-browned Portuguese who went out with the fishing fleets. He got his knowledge out of books, and strange books they were, and strange knowledge.

Up on the hill, in a little white house, lived Dr. Manning, who had been a fixture there for decades. Dr. Manning spent his days puttering around in his garden and writing an interminable autobiography that would never be published. He liked Pete because the boy was quiet, and very often Pete could be found squatting cross-legged in some corner of the little house, turning over the pages of Manning's books. He dipped into them, tasting briefly, racing on, but always pausing over the colored plates by Rackham and Syme and John R. Neill, with their revelations of a world that was too bright and fascinating to be real.

And at first he knew it wasn't real. But the daydreams grew and grew, as they will when a boy spends the lazy days idling in hot tropical sunlight by the canals with no one to talk to who thinks the thoughts he thinks. And pretty soon they were real, after all. There was an enormous map Dr. Manning had on the wall, and Pete would stand before it and trace imaginary voyages to the ports that fitted those glamorous pictures Rackham and Neill had painted.

Yes, they were real, finally.

Cartagena and Cocos, Clipperton Island and Campeche; he chased them down the alphabet he'd unwillingly learned at school, and they were all enchanted places. Clipperton was the haven of old ships. It couldn't be really an island, just hundreds and hundreds of the great Yankee clippers, with sails like white clouds, rails thronged with sailormen who hadn't died for good.

Not that Pete had any illusions about death. He'd seen dead men, and he knew that something goes out of a man — the soul goes out — when the lips slacken and the eyes stare emptily. Still and all, they could come back to life in Campeche and Cocos and in thunder-haunted Paramaribo, where dragons lived. But Paramaribo dragons could be killed by arrows dipped in the shining venom of the upas tree, which grew in a certain grove he'd discovered in a daydream.

Then he found the toad. He was trailing his father, Manoel, one time, to make certain the old man didn't get too drunk and fall in one of the canals. It was Saturday night, when all good fishermen drink as much as they can hold, sometimes a little more. And Pete, a slim, silent watcher, would follow his father, darting through the shadows, ready to catch the unsteady figure if it lurched too close to the dark waters, or to yell for help if he couldn't.

184

Pete was thinking about a certain town he'd heard of named Juba, where there were — he could see them now — huge sleek black figures on golden thrones, and leopard skins, and he could hear the rolling drums deep inside his head. His bare feet scuffed the dust through shafts of light that angled out from the windows, and discordant music came faintly from the Shore Haven down the road. Manoel had stopped and was kicking at something on the ground. It moved a little, and Manoel pursued it.

Pete edged closer, his eyes alert and curious. A small dark blotch hopped laboriously away from the drunken man's feet. Pete might have let his father crush the toad, but somehow he didn't, though he was no kinder than the average boy. It was Manoel's drunkenness that made Pete run forward. It was an idea, half-formulated in his mind, that a drunken giant could stamp out life into oblivion, and, maybe, that up in the starry sky were bigger giants who might get drunk some time and send their feet crashing down on men. Well, Pete had funny ideas.

The important thing is that he ran in behind his father, sent the old man sprawling with a quick shove, and snatched up the toad. It was a cool, smooth weight in his hand. Manoel was yelling and cursing and trying to rise, but he thought that a coast guard patrol had run him down and tiger sharks were coming in fast, smelling the blood. Pretty soon he discovered the blood was only red wine, from the broken bottle in his pocket, and that distressed him so much he just sat there in the road and cried.

But Pete ran home with the cool, firm body of the toad breathing calmly in his hand. He didn't go into the shack where his mother was boiling strong coffee for Manoel's return. He circled it and went into the back yard, where he'd made a tiny garden by the fence. It would be nice to tell about how Pete loved flowers and had a bed of roses and fuchsias glowing amid the squalid surroundings, but as a matter of fact Pete grew corn, squash, and tomatoes. Manoel would have disapproved of roses and clouted Pete across the head for growing them.

There were some rocks piled up near the garden, and Pete put the toad among them. And it was a funny thing, but Pete stayed right there, crouching on his knees, looking at the toad for a long time. There are little lights in a toad's eyes that flicker like lights in a jewel. And maybe there was something more in this toad's eyes.

You'll say it was dark in the back yard and Pete couldn't even see the toad. But the fact is he did see it, all right, and old Beatriz, the *gitana,* who knew more than she should have known about witches, might have explained a little. You see, a witch has to have a familiar, some little animal like a cat or a toad. He helps her somehow. When the witch dies the familiar is suppose to die too, but sometimes it doesn't. Sometimes, if it's absorbed enough magic, it lives on. Maybe this toad found its way south from Salem, from the days when Cotton Mather was hanging witches. Or maybe Lafitte had a Creole girl who called on the Black Man in the pirate-haven of Barataria. The Gulf is full of ghosts and memories, and one of those ghosts might very well be that of a woman with warlock blood who'd come from Europe a long time ago, and died on the new continent.

And possibly her familiar didn't know the way home. There's not much room for magic in America now, but once there was room.

If you're thinking the toad talked to Pete in a voice he could hear, you're on the wrong track. I'm not saying something out of the ordinary didn't happen. It's possible that the toad looked into Pete's mind with its tiny, cool, quiet mind, and asked a question or two, and it's also possible that a little magic started working there in that dark, fish-smelling back yard, with the tin-pan music of Cabrillo's bars murmuring through the night. But I'm not saying it's so, either.

All that happened was that Pete went into the house and got slapped for leaving Manoel. Margarida, a short, fat woman with worried dark eyes, said that Manoel would certainly fall into a canal and be eaten by barracuda, and Manoel's family, including Pete, all his five brothers and sisters, and Margarida herself, would starve miserably. She worked it out in great detail, gesturing wildly. Then the coffee boiled over, and she rushed to save it and then gave Pete a cup.

Pete drank it and grinned at Gregorio, who was trying to sharpen a gaff with all the dexterity of his six-year-old hands.

"The father will be okay, *minha mae*," he told Margarida. "He is not so drunk."

"Pedrinho, Manoel is not young any more. You must go out on the boats yourself someday soon."

"Good!" Pete said, thinking rapturously of Campeche and Tampico. Perhaps Tampico did not really have magicians, after all, but the truth would be even more glamorous. Margarida looked at the boy and bit her lip. Well — *basta*, apron-strings have to be cut some day. It was not as if the boy were not always talking about sailing the Caribbean.

"Put the *criança* to bed, Pedrinho," she ordered, turning to the stove. So Pete collected Cypriano José, a chuckling, fat baby, and herded Gregorio before him into the next room.

In the dark, by the rock pile, the toad sat quietly, staring into the shadows with eyes that glittered like strange jewels.

For a while that night Pete lay awake, his mind racing with vivid pictures of ships driving majestically through the oceans of the world. Someday he'd be on his way to Cartagena and Juba, Juba where heavy golden bracelets shone against satiny black skin, where great processions moved with palanquins and purple banners to the clash of cymbals and the mutter of drums. Cocos and Campeche and the Isle of Pines, where red-sashed pirates grinned in their beards and sang bloody songs. Tampico, where turbanned men called up afrits and jinn, and sleeping princesses lay in palaces of pearl. Clipperton of the white sails, Belem, where each white house had a bell-tower and the sweet chimes sang out forever in the peaceful valley . . .

Pete slept.

And then, somehow, the bed was revolving slowly. In Pete a dim excitement rose, and a consciousness that something was about to happen. As he slipped sidewise into mid-air he glimpsed rolling water below, and instinctively brought his hands together and straightened his knees. He cut the surface in a clean dive. Down and down he went, while his vision cleared and he saw, through a rush of bubbles, a clear, blue-green light.

He went slower and slower, turning his hands to slant to the surface, but not rising very fast. He had been holding his breath. Now, as a barracuda came nosing toward him through a forest of wavering weeds, fear made him kick out convulsively and he sucked in a gasp. He expected strangling water to gush into his lungs, but there was no discomfort at all. He might have been breathing air.

The barracuda swam up after him. One of his flailing hands struck the fish, and it darted away. Pete saw its torpedo body dwindling down the long, blue-green vista. Hanging there, automatically treading water, he began to realize what lay around and beneath him.

This was the southern sea. The colors that fade when coral is drawn out of its element were garishly bright here, intricate and lovely labyrinths on the bottom. Among the coral, fish went darting, and overhead a sea-bat, a devil-fish, flapped slow wings past, its stingaree tail trailing. Morays coiled by, opening their incredible, wolfish mouths at him, and many-limbed crabs scuttled sidewise over the rocks and little sandy plateaus of the bottom. Groves of seaweed and great fans of colored sponges swung with hypnotic motion, and schools of tiny striped fish went flashing in and out among them, moving all together as if with a single mind.

Pete swam down. From a cavern among the brown and purple rocks an octopus looked at him out of huge, alien eyes. Its tentacles hung and quivered. Pete swam away, hovering over an expanse of pale sand where the light from above shimmered and ran in rippling waves, his own shadow hanging spread-eagled below him. In and out of it many little creatures went scuttling busily on their underwater errands. Life here was painted in three dimensions, and there was no gravity. There was only beauty and strangeness and a hint of terror that sent pleasurable excitement thrilling through Pete's blood.

He swam upward, broke the surface, shaking water from his eyes and hair. The air was as easy to breathe as the water. He rode lightly on the rise and fall of smooth waves, looking about him. A forested shore lay half a mile away, across a blue, sunlit sea, and mountains rose behind the dark slopes. The ocean lay empty except for . . . yes, it was there, a clipper ship, sails furled, masts swaying back and forth as the vessel rocked in the trough of the waves. Its clean, sweet lines made Pete's throat ache. He could imagine her under sail, leaning forward into the waves, white canvas straining in great billowing curves, and the sharp bowsprit with its gilded girl's image driving into the spray.

The clipper lay at anchor; he could see the chain. And he could see movement on the deck. Perhaps . . . He swam toward the ship. But the waves were growing troubled. They slapped at him, slapping his cheeks . . .

"Minho filho! Pedrinho — "

And — "Pedro!" his father's deeper voice rumbled, with worried urgency in it. "Wake up!"

He felt a cool, dry hand laid on his forehead, and something warm and electric seemed to dart through his head. He heard words he did not understand, but they were calling him, summoning —

He opened his eyes and looked up at the little shrunken face of the gipsy, Beatriz Sousa. For a long, long moment her incredibly bright black eyes stared down at him, and the toothless mouth whispered a word or two more. Then she nodded as though satisfied and drew back, giving Margarida room to fling herself forward and hug Pete's head roughly to her capacious bosom.

"Ai-i! Pedrinho, coelzinho, my little rabbit, do you hear me? You are awake now?"

"Sure," Pete said, yawning and blinking as he tried to

wriggle free. "What's the matter? Why was the Senhora Beatriz —"

The old *gitana* was stuffing strong black tobacco, heavy with perique, into her battered pipe; her eyes were hooded by wrinkled lids. She seemed to have shrunken into a smaller person, now that she was not needed in the house. She did not look up when Manoel gave her a resentful glance and growled, "Your *mae* ran out and got the old woman. I say it is foolishness. Now get up, boy. At once!"

Margarida sidled into the kitchen, pulling Beatriz Sousa with her, whispering to the old woman to ignore Manoel. "He is a good man, Senhora, but he thinks a slap will cure all ills."

Under Manoel's baleful and somewhat bleary eye, Pete shucked his pajamas and got into patched underwear and worn denim shirt and trousers. He was hoping Manoel would say nothing. But a calloused hand reached out and gripped his shoulder as he turned to the door. Manoel scowled down into the boy's face.

"It is past noon," he said. "What sort of sleep is this? Your *mae* could not wake you. She came in crying to me, and *I* need my sleep." That was true, Pete thought, examining the telltale symptoms of bloodshot eyes and the circles under them.

"I hope you did not fall into the canal last night, *meu pai*," he said politely.

"That is as may be," Manoel growled. "Now listen to me, *rapaz*. I want you to tell me the truth. Do you know the white powder that Beberricador sells at night, by the docks?"

Pete said very firmly, "I have never touched that powder, *meu pai,* or anything else that Beberricador sells. Never in my life."

Manoel leaned forward and sniffed doubtfully. "You do not lie often, Pedro. Your breath does not smell of wine, either. Perhaps you were simply tired, though — there is something wrong when not even blows will waken a sleeping boy. What am I to think?"

Pete shrugged. He was ravenously hungry and anxious to escape from this inquisition. Besides, what was wrong? He had slept too long; that was all. And Manoel was ill-tempered at being awakened while the clangor of a hangover still beat in his grizzled head.

"Come, Pedrinho," Margarida called from the kitchen. Manoel pushed the boy away and Pete, glad to be released, hurried into the next room. He heard his father's body drop heavily on the bed, and knew that within minutes he would be snoring again. He grinned, winked at young Gregorio, and turned toward his mother at the stove.

"Pedro — " Beatriz Sousa was beside him, staring very intently into his eyes.

"*Sim*, Senhora?"

"Pedro," she whispered, "if you are troubled — come to see me. Remember, I can look through a stone wall farther than most. And don't forget there are many kinds of dreams." Her toothless jaws clamped; she hobbled past him and straight out the doorway, her black skirts whisking. Pete looked after her, baffled. He didn't quite know what to make of Beatriz. All this fuss because he'd overslept. Funny!

"You scared me, Pete," Gregorio said. "I thought you were dead."

"Do not use such words, spawn of the devil," Margarida squealed, spilled stew hissing on the hot stove. "Go and make yourself useful for a change, nasty one. Look, Cypriano José is at the garbage. Pedrinho, eat your stew. It will strengthen you."

Pete didn't feel particularly weak, but the stew was rich and spicy, and he ate fast. Afterward, remembering the toad, he went out to look in the rock-pile, but it had hidden itself somewhere in the cool, dark recesses and he could not see even a glimmer of the strange, bright, tiny eyes. So he took a homemade rod and headed for the canal.

On the way Bento Barbosa, who was rich and owned ships, waved a sausage of a finger at him and called him a *sonambulo,* so Pete knew that somebody, probably Gregorio, had been gossiping. He made up his mind to clout Gregorio's head later. But Bento Barbosa thought it was a good joke, and he twirled his raven mustachios and sent jovial laughter after Pete's retreating form. *"Mandriao!"* he shouted happily. *"Preguiçoso!* Lazybones!"

Pete wanted to throw a rock at him, but he thought he had better not. Bento Barbosa had ships, and it had been in Pete's mind for some time that he might one day be lucky enough to sail in one of them. Cartagena and Cocos and Clipperton . . . So he just went on walking through the hot Florida sunshine, his bare feet scuffing up the sandy dust, and thought about the dream he'd had. It was a good dream.

The canal was quiet. While Pete fished he was in a backwater where nobody else existed. He waited for the fish to bite, and wondered when he'd be on a boat, sailing out across the Gulf. Tampico and Juba called him, and he heard the thunder rolling, heavy and ominous, above Paramaribo, where dragons lived. Mailed in shining green and silver they swept in sinuous flight against the blue, their enormous wings darkening the sun, their scaly armor clashing. And Campeche, and the Isle of Pines with its marble temples and its laughing, bearded pirates. Well, and there was Cartagena too, and Cadiz and Cochabambo, and all the enchanted ports. They were real enough to young Pedro Ignacio da Silva Coutinho, and his brown toes wriggled with excitement above the still green water of the canal.

Oh, nothing much happened to Pete that Sunday. He sauntered home in the evening, his head full of shining pictures, and he heard little of the noisy family life boiling around him as he ate his supper.

Out in the stone-pile the toad squatted with its glowing jewel-eyes and, maybe, its memories. I don't know if you'll admit a toad could have memories. But I don't know, either, if you'll admit there was once witchcraft in America. Witchcraft doesn't sound sensible when you think of Pittsburgh and subways and movie houses, but the dark lore didn't start in Pittsburgh or Salem either; it goes away back to dark olive groves in Greece and dim, ancient forests in Brittany and the stone dolmens of Wales. All I'm saying, you understand, is that the toad was there, under its rocks, and inside the shack Pete was stretching on his hard bed like a cat and composing himself to sleep.

And this time the bed began to revolve right away, and spilled him out into darkness. He was expecting it, somehow. He didn't worry about being able to breathe now, he just relaxed and let himself sink, while his eyes accustomed themselves to the green gloom. It wasn't gloom at all, really. There were lights and colors. If it hadn't been for the feel of the water gliding by against his skin he might have imagined himself up in the sky, with meteors and comets blazing past. But these were sea-things, shining in the dark, the luminous life that blazes beneath the southern sea.

First he'd see a tiny twinkling speck, like a star, and it might have been next to his face or a mile away, in that immense, featureless void, with its faint hint of green. It would grow larger. It would turn into a radiant sun of purple or crimson or orange and come rushing at him, and swerve aside at the last moment. There were sinuous ribbons of fire that coiled into bright patterns, and there were schools of tiny fish that flashed by like sparks. Down below, in the deeper abyss, the colors were paler, and once an enormous shape blundered past down there, like the sea-bottom itself moving heavily. Pete watched awhile and then swam up.

Under a thin new moon the sea lay quivering with silver. Beyond him was the silent isle, and a rakish, sweet silhouette hung at anchor in the lagoon, the Yankee clipper, its bowsprit pointing now at the sky, now at the sea. To and fro it rocked, and Pete, rising and falling upon the same rhythm, was glad that he shared the waves with that lovely shape. Pete knew ships and loved them, and this was a dream of a ship. What he wanted more than anything was to see her under sail, with white canvas straining full of the breeze and a creamy wake parting behind her stern.

He began to swim toward the silent clipper, and he was almost at the anchor chain when a marlin drove up to the surface and tore at him, and a stabbing pain went through his arm. The marlin had a man's face. It was very serious and thoughtful, and it was holding a glass tube tipped with a long sharp needle, and it wasn't a marlin after all. It was old Dr. Manning, come down from his little hilltop house . . .

There was a strange taste under Pete's tongue. He blinked up at Margarida's worried fat face. *"Minha mae — "* he said, puzzled.

"Thank the good God!" Margarida cried, enfolding Pete in a hysterical hug. "My Pedrinho — *ai-i gracas — "*

"Thank the good *doutor,* rather," Manoel said grumpily, but he too looked troubled. Margarida didn't hear. She was busy smoothing Pete's hair and then mussing it up again, and Pete didn't know what the fuss was all about. Dr. Manning was snapping his black bag shut. He blinked doubtfully at Pete, and then sent Margarida and Manoel out of the room. After that he sat down on the bed and asked Pete questions.

It was always easy to talk to Dr. Manning, and Pete explained about the pirate islands with their magical names, and about the southern sea and the ship. It was a wonderful dream, Pete said, watching the *doutor's* puzzled eyes. He hadn't been taking any drugs, no. Manning was especially inquisitive on that point. Finally he told Pete to stay in bed awhile, and went into the kitchen. Though he kept his voice low out there, Gregorio managed to slide the door open a crack, and Pete could hear what was being said. He didn't understand all of it.

Dr. Manning said he'd thought at first it might be sleeping sickness, or even narcolepsy, whatever that was, but — no, Pete was healthy enough physically. Manoel growled that the boy was bone-lazy, spending his time fishing and reading. Reading! No good could come of such things.

"In a way you're right, Manoel," Dr. Manning said hesitantly. "It's natural for a boy to daydream now and then, but I think Pedro does it too much. I've let him use my library whenever he wanted, but it seems . . . h'm . . . it seems he reads the wrong things. Fairy tales are very charming, but they don't help a boy to cope with real life."

"*Com certeza,*" Manoel agreed. "You mean he has crazy ideas in the head."

"Oh, they're rather nice ideas," Dr. Manning said. "But they're only fairy tales, and they're beginning to seem true to Pete. You see, Manoel, there are really two worlds, the real one, and the one you make up inside your mind. Sometimes a boy — or even a man — gets to like his dream world so much he just forgets about the real one and lives in the one he's made up."

"I know," Manoel said. "I have seen some who do that. It is a bad thing."

"It would be bad for Pete. He's a very sensitive boy. If you live too much in dreams, you can't face real life squarely. And Pete will have to work for his living."

"But he is not sick?" Margarida put in anxiously.

"No. He's thinking the wrong way, that's all — for him. He should get out and have more interests, see what the world's really like. He ought to go to Campeche and Tampico and all these other places he makes up dreams about, and see them as they really are."

"Ah," Manoel said. "If he could go out on the boats, perhaps —"

"Something of the sort." Dr. Manning nodded. "If he could go on the *Princesa* for instance, tomorrow. She's bound to Gulf ports, and Pete might ship as a cabin boy or something. The change and contacts would be just what he needs."

Manoel clapped his hands together. "Bento Barbosa owns part of the *Princesa*. I will talk to him. Perhaps it can be arranged."

195

"It would be best for Pete," Dr. Manning said, and that was the end of the conversation, except that Pete lay quivering with excitement at the prospect of seeing the Gulf ports at last.

He went to sleep again, but he did not dream this time. It was a lighter slumber, and he drowsed for hours, waking once in a while as voices came to him. Manoel, in the kitchen, was talking angrily, while Margarida tried to quiet him.

Slap! and Gregorio began to wail. "You will keep your tongue still after this!" Manoel shouted. "There is no need to run gossiping down the street. This is a private matter."

"He is only a *menino*," Margarida pleaded, but Manoel roared at her angrily.

"His tongue wags night and day! Just now Bento Barbosa asked me what was wrong with Pedro and said he could not send a sick boy on the *Princesa*. I had to talk to him a long time before he would agree to take Pedro. There must be no more of these — these — " Manoel cursed. "It is too hot here in Cabrillo and the air is bad. Once Pedro is out on the water he will freshen up. *Deus,* do you think I would send him away if he were really sick, woman?"

A door slammed and there was silence. Pete dozed again, and remembered Cocos and Cartagena, and the dragons sailing over Paramaribo, and finally he decided he was awake. So he got up, drank the coffee Margarida forced on him, and went out. His arm was still sore from Dr. Manning's hypodermic needle.

He took a circuitous route to avoid passing Bento Barbosa's store, and this brought him past the *gitana*'s gate. The old woman called to him, and he couldn't pretend he hadn't heard; you couldn't fool Beatriz Sousa's sharp black eyes. So he went uneasily into the garden and up to the porch, where the Senhora sat shuffling the tarots on a flimsy table.

"Sit down, Pedro," she said, pointing to the creaky cane chair opposite her. "How are your dreams today, *meus neto?*"

It was funny that she'd never called him grandson before. It was funny, too, that she hadn't once looked up at him since he'd opened the gate. The wise, bright eyes were focused on the cards as they slapped softly down. Flick — flick — and a nod; flick, flick, and now the silvery head lifted and the bright black eyes looked straight into Pete's.

"A long time ago I lived in Lisbon," she said, in softly slurred Portuguese that made the name of the city *Leeshboa*. "But before that, *meus neto,* my tribe was in the mountains where there are only old things, like the trees and the rocks and the streams. There are truths to be learned from the old things — " She hesitated, and her brown, shrunken claw closed over Pete's hand. "Do you know the truth, Pedrinho?"

Puzzled, he met her bright stare. "The truth about what, Senhora?"

A moment longer she searched his eyes. Then her hand dropped and she smiled.

"No. Never mind. I see you do not. I had thought perhaps you might need advice from me, but I see you need nothing. You are safe, *menino*. The old magic is not all evil. It may be very bad for men in towns, but a gift is not offered to one who has no use for it."

Pete did not understand, but he listened politely. "*Sim,* Senhora?"

"You must decide," she said with a shrug of her narrow shoulders. "You need no help from me or anyone. Only remember this — you have no need to be afraid, Pedro, never at all." The toothless jaws worked. "No, do not look at the tarots. I will not read your future for you. Your future . . ." She mumbled something in the gipsy tongue. "Go away now. Go."

Pete, feeling that he had somehow offended the old woman, got up reluctantly. She did not look after him as he stepped down from the porch.

Even when he got home that evening and found Margarida busy packing the gear that he would need and hovering between pride and tears, he could not quite believe all this was for Pedro Ignacio da Silva Coutinho. Manoel superintended, sitting by the stove and scornfully rejecting dozens of articles his wife wanted to put in the sea-bag. The children were delirious with excitement, and neighbors kept dropping in with good advice. Within an hour Pete had been given twenty assorted crucifixes, charms, and amulets, all designed to protect him from the dangers of the sea. Manoel snorted.

"A strong back and a quick eye are better," he declared.

Margarida threw her apron over her head suddenly and burst into sobs. "He is not well," she wept. "He will die, I know."

"You are a fool," Manoel told her. "The *doutor* said Pedro is healthy as a jackass, and as for you, stop acting like one and bring me more wine."

As for Pete, he went out into the yard and looked around it with new eyes, now that he was leaving. All the ports of the world lay open to him, Tampico and Campeche and a thousand more, and the pirates were singing on the Isle of Pines, and over Paramaribo the dragons were flying with their mailed and clashing wings.

When Pete went to bed that night he was quite sure he wouldn't oversleep again. Not with the ports of the world beckoning to him. Through the open windows beside him came the faint sound of song and music from the Castle and the other waterfront taverns, the last sounds he would hear from little Cabrillo on the Gulf before he sailed away on the *Princesa* into a beckoning world.

What he'd find there, of course, was up to Pete. But he was sure there were magicians in Tampico and leopardskins and golden thrones in Juba. Dragons and pirates and white temples where magic dwelt. And best of all, the places he didn't know about yet, the ones that would come as surprises. Oh, not entirely pleasant surprises. There should be a hint of peril, a touch of terror, to emphasize the brightness of adventure . . .

Tampico . . . Tampico . . . Juba and Campeche . . .

Paramaribo . . . Cocos and Clipperton and Cartagena . . . They blended into a singing silence in his mind.

In the dark stones the toad sat breathing softly, its eyes looking not at the night, but at something far away.

In a blue brightness Pete went whirling and spinning down, the southern sea taking him eagerly to its depths. Below, the coral blazed with rich colors, and a tiger-shark curved away and was gone.

He swam upward. His head broke the surface and the blue sea lay under a blue sky, cradling the forested isle in the immense plain of waters. Beyond the lagoon lay the clipper ship. A rattling and a clanking came to Pete's ears. The anchor was rising, white sails mounting on the masts. The wind caught the canvas and billowed them, and the ship heeled over a little as they filled taut and strained against the blue.

The ship was sailing . . .

Sudden desolation struck through Pete. He was afraid, abruptly, of being left alone on this enchanted ocean. He didn't want to watch the clipper dwindle to a speck on the horizon. With desperate haste he began to swim toward the vessel.

In the translucent blue depths beneath him bright shapes moved. A school of dolphins broke the surface with their precise, scalloping play all about him. Showering silver rolled from their sleek hides as they leaped. But ever the rattling of the anchor-chain grew louder.

Almost articulate . . . almost understandable . . . altering to a harsh voice that commanded — what?

Waken — waken . . .

Waken to morning in Cabrillo, Pedrinho; waken to the tide that will take the *Princesa* out across the Gulf. You must go with the tide. You must see Tampico and Campeche. You must look upon the real Tampico, with its black oil-tankers in the oily water. You must see the ports of the world, and find in them what men always find . . . So waken, Pedro, waken as your father's hand closes on your shoulder and shakes you out of your dream.

199

Not for you, Pedro.

Out of nowhere, a cool, small, inhuman voice said softly, "A gift is offered, Pedro. The old magic is not all evil. Reach up quickly, Pedro, reach up — "

Pete hesitated. The ports of the world — he knew how wonderful they were to see, and the *Princesa* would be waiting for him. But the chain of the clipper's anchor was almost within reach. He heard the cool little voice, and he gave one more strong stroke in the water and reached up with both hands. The slippery wet surface of the anchor-chain met his dripping palms. He was drawn up out of the sea.

Behind him voices faded. He thought he could hear dimly his mother's cry, and the shrill tones of little Gregorio. But they dwindled and were gone in a new sound from deck, the sound of deep song rising above the shuffle of bare feet.

"As I was a-walkin' down Paradise Street . . ."

Hands were helping him over the rail. He saw grinning sailors pacing around the capstan, bending above the bars, singing and singing. He felt the sun-warmed deck beneath his feet. Overhead canvas creaked and slapped and the ship came alive as wind took hold of the sails and billowed them out proudly, casting sudden translucent shadows over the deck and the grinning men. The clipper's bowsprit dipped once, twice, and spray glittered like diamonds on the gilded figurehead. He heard deep, friendly voices that drowned out the last faint, dying summons from — from — he could not remember.

Thunder rolled deeply. Pete looked up.

Mailed in shining armor, its tremendous wings clashing, a dragon swept through the sunlit air above Paramaribo.

ROBERT BLOCH, creator of such modern masterpieces of horror and the supernatural as *Psycho* (the novel made into the suspenseful Alfred Hitchcock film), was born in 1917 in Chicago. He sold his first short story to *Weird Tales* in 1935 just two weeks after high school graduation. His early work, much of it reprinted in *The Opener of the Way* (Arkham House, 1945), was strongly influenced by H.P. Lovecraft; but he soon developed his own distinctive style, crisp and fast-moving and discovering horror in today's white-tiled hospital halls and neon-lit city streets — a style typified by stories like his famous "Yours Truly, Jack the Ripper." The huge success of the film *Psycho* enabled the Chicago-born and -based Bloch to move to Hollywood, where he has since done movie and television scripts, many based on his own stories. Recently he has stepped up his production of fiction, his latest novels being *Psycho II* and *The Night of the Ripper*. His *Selected Stories* have been issued in three large volumes by Underwood/Miller.

Most writers are fortunate to find fame at all, but **AUGUST DERLETH** attained it in three different fields. Author of more than 120 books (not to mention editor of some 32 anthologies), Derleth was born in Wisconsin in 1909 and graduated from the University of Wisconsin with a B.A. in 1930. He was only fifteen when he sold his first story, a vampire tale called "Bat's Belfry," to *Weird Tales*. Derleth soon gained a growing reputation as a writer of supernatural and horror fiction, often with quiet, realistic small-town backgrounds, many in the vein of H.P. Lovecraft. Notable collections of these include *Someone in the Dark* (1941), *Lonesome Places* (1962), and *Mr. George and Other Odd Persons* (1963, published under the pseudonym Stephen Grendon). His *Sac Prairie Saga,* a multi-volume account of Wisconsin past and present, made him a prominent regional writer, and his present fame as founder and first editor of Arkham House is rapidly growing as well. The firm was originally formed to publish Lovecraft's work in hardcover books for larger audiences. Soon it was doing the same for such now-famous writers as Robert E. Howard, Ray Bradbury, Robert Bloch, and Fritz Lieber, in handsome editions in a distinctive black and gold binding. It issued a posthumous memorial edition in two volumes, slipcased, of *The Solar Pons Omnibus,* Derleth's Sherlock Holmes pastiches, in 1982. Derleth died in 1971 in his home town of Sauk City, so often celebrated in his work.

Gentle and genial **WASHINGTON IRVING** created two imperishable figures of American legend — Rip van Winkle, who fell asleep one thundery afternoon in the Catskills and woke to find that twenty years had passed; and the Headless Horseman of Sleepy Hollow. Born in New York in 1783, Irving began a law practice at sixteen while providing stories for his brother's newspaper, which he gathered into his first book, *Salamugundi.* His second, the humorous *Knickerbocker's History of New York,* made him rich and famous, one of the first Americans to gain international respect for American letters. Irving quit law and business to write abroad, largely in England. He served as U.S. Ambassador to Spain from 1841 to 1846 and then returned home. His remaining works were historical and biographical — among them his *Life of Washington,* which Irving finished shortly before his death in 1859.

CARL JACOBI, one of the prominent writers showcased by that famous magazine *Weird Tales,* was born in Minnesota in 1908. Graduating from the University of Minnesota in 1930 in the Great Depression, he worked briefly as a reporter for the *Minneapolis Star* while writing fiction for the pulps to help support his ill and aging parents. His stories were colorful, meticulously researched, often set in far-off places like Borneo or the Carribean; his best were tales of the supernatural, collected in *Revelations in Black* (1947), *Portraits in Moonlight* (1964), and *Disclosures in Scarlet* (1972). A biography, *Lost in the Rentharpian Hills* by R. Dixon Smith, was published in 1985.

A major figure of science fiction's golden age, the astonishingly prolific **HENRY KUTTNER** wrote under so many pen-names that his full influence has yet to be correctly estimated. Born in Los Angeles in 1914, he sold his first story, "The Graveyard Rats," a grim horror tale, to *Weird Tales* in 1936. Sales came rapidly in every field — air-war, mystery, adventure — but his best work was in the supernatural genre until the '40s, when he turned to science fiction, married fantasy writer C.L. Moore, and wrote a large number of high-quality stories for such magazines as *Astounding Science Fiction* (including the classic "Mimsy Were the Borogoves") and *Startling Stories* ("The Time Axis"), under such pen-names as Lawrence O'Donnell (*Fury*, 1950) and Lewis Padgett (*A Gnome There Was*, 1950). Much of his work was done in collaboration with his wife. Finishing a brief term of service in the Medical Corps in 1945, Kuttner turned to writing mysteries. He went to the University of Southern California from 1950 to 1954 for his B.S. and died in 1958 from a sudden heart attack.

Almost unknown in his own lifetime, **H.P. LOVE-CRAFT** is recognized widely today as a master of the macabre and supernatural. Born in Providence, Rhode Island, in 1890, Howard Phillips Lovecraft was kept from school by illness and turned to his own imagination for company and largely educated himself by omniverous reading. He turned early to writing; articles and stories in amateur magazines soon led to his first professional sale, "Dagon," to *Weird Tales* in 1923. This magazine was the largest (almost the only) outlet for his writing life, and he soon became one of its top writers. Much of his work had a common background: alien, monstrous beings from strange dimensions, who lived on beneath the seas, hoping to regain control of Earth when "the stars were right" and their hordes of alien followers could appear. In fact, Lovecraft's best work — the novelettes "The Dreams in the Witch-House," "The Shadow Out of Time," and "The Haunter of the Dark" and *The Shadow*

Over Innsmouth (1936) used this concept. His style, not only in writing but in life, was that of an eighteenth-century gentleman. After he died of cancer in 1937, his friends August Derleth and Donald Wandrei formed Arkham House to publish his works. The first volume, *The Outsider and Others* (1939), is now a collector's item. A major biography by L. Sprague de Camp appeared in 1975, and Lovecraft's major works have recently been reissued in three thick volumes: *Dagon and Other Macabre Tales, The Dunwich Horror and Others,* and *At the Mountains of Madness.*

"I must go down to the seas again, to the lonely sea and the sky, / And all I ask is a tall ship and a star to steer her by. . . ." These lines, from the poem "Sea Fever," are perhaps the best-known work of **JOHN MASEFIELD,** born in England in 1878. A lawyer's son who sailed as a seaman aboard a windjammer around the Horn to Chile, he resigned as Sixth Officer of the *Adriatic* to become a writer. *Salt-Water Ballads,* his first book, was published in 1902; other poems and plays followed. His World War I service with the Red Cross was recounted in a powerful book, *Gallipoli* (1916). In England after the war he received an L.L.D. from the University of Aberdeen and an honorary D.D.Litt. from Oxford, both in 1922. In 1930 he was appointed Poet Laureate of England, a post he held until his death in 1967.

"None strikes the note of cosmic horror so well" as **CLARK ASHTON SMITH,** according to H.P. Lovecraft. Born in California in 1893, Smith had little formal schooling due to childhood illnesses. He largely educated himself, learning Latin, Spanish, and French and reading Webster's *Unabridged Dictionary.* His first story, "The Malay Kris," appeared in the *Overland Monthly* in 1910. Most of Smith's output was poetry, but in 1925 he turned to fiction to help support his aging parents, selling "The Abominations of Yondo" to *Weird Tales.* Strongly influenced by Edgar Allan Poe and the Arabian

Nights, his stories are colorful, grim, and fatalistic in mood, set in gorgeous, exotic worlds whose names became the titles of later collections, including *Zothique* (1970), *Xiccarph* (1972), and *Poseidonis* (1973). Harlan Ellison and Ray Bradbury later stated that his story "The City of the Singing Flame" inspired them both to become science fiction writers. Smith's best fantasy fiction appeared in *Out of Space and Time* (1942) and *Lost Worlds* (1943). A series of strokes led to his death in 1961. An omnibus volume of his work, *A Rendezvous in Averoigne,* has just been published.

LADY ELEANOR SMITH came of a colorful ancestry reflected in her vivid fiction: her father was the Lord Chancellor of England, noted lawyer F.E. Smith, first Earl of Birkenhead, and other forebears of hers were gypsies. Born in England in 1902, Lady Eleanor spoke Romany, was educated by French governesses and in English schools, and at seventeen became a society reporter for London newspapers. An expert swimmer and rider, she worked as publicist for a circus for months and often rode in the ring, an experience used in her title story in *Satan's Circus and Other Stories* (1932). Her books include the fantasy novels *Lovers' Meeting* (1940) and *The Man in Grey* (1941), which was made into a film with James Mason the year of her death, 1945.

HENRY S. WHITEHEAD was born in New Jersey in 1882. He graduated from Harvard in 1904 with an A.B. degree and injuries from the football games he played there that were to shorten his life by a decade. He worked as a reporter, decided on a career in the Episcopal ministry, attended Berkeley Divinity School, and was assigned to the Virgin Islands as acting archdeacon from 1921 to 1929. Here he wove colorful Carribean legends of voodoo and buried treasure, pirates and monsters, into gripping eerie tales told in a solid, convincing manner. His supernatural stories are gathered into two volumes:

Jumbee and Other Uncanny Tales (1944) and *West Indian Lights* (1946). Whitehead died in New England in 1932.